the

infidelity

pact

the

infidelity
pact

Carrie Karasyov

Broadway Books

New York

BROADWAY

PUBLISHED BY BROADWAY BOOKS

A hardcover edition of this book was originally published
in 2007 by Broadway Books.

Published in the United States by Broadway Books,
an imprint of The Doubleday Publishing Group,
a division of Random House, Inc., New York.
www.broadwaybooks.com

BROADWAY BOOKS and its logo, a letter B bisected
on the diagonal, are trademarks of Random House, Inc.

Book design by Donna Sinisgalli

Library of Congress Cataloging-in-Publication Data
Karasyov, Carrie, 1972–
The infidelity pact / Carrie Karasyov.
p.   cm.
1. Housewives—Fiction. 2. Adultery—Fiction.
3. Los Angeles (Calif.)—Fiction. I. Title.
PS3611.A7775I64 2007
813'.6—dc22
2006100683

ISBN 978-0-7679-2704-8

PRINTED IN THE UNITED STATES OF AMERICA

1 3 5 7 9 10 8 6 4 2

First Paperback Edition

To my dear friend Lesbia

Without whom this book could never have been written

The Brie was heaving, the wind was howling, and the doorbell kept ringing. It was the second Saturday in January, and Eliza and Declan Gallahue were hosting one of their small but chic cocktail parties at their small but chic house on Via de la Paz. The party was entering its second hour. Most of the guests had already arrived and had a drink in hand and a canapé in mouth. The room glowed with the warmth of the twenty-five-watt bulbs that Eliza had painstakingly put in every lamp in her living room, having extracted the usual seventy-five-watt bulbs that she favored, tucking them into a drawer for the night on the advice of her favorite decorator friend who said that it was the best way to create a festive atmosphere. Besides, didn't everyone look so much better in the dimmer glow? It seemed to do the trick. People were relaxed, the chatter had reached a comfortable din, and most guests were already on their second drink.

Eliza tried to suppress the anxiety she'd been feeling since even before taking on the job of hostess. If only she could relax and have a good time, especially since the party was going well. But somehow she was still too edgy to enjoy her success. She tried to talk herself into it. The house looked good—she had asked her housekeeper to come early that morning to attend to all the miscellaneous upkeep, like shining the silver picture frames and ironing the monogrammed linen cocktail napkins that had seemed like such an irrelevant wedding gift but actually came in handy. In a last-minute pre-party frenzy, Eliza had run around pulling errant feathers out of deflating pillows, realigning the George Smith armchairs so that they were perfectly symmetrical, picking droop-ing leaves off potted plants and rearranging the small collection of Halcyon Days enamel boxes that she kept on a side table. Minor details, but now no one would say the house was anything other than immaculate. When she was nervous, no one cleaned up like Eliza Gallahue.

Eliza also knew that she looked good: after a stressful morn-ing she had cleared her afternoon and gotten a blowout for her shoulder-length hair at Frederic Fekkai, then splurged for a ses-sion with the makeup artist. (That was one thing Eliza could never master: makeup application. Her husband always teased her about it, and begged her to get a lesson; she was so inept with an eyeliner brush that it was almost comical. Her mother had told her at quite an early age that she was hopeless with small mechan-ical skills, so Eliza figured there was no point in trying to get bet-ter.) And the sessions with the trainer had paid off: finally Eliza had the post-baby body that she had dreamed of. It was the first time in about four years that Eliza felt like she had returned to her old teenage self, and it had been the most grueling work of her life. She had cut the carbs, forgone desserts, put in four hours a week on the treadmill, and done more downward facing dogs than she ever thought possible. But the results were in, and now there were no inches of flab to be pinched around her waist, a ma-jor achievement. In celebration, Eliza was wearing the slinky black cocktail dress with a slit on the side that she had been sav-ing since Michael Kors's 50-percent-off sale, and the new Jimmy Choos that were her Christmas present to herself. Eliza usually kept things very simple and very California with her wardrobe— Gap khakis, cute skirts, and oxfords, but every now and then she would splurge and take things in a higher direction.

She looked across the room. Declan, her dark-haired, green-eyed husband, who hadn't seemed to age in the ten years that she'd known him, was chatting amiably with Ron Freedman and Stan Smith, who were both looking very aware of the fact that they were about a foot shorter than he. Declan was a towering six-four. Eliza was pleased, though, because she had wanted Declan to get to know Stan. His wife, Pam, was on the board of Brightwood School, and besides being nice might actually be of use one day. Eliza found it scary to think that everything came down to networking, even where your kids were concerned. Getting them into the right schools, let alone getting yourself into the right clubs, etc., was daunting. But it was a simple fact of life.

Eliza had hired a bartender and enlisted their housekeeper, Juana, to pass hors d'oeuvres for the night, but she'd still rushed around refilling drinks, tactfully placed coasters under perspiring tumblers, and made sure there was enough cocktail sauce to accompany the shrimp. Frank Sinatra (Declan's favorite) was playing softly on the stereo system. The Gallahues' adorable toddlers, three-year-old Donovan and one-year-old Bridget, made the sweetest cameo appearance in their footed pajamas to wish the guests hello and good night. On the surface, it seemed like yet another successful cocktail party in the Pacific Palisades. On the surface.

Just then Eliza spotted Justin Coleman molesting the Brie platter. He'd arrived in one of his moods, still in a striped Armani suit and Gucci tie that was his uniform at work, and Eliza could tell that he and Victoria had been fighting on their way over. It didn't take too keen an observer to notice, since they usually fought, but this particular fight had Eliza worried. There was just too much at stake for all of them. When Eliza had opened the door, Justin had pecked her on the cheek and immediately scanned the room to see if anyone he deemed important and ass-kiss-worthy was there, and when he didn't find anyone his face fell in disappointment and he beelined for the couch, where he plopped himself in the middle of Eliza's recently fluffed Fortuny silk pillows and began to scarf down the cheese platter. Eliza couldn't help but be repulsed watching his small white hands work furiously to extricate the creamy center of the Brie without getting any mold. She hated the assholes who did that. Just suck it up—is some mold going to *kill* you? she thought. After every scoop, which he scraped onto a Carr's cracker and popped into his mouth, he returned to the Brie and dug deeper and deeper into the center, causing it to heave as if on life support, until the outer white shell finally drooped in exhaustion and the entire cheese collapsed. The once tastefully arranged platter now looked like the remnants of a pie-eating contest. Brie always was messy, Eliza thought with a sigh. Why did it remain in the cocktail party canon?

"As you can imagine, he didn't want to come," Victoria had said tautly. Although she was stunningly beautiful, with stick-straight long blond hair, piercing blue eyes, and a figure to kill for, Victoria had been increasingly irritated and stressed of late, which did little to enhance her looks.

"I'm frankly surprised he showed," said Eliza. "I'm surprised that any of us showed the way things are going."

Victoria and Eliza exchanged knowing looks. But before they could continue, Pam Smith, the whippet-thin neighborhood activist, came over and interrupted.

"Eliza, the house is *adorable*! You have such great style," she said genuinely. Eliza flushed with pride. Then Pam turned and looked at Victoria. "And how are you? I haven't seen you or Justin in the longest time."

"I know, it's been a while," said Victoria tersely, taking a glass of champagne from the passing bartender. Her gold bangles clanked down her arm one by one when she took the glass, and then clanked back up when she took a sip.

"Oh, well, I know you're busy, with your two adorable boys," said Pam, surprised at how cold Victoria was being. Eliza immediately felt embarrassed and jumped in.

"Justin's just been working day and night lately, and Vic as usual has been running around doing everything from chairing the St. Peter's benefit to kicking butt on the tennis team, so I think they're both exhausted," Eliza said, trying to deflate the tension.

"Yes. My husband is really busy these days, being every coked-out wannabe actor's lackey," said Victoria, grimacing before she motioned toward Justin. "Which is why he's sitting over there refusing to talk to anyone. His ball and chain summoned him to dinner at Koi tonight, and when I told him he couldn't go he pouted all the way."

She was referring to Tad Baxter, one of the "It" actors of the moment and Justin's biggest client. Justin was just supposed to be his agent, but he was more like valet, pimp, drug dealer, and whipping boy. It drove Victoria crazy that her husband had to take so much abuse from a guy who had been working the drive-through at Taco Bell less than two years ago.

"Oh, I see," said Pam, not seeing at all and not sure what to say. Although she lived in Los Angeles, she remained untouched by anything to do with Hollywood. Any of the depraved trappings and idle gossip of the entertainment world were of no interest to her, and she always seemed surprised when people brought them up.

"Sorry," said Victoria, finally turning her attention to Pam and realizing that she was speaking cryptically and being rude. "It just gets really hard when you work with celebrities. They think they own you."

"I can imagine." Pam nodded.

"So Pam, please tell us about what's going on in the world of illegal aliens," said Eliza, desperate to change the topic. "I mean, that came out wrong, but tell us what's going on with your work. Victoria, Pam is on the board of Human Rights Watch and very active in trying to prevent the wrongful imprisonment of under-age Latin Americans."

"Fascinating," said Victoria flatly.

"It is, but also so tragic . . ." began Pam, and then proceeded to launch into the ins and outs of all the incredibly generous and philanthropic ways she was assisting the cause. Eliza and Victoria were both totally distracted and put themselves on autopilot, "Mmm-hmming" at appropriate moments, nodding sadly when Pam's voice got tight with emotion, and gasping at dramatic pauses.

Eliza's mind was on other things, unfortunate things that had more of a pressing impact on her life. The fact was, everything was getting out of control and she didn't know how she could possibly fix it. Victoria in particular was becoming a loose cannon. Eliza had always counted on her to be the composed one, the friend who would never lose her cool and never cause a scene. Appearances were so important to Victoria, and she was so righteous in her decisions that she never wanted anyone to get a glimmer that there was anything else bubbling beneath the surface. But the past few months had changed everything. Victoria was getting reckless and volatile. And Justin, who was always a jerk in every aspect of his life—from his designer suits and slicked-back hair, to the silly Porsche that he drove and insisted on calling "Porsh-a"—was prepared for battle. Nowadays, they had become messy fighters, meaning that they didn't care who knew they were fighting or what about.

"The wind is going *craaaazy* out there," said Brad Adams, who had just been let in the front door by Juana and made his way over to greet his hostess. A high school football star whose brawny good looks had once made him quite a catch, Brad had now slipped into middle age—well, almost—and although he still had a mischievous glimmer in his sparkling blue eyes, there was little else about him that was remarkable. His once chiseled brow had begun to slide and now his eyes peered out from doughy rolls; his receding dusty blond hair also contributed to his everyman appearance. But Brad didn't seem to care—he still had that preppy insouciance and frat-boy demeanor that made people forget that he was pretty ordinary. Eliza was both shocked and relieved that he had come and immediately looked around the room to see if Brad's wife, Leelee, had noticed his entrance. Of course she had; she had been staring at the door longingly all night. Leelee, who had nearly bitten her cuticles down to the quick while waiting to find out if her husband would show, looked both exalted and afraid on the other side of the room.

"I know, the Santa Anas are having a field day out there," said Eliza, returning the casual peck on the cheek that he had greeted her with. As Brad made his way, kissing hellos to Victoria and Pam, Eliza shot Leelee a wide-eyed look of surprise and confusion.

"Global warming. It's all our fault," Pam was saying sadly as she nervously played with the wooden prayer beads around her neck, and shook her head. She seemed genuinely troubled by the state of the world, and her hazel eyes began to mist. Finally she snapped out of it. "Which reminds me, I see John York over there and I have to go talk to him about Ocean Watch—we need him to donate a round at Riviera for the silent auction," said Pam, excusing herself.

Victoria and Eliza both looked at each other curiously and then turned to Brad.

"So how are things, Brad?" asked Victoria, trying to be casual but sounding more like a psychiatrist talking to a patient who had just attempted suicide. Eliza shot her a look of daggers, but Victoria pretended not to notice.

"Things are great, Victoria," said Brad, smiling at Victoria's seriousness. "Although I was trapped in a conference room in Irvine all day with no service on my cell phone. The guy at my lunch yesterday spilled white wine all over it and now it's totally trashed."

Eliza and Victoria looked at each other in shock. So that's why he's been MIA, they both thought.

"That is such a bummer!" said Eliza, with a little too much enthusiasm.

"That's awful!" said Victoria, with buoyancy in her voice.

Brad gave them both a strange look. "So, have you seen my wife?"

"She's over there," said Eliza, pointing to Leelee, who was making fake conversation with the bartender. "She'll be glad to see you."

"Thanks," said Brad, who then walked over to Leelee, his wife of ten years. Brad and Leelee could pass for brother and sister. They were both semi-stout and blond, with pleasant rosy faces that had been more striking in their youth, giving them the appearance of former prom king and queen of a large suburban high school.

Eliza and Victoria both waited a beat to make sure he was out of earshot before shaking their heads.

"God, Leelee's going to be so relieved. All that freaking for nothing," said Eliza.

"Do you really think he's clueless? Maybe he's faking," suggested Victoria.

"Unless he's an Academy Award–winning actor, he has no idea," said Eliza with certainty.

They both turned to watch their friend greet her husband. Across the Provence-inspired blue living room, they saw Leelee tentatively greeting her husband, Brad presumably explaining why he hadn't returned her calls, and Leelee realizing that her life was not over.

Suddenly, Eliza felt flooded with relief and joy, even gratitude. She glanced around the room, where her friends both new and old were making themselves at home, all having a nice time. Her kids were asleep, her husband was happy, and it was Friday. What could be better? Maybe they would actually come out of this mess unscathed.

Her reverie was interrupted by the soft ping of the doorbell. Eliza sent Victoria over to the sideboard to check out her newly purchased Georg Jensen candlesticks that she'd scored on eBay, and made her way over to the door. As she turned the knob, a large gust of wind blew into the room, carrying along a few scattered leaves. Standing on the threshold was Helen, the fourth member of the close-knit gang that included Eliza, Leelee, and Victoria.

"Hey, I was wondering when you would get here. What took you so long?" asked Eliza, kneeling down to pick up the leaves. They somehow had managed to land in every corner of the entrance hall, so Eliza had to use all of her yoga flexibility to reach from one end to the other without flashing everyone her underwear underneath her skirt. Helen remained motionless and silent.

Eliza looked up at her. Helen was an attractive Korean American in her early thirties, whose honest features were completely unable to conceal exactly how she was thinking when she was thinking it. And right now, she was looking frightened. Eliza immediately knew. Something was very wrong.

"What?" asked Eliza.

"Anson Larrabee is dead."

·· *2* ··

The Gallahues' house was located on a street that was a dead end in more than one sense of the word. Situated in the area of the Palisades known as The Bluffs, it was the westernmost part of town, and the closest to those spectacular and coveted ocean views. The closer you drove toward the ocean, the more expensive the properties were. However, if you kept going, you would fall sharply down the craggy cliff onto the Pacific Coast Highway. It was a fantastic vista, but a potentially tragic fate. And because of its proximity to the water, it could get breezy to say the least. On this particular night, as several of Eliza's guests had commented, the winds were picking up speed, and were rattling the windows in the Gallahues' kitchen.

After her initial shock at the news of Anson's demise, Eliza quickly rallied and had gathered Helen, Victoria, and Leelee for a strategy session in the pantry. She knew that it was rude to leave the rest of her guests, but she had no choice.

"Okay, start from the beginning and tell us everything," demanded Victoria, her voice stern and all business. Victoria, who had an MBA from Stanford, had run a major division of Fox Studios before chucking it all a few months after the birth of her twin

sons, Austin and Hunter. She had never fully been able to recon-
cile her advanced degrees with carpools and tennis lessons, and
she often slipped back into boss mode. Eliza imagined this was
the voice she'd used with her subordinates when she was a big-
deal studio executive.

Helen pushed her wavy dark hair out of her face and took a
deep breath. "I don't know, I don't know . . . I went over to pick
Anson up, as we all agreed"—she said this last part looking at
them accusingly—"and then when I got there, there were a ton of
cop cars and an ambulance with flashing lights—"

"I heard the sirens!" interrupted Leelee.

"Shhhh . . . let her finish," reprimanded Victoria.

"And, okay, so I drove up to the first cop. He was directing
traffic away, and I said 'What's going on?' and he said 'Nothing,
ma'am' and I said 'I need to know, my friend lives there' and he
said 'I am not at liberty to say.' He was all blow-offy and, like, *Get
lost*. And then I saw . . . oh God, I saw a stretcher being carted out
of his house—"

"Just like on *CSI*!" said Leelee.

"Totally, and I was like, 'Oh, God, is that Anson?' and he
was like, 'I'm not at liberty to say,' and then I like, freaked out,
because this is a joke! I mean, for all he knows, Anson and I are
inseparable BFFs. So I start getting mad, and then finally another
cop comes over and says yes, it is Anson, and I say 'What happened?' and he's like, 'We're not sure yet, looks like he fell down
the stairs' and I said 'Was it foul play?' "

"You said *what*?" snapped Victoria.

Helen stopped talking and looked worried. "I asked if it was
foul play," she said softly, fear creeping across her face.

"Why in the world would you put that thought in his head?"
asked Victoria, enraged.

Helen looked like she might cry. "I don't know . . . I guess I've seen too many episodes of *Law & Order*."

Eliza put her arm around Helen. "Don't worry. I'm sure you didn't put anything in the policeman's head. He's a cop, for lord's sake. He sees crime scenes all the time."

"In the Palisades?" asked Leelee skeptically.

"What did he say?" insisted Victoria.

"He said he wasn't sure yet. Too early to tell," said Helen.

"So it might be murder," said Leelee.

"I guess, yes, it might be murder," said Helen.

The other three women were speechless, which for them was unusual. Eliza looked at each one of her friends and took a deep gulp. Leelee, the preppy mom who always had something dirty and outrageous to say to shake things up, was quiet. Victoria, the formerly cool and collected leader, just shook her head in disbelief. Helen, who had a propensity to look at everything from an existential or otherworldly angle, seemed shaken to her core. And Eliza herself, the reliable, steady voice of reason, was left totally stunned.

"Um, okay, I have no idea what to say," she said.

"Me neither. But come on, are we certain he said he wasn't sure if it was *foul play*?" asked Leelee.

"I wouldn't lie," snapped Helen.

"This cannot be happening," said Leelee.

Just then Juana entered the pantry. She stopped abruptly; surprised to see them all huddled in the corner.

"Sorry, Missus, I need more napkins," she said apologetically.

"Sure, Juana," said Eliza, sliding over to the cabinets and pulling a stack of toile cocktail napkins out of the drawer. Paper would have to do; she couldn't be bothered to find the additional linen napkins.

"Thanks, Missus," said Juana, giving them all one more strange look before she reentered the living room.

"You guys, we can't really do this now, in the middle of the party. People will be suspicious," said Eliza.

"Suspicious?" asked Helen with alarm. "You don't think that anyone will think we had anything to do with this?"

Before Eliza could say anything, Victoria jumped in.

"Eliza's right," said Victoria. "Let's all go back in, pretend everything is okay, and then regroup later tonight."

"God, just when I thought this whole thing was going to be over . . ." began Leelee, her voice tight.

"It is over, in a way," said Victoria, sternly.

"But not the way we thought," said Helen.

"But the way we all hoped," said Victoria. They all turned and looked at her. She was right. They had never actually articulated it to one another, but in their daydreams, this was the best-case scenario. What could be better than to have Anson Larrabee, their nemesis, dead?

For the rest of the evening, they all played their parts, all the while clenching the stems of their white wine glasses and praying for the night to be over. It was time to end this, once and for all. Their pact had taken a nefarious turn for the worse, leading them on an insidious course, slithering through every aspect of their lives, wreaking havoc on their marriages, driving them insane. If Anson had died from natural causes, they might have some peace. But if he was murdered . . . it could be the beginning of the end for all of them.

·· 3 ··

On an overcast Wednesday night in July, approximately eight months before Anson's death, Eliza, Victoria, Helen, and Leelee had gathered at the Pearl Dragon for Girls' Night Out. The sad irony that they were no longer girls was not lost on them, but they all thought if they changed the name to Women's Night it would sound like some sort of angry feminist convention, and Ladies' Night had a little bit of a porno twist to it. They all *felt* like girls, so while recognizing the misnomer, they made no attempt to change the name.

The Pearl Dragon was mostly a sushi restaurant, but it also had the only full bar in the Palisades. This meant that on summer nights there was usually a throng of college-age students clad in miniskirts (females) and baseball hats (males), hanging out at the bar, trying to pick up members of the opposite sex. Eliza and her gang stayed toward the back, attempting to pay little attention to the pheromones flying in the front, distracting themselves with spicy tuna rolls, shrimp tempura, and baked cod. The four best friends saw each other often, but it was mostly on the fly, when they were picking up or dropping off their children at classes, grabbing coffee at Starbucks, or doing shoulder stands in yoga class. These nights were their chance to catch up sans diaper bags, attention-demanding kids, and husbands who had little interest in dissecting the latest issue of *Us Weekly*.

"We're so old," lamented Leelee, glancing at the Jessica Simpson wannabe in the skintight lowrider jeans who had just planted herself on the bar stool, exposing her lacy pink thong to the entire restaurant.

"It's sad," said Eliza, sucking the beans out of the edamame. "We could be their moms."

"No, we couldn't!" protested Victoria.

"In Oklahoma," insisted Eliza.

"If we were babies having babies, shopping in preteen maternity," said Victoria dismissively. Victoria was a fact person. She had little use for exaggeration or drama.

"I got my first gray hair the other day," said Helen, picking the olive out of her dirty martini and taking a bite. "I'm thirty-three. I'm having a metaphysical crisis. Gray hair equals death to me. It's all downhill from here."

"Come on!" said Eliza. "It does not equal death."

"Hey, they say the sex gets better when you're older," said Leelee, with a twinkle in her eye. Leelee adored talking about sex, which was odd considering she usually dressed like a forty-five-year-old who had just gotten off the golf course and was on her way to her second gin and tonic. But she had informed her friends again and again (almost too much) that underneath her prudish cashmere sweater sets she wore slinky black lingerie, the really raunchy kind with garter belts.

"I don't feel sexual," sighed Helen. "I can't even think that way. I mean, Wesley and I would rather watch a good episode of *Lost* than do it. It's sad. And it's a real crisis now that it's summer. There's no good TV on, all reruns and reality shows. I can't wait for the fall season to start."

"Spice it up! Get some toys!" said Leelee mischievously. She swirled the chardonnay in her glass and took a large gulp. She had a large cache of sex toys in a box tucked away in the back of her closet. The truth was, she hadn't used any of them in ages. The only thing that got any workout these days was her dildo, but that was when she was alone. And she would never tell her friends that.

"Yeah, right. With Wesley? Don't forget, my husband was raised in British boarding schools. I think I'd give him a heart attack if I whipped out handcuffs," said Helen.

Eliza and Victoria laughed, shuddering at the image of Wesley Fairbanks IV, Helen's pale husband, who was twenty years her senior, chained to a bedpost.

"Have you ever tried?" asked Leelee.

"Ask Wesley? No, Wesley and I don't even seem to talk to each other anymore," said Helen, reaching over and picking up a piece of edamame. She played with it a little but didn't put it in her mouth. "My husband and I are like two ships passing in the night. Friendly ships, but just . . . separate."

Helen became quiet. She thought about her home life and a dull numbness engulfed her. She was so used to the silence and the detachment that sometimes she had to remind herself that this was probably not how it should be. At the very least, it was not how she'd pictured married life should be. Maybe she should have married someone closer to her in age. Maybe they would have more in common. She looked up and saw her friends staring at her with concern. She didn't want to be the downer. "So, what, do you all use toys?"

"No," said Eliza abruptly. "I mean, I'm not opposed. I have." Eliza was evasive about her sex life. She would engage and talk about sex in the past, but now that she was married she felt protective of her husband. All that sanctity of marriage stuff had actually rubbed off on her. She knew that if she said something negative about Declan—related to sex or not—her friends would file it away and always have it in the back of their minds (the way she did when she heard their confessions). She didn't want to let anyone have that over her. It was better to deflect.

"You gotta do your hubby right, or he'll get it somewhere else," said Victoria firmly. Victoria talked about sex the way a man would. There was a certain hardness there, an anger. The others knew that Justin was a bit of an asshole. They figured that's why Victoria was so blunt. It was as if by disengaging, not thinking her sex life could ever be a love life, she was launching a preemptive strike. She also liked to be in control of everything.

"Isn't it so sad that we just get older and fatter and less desirable, and men, even if they get older and fatter, get *more* desirable?" asked Eliza. "We're saddled with baby weight, gray hair, and wrinkles, and we're expected to have these kids, take care of them, work out like a maniac, get Botox, have a career . . ."

"Well, you're the only one with a career," interrupted Leelee.

"That's because she's the only one who had a career that could accommodate kids," snapped Victoria. She was still bitter about leaving her job and saw it as some kind of failure. Why had she wasted all that time getting an MBA when she had no time to use it? She regretted that she hadn't chosen a career in something like journalism. Something portable that she could do on her own schedule. If Eliza could do it, she was sure she could. But it was too late. She had chosen business because she wanted something intense and masculine. Something that depended on facts, where she could compete with the best of them. But she had learned the hard way that no matter how smart you are, the corporate world was just not set up for women with kids. And all that feminist progressive propaganda they shoved down your throat? Bullshit.

"Honey, I don't miss having a career, although I never really had a career, just a job," laughed Leelee. "Let Brad do all the work, and show me the money!"

Money was a sore subject with Leelee. She had married Brad when he had more of it, but then it all had come crashing down and Leelee was locked into a life that was—while still privileged—not exactly what she had in mind.

"Declan doesn't seem like the type who's hard on you about weight and work and all that," said Helen to Eliza.

"No, he's not. But come on, there's pressure. I'm surrounded by some of the thinnest women in the world in this town. No way could I show up looking like a heifer," answered Eliza.

"But what are you talking about anyway? You've got a hot bod now, missy," said Helen. Eliza protested but inside she burned with flattery. Finally someone had noticed her toned arms!

"Isn't it odd that this is our life?" asked Victoria, with sudden seriousness. "I mean, we are all basically suburban moms—I know the Palisades are technically part of L.A., but come on, we all drive SUVs with baby seats and hang out in playgroups and at the country club. There's the tennis team, all that mundane crap. I went to an Ivy League college! I was third in my class at Stanford Business School! And now I'm organizing the charity bake sale at St. Peter's? It's bullshit."

All of the women looked at one another in commiseration. "It's so true," said Eliza.

"But I mean, what do you miss the most about being young? What are you unhappy about? Is it that you miss things, or just that you want additional things?" asked Helen. Helen loved to dissect topics, look at everything from different angles, especially supernatural, spiritual, and existential. She was the master at asking probing questions that weren't offensive, and her greatest quality was that she liked to hear the answers. This is a person who listens, thought Eliza the first time she met her. That's so rare in this day and age. The funny thing was that she asked all the pertinent questions to everyone else and not to herself and her husband.

"Oh, I can answer that one," said Leelee, carefully aligning her third glass of chardonnay with her placemat. "I want to turn back time. To do it all over again. I want to do some things differently."

Leelee's drunken honesty made everyone a bit sad. Without alcohol, she was usually evasive about personal issues, especially her disappointment with Brad, whom she had probably married way too young. But hints of anger came spilling out—just little glimmers—when she imbibed. She always tried to cover them up by being breezy and casual, but no one bought it.

"What would you do over again?" asked Helen.

"Oh, I don't mean Brad or anything," she said, although everyone knew she really probably did. "I just mean I'd get a lot busier before I got married. I would bang up a storm!" she said, trying to use humor to deflect the seriousness of her remarks.

"So it's a sex thing with you?" asked Victoria. She wanted the facts.

"Don't you think?" asked Leelee. "It's great to be married, but it would be great to be given carte blanche to have sex with more people."

Leelee talked a big game, but again, no one thought it was sex she was after.

"What do you think?" asked Victoria, turning to Eliza and Helen.

"My sex life is pretty nonexistent," said Helen, matter-of-factly. "I used to be quite wild in my younger days, if you can believe that." Everyone could. "It's funny because I've been thinking about that a lot lately. How it was so exciting to discover a new position, or explore a new person's body. I loved those first moments of running my fingers over a man's stomach, someone I had never slept with before, and just tracing the outline of his abs or his nipples. I love the tactile part of sex. I miss the novelty, and I guess the variety. There's something so exciting about making new human connections."

Everyone was quiet for a minute.

"Not to mention that I'd love to do it with someone who cares," added Helen. Unlike Wesley, who seemed to care only about hiking, smoking pot, reading scripts, and finding his next movie to direct.

"What about you, Eliza?" asked Victoria. When she warmed to a topic she'd grill everyone as if they were witnesses and she was the prosecutor in a death-penalty case.

"My sex life is fine. I don't have any complaints," said Eliza.

Victoria was not going to let her off the hook. "You're totally happy at the place you are now? You look at those girls over there," she said, motioning to the scantily clad nineteen-year-olds, "and you feel great."

"No," sighed Eliza. She didn't think anyone could feel great next to those toothpicks. "Those are two different questions. Yes, it's a bummer that we don't look like them, but I am happy in my life now."

"You wouldn't change a thing?" asked Victoria in disbelief.

"That's not what I'm saying," said Eliza. She leaned in. "Okay, nothing to do with my husband, whom I worship, and all those disclaimers . . ."

"Yeah, yeah," said Leelee, waving them away in the air.

"But I miss being *coveted*. It sounds lame, but I just can't remember when I walked down the street or went to the grocery store and some hot, or even semihot, guy gave me a look like he thought I was attractive. I don't even want a jump-your-bones look. Not sexy. Just romantic." Eliza's fantasy life was compartmentalized. She was happy with her husband and children, but perhaps because she was a writer, she had grandiose daydreams about being plucked from obscurity by knights in shining armor. It was as far as she would go.

"I know what you mean," said Helen. "The other day I was at Starbucks and this cute guy kept staring at me, and I thought, Wow! I got it going on! And then when I left and got in my car I noticed in the rearview mirror that I had a foam mustache."

"Embarrassing," said Leelee.

"Totally."

"I don't even go there. If someone gives me a curious look, I assume I got my period all over my pants or something horrible like that," said Leelee.

"There's just too much competition out there, and they're all younger and have better metabolisms," said Eliza.

"And breast implants," said Leelee.

"And brains the size of peanuts," said Victoria.

"What are you talking about? None of us look half bad," said Helen.

"It doesn't matter. Youth is wasted on the young, or whatever that phrase is," sighed Eliza, sipping her margarita.

"So you want someone to want you?" asked Victoria, clarifying.

"Yes, Victoria. I want someone to want me," answered Eliza, resigned. "I mean, I'd just like one look, a sort of glance my way. Sometimes I imagine it. Like when I walk out of the nail salon, wearing those weird rubber sandals they give you so you don't mess up your pedicure, and I'm like in my sweats, my hair is back in an elastic because I didn't blow dry it straight, and I look like a mess. And I want a hot guy to walk by and say hey, or just give me a look like, *Hey.* But the thing is, it's not only a sexual look. It's like I'd love it if he could see through to my mind and recognize that I am a unique and interesting person, someone special, and not just some *mom* who has to pick up her dry cleaning and lose ten pounds." Eliza stopped, worried that she had said more than she wanted to. But it was all true. And they all felt it.

"You don't need to lose ten pounds," said Helen. "Would you stop with the weight thing? It's getting annoying!"

"You should see the bread belt . . ." Eliza protested.

"I don't believe you, so shut up," said Helen.

"So get a trainer," snapped Victoria. It bothered her when people would complain about things that they were too lazy to fix.

"I know, I should, and talking about weight is so boring. So what about you, Victoria?" asked Eliza.

Victoria leaned back. "I miss the chase. You know, going after a guy, and getting him. I liked figuring out what he liked and didn't like, and orchestrating the whole affair, but letting him think he had the upper hand. That was all the fun."

Everyone knew that Victoria had done everything she could to get Justin—even breaking up his first marriage. They both lost interest in each other soon after.

"Well, the grass is always greener," lamented Eliza.

The conversation moved on. There was a half hour discussion of what had caused the recent breakup of a celebrity couple, done with as much analysis as an episode of *Crossfire.* There was some gossiping about the people who had bought that ugly monstrosity on Embury Street, and a complete analysis of the new bitchy blonde on the tennis team. Everyone talked about their children and what activities they were doing this summer. Some had outgrown their "Mommy and Me" classes at Happy Child, others were ready for soccer. It was the usual banter for one of these evenings.

And yet. In the car on the way home from dinner (which was only a four-minute ride—it took longer to walk to the parking lot than to drive home), Victoria was seized by a thought. Things could be different. They could all get their wishes. There was no time to waste. The next morning she called the girls and arranged for another Girls' Night Out. Helen was busy with her yoga classes, Leelee blabbed about some committee meetings she had for a cancer benefit, and Eliza mentioned some dinner she had planned at the Brentwood. Victoria hadn't really wanted a rundown of her friends' social calendars, just to set a date for the next girls' night. She ultimately learned that the closest date they were all available was the next Friday. Victoria hated to wait—she was running out of time herself—but it would have to do. It was probably a good thing to have a one-week waiting period before you encouraged others to change the course of their lives.

·· *4* ··

The following evening, as Victoria sat in the passenger's seat of her husband's idiotic sports car, mapping out her plan in her mind was all that could keep her from going insane. If she had been emotionally invested in the conversation that she was having with her husband, she would have been alternatively enraged and disgusted. Now that she had a scheme as to how to extricate herself from her situation, nothing really mattered. Not even Justin's petty admonishments.

"You should have worn that light blue dress, the one with the halter top. That looks much better on you," he said, giving her a sideways appraisal.

"Right," Victoria said, barely opening her lips to enunciate. Eliza would be the hard nut to crack, she decided. Helen was pretty open-minded, and Leelee always succumbed to pressure, but Eliza would be the holdout. One holdout mattered; she needed them all on board or it wouldn't work. They were all so dependent on one another that if one was doing it and the other wasn't, they'd all get panicky.

"I think it's by Ralph Lauren? Yeah, the one Gwyneth Paltrow wore to the premiere of her last movie," he said, making a right onto Sunset and heading toward Bel Air.

"It's so gay that you know that," said Victoria.

"What, you're offended? Don't you want to look good?" said Justin, his voice rising and warming up for a fight. "It's my client's party. I need you to look the part. Didn't you sign up for this?"

"Whatever," said Victoria. She knew she sounded like a sullen teenager, but she didn't care.

"Oh, so it's going to be *that* tonight. That's great, just great, Victoria," he said with irritation.

"I don't know what *'that'* is, but if you're trying to pick a fight, don't bother."

"Why can't you just be normal, for once? Why do I have to beg you to put on a happy face when we go out? The other wives are there, smiling, chitchatting, and you just stand there tensely chugging your white wine and letting everyone know that you're having a miserable time. Couldn't you just be supportive for once?" he hissed.

Victoria thought he looked like a yappy dog when he got

mad. His small mouth and almost invisible lips seemed to snap up and down the way some irritating rat-dog's would.

"I am supportive. I go, don't I?" she seethed. "Unlike you, I may add. You never showed up at *my* work events, and now you never show up at any events for the school or the boys or anything. Unless of course there's some VIP there that you need to *dazzle*." She said the last word with utter contempt.

I like to dazzle my clients. That was Justin's selling point when he was trying to lure a young actor or actress into his fold. *Let me dazzle you.* He had said that to Victoria when he proposed to her. Dazzle was Justin's way of closing the deal.

Justin looked over at Victoria and glared, then pressed down harder on the accelerator. She could be such a bitch sometimes. Most of the time. Like she was on the rag every day of the goddamn week. He didn't need that crap. She should kiss his ass. He'd thought she was a classy broad when he married her, but now he wasn't so sure. Wouldn't someone with manners and class attempt to be polite at parties?

"You can be so charming, Victoria, when you want to be. Couldn't you try to do that tonight?" he asked finally.

"We'll see," she answered.

"You know what? Don't talk to me all night. Just stay away from me," he said.

"With pleasure," she said, a small smile finally coming to her finely glossed lips. That was an order she could obey.

The house was a sprawling Mediterranean that took up every inch of the less-than-one-acre property it sat on, except for a small strip of yard that had a patio. Valets ran up to their car and helped them out as briskly as firemen escorting victims from a burning building. Justin, seeing people that he knew pull up in a

Mercedes behind them, held out his hand for Victoria and put on a big smile as he led her up the stairs to the front door. Appearances, must keep up appearances.

The door, as was customary at these events, was opened not by the host but by a caterer, who offered mineral water or white wine and then sent them on their merry way into the living room to fend for themselves. There was little formality at these parties; sometimes guests didn't even see the man or woman of the house the entire evening. Most people came in with an agenda and already knew who they wanted to talk to, how long they wanted to stay, and who they wanted to walk with to the door, and left little margin for surprises. Justin, who was more adept at scanning a room than a Secret Service agent, immediately located the reason he was there—Hadley Whitaker, a twenty-three-year-old blonde who had just unexpectedly won the female lead in George Clooney's next movie and who was currently between agents—and set off to introduce himself, leaving Victoria alone without so much as a word. It didn't matter; she was used to this, and actually she preferred to maneuver through these parties by herself.

It never intimidated her to be left alone, and it amused her how some of the other wives and women she knew panicked when that happened. They looked like fools. Victoria knew that her confidence prevented anyone from regarding her with pity. People in L.A. were so lame that she was often glad not to have to interact with them, and it was fun for her to analyze everyone from afar. It was amusing to her that she and Justin could be at the same place and if they were to discuss it later, he would have noticed only what stars or movers and shakers were there, whereas Victoria would be able to give a complete description of the main rooms of the house and inform her husband who was now sleeping with whom, based on the subtle body language and eye contact that she had been witness to. It was to her benefit that Justin didn't ever pick up on any of those sorts of signals. He was so self-involved that if he was at a dinner talking to someone he wanted to impress, a couple could be copulating next to him and he wouldn't notice.

Victoria sighed as she walked along the west side of the room, toward the windows, taking in the decor as she strode. The owners of the house were clearly enamored of the Gothic style, probably Tim Burton fans, she surmised, and had spared little expense putting together every piece of Gothic furniture that they could get their hands on. The side chairs scattered around the room were heavy mahogany pieces with intricate undulating curved designs, and the large sofa was an incised oak piece covered in a very pretentious cabernet silk damask. All of the furniture was that dark, heavy wood that should feel sturdy and yet somehow managed to appear completely uncomfortable. But like set designers, the owners had committed themselves to the time period. There were few lamps, and instead candles flickered in a plethora of bronze candelabras mounted in the wall, spliced between the four large mahogany mirrors that captured their dancing reflections. Victoria could never live there, and yet she wondered if she would be happy anywhere.

Her life was not going the way she wanted it to. Well, that wasn't completely true; she did have her boys. And she loved her boys; first and foremost, she loved the fact that she had boys. She could never have dealt with girls. They were too moody, too whiny, too clingy, and if that wasn't enough, one day you'd have to tie their legs together so you wouldn't become a grandmother at forty-five. No, girls were not for her. In fact, she'd always been a boys' girl, never going in for that Hello Kitty crap. Everyone said that boys were more difficult to raise when they were young because they were so active, but then they were much easier when they were older because they didn't hate you. But Victoria felt as though her boys were easy now. Austin was a natural athlete who at age two could throw a ball better than most six-year-olds. She already had talked his way into Peewee Hoopsters even though the age requirement was three, and he was excelling. And Hunter had started to read. Yes. No one believed her, but he had. She'd known he was brilliant when, at seven months, he picked up a book that was upside down and turned it around to look at it. That's advanced. Some mothers don't know that, but they don't read up on that stuff the way Victoria did. As soon as she'd found out she was pregnant she ordered every well-regarded baby hand-book on Amazon and pored over them all as if they were chem-istry textbooks. If she was going to be a mother, she was going to be the *best* mother, just like she had been the best junior execu-tive at Fox. Her encyclopedic knowledge of motherhood had en-abled her to identify every benchmark that her sons breezed past way ahead of schedule. But she couldn't really brag about that to anyone—all those mothers were so *sensitive.* They were raising pussies. They were so worried that little Jack would get a bruise that they didn't teach him how to put his fists together and fight back. There would be no wimps on Victoria's watch. No sirree.

But Hunter and Austin aside, the rest of Victoria's life was like a wild mushroom wilting and shriveling in the sun. In fact, it was getting messy and dangerous, and she was nervous—and nervousness was not something Victoria was used to experienc-ing. She never ruminated about the choices she had made, be-cause she was not impulsive or emotional by nature. And if the outcome wasn't what she had planned, she never questioned the reasons that she had made the choices that led her there. Victoria was decisive and did what she wanted. If she realized later that she hated her job or the man in her life was a jerk, she didn't make herself miserable by wallowing in "Why me?" self-pity. She did something about it.

But now, as she walked along the long wall of glass doors at the back of the living room and looked out at the view of the hills dappled with lit-up mansions, she was worried. It was perhaps the first time that she began to question her decision. Why had she let this man into her life? He was making her miserable, threatening to ruin everything she had built, and, worst of all, made her doubt herself and her taste. She had been increasingly despondent over the past few months and was on the verge of asking her friends for help. And for Victoria, whose greatest pride was her self-sufficiency, this concept was anathema. She was a grown woman! She didn't want anyone to feel sorry for her, or to see any cracks in her armor. Yes, Eliza, Helen, and Leelee were her friends, but could you ever really trust your friends? And even if she did, would she want them to pity her? It made her shudder. But the other night, just when she was about to break down, a brilliant idea came to Victoria, and now she realized that she didn't really have to tell her friends anything. She would enlist them, and they would all plunge forward as a team on equal footing.

·· 5 ··

While Victoria was whiling her time away at a party in Bel Air, Helen was sweating out a day's worth of yogurt and granola at a Bikram yoga class. As she twisted from pose to pose in the ninety-five-degree room, she felt the toxins in her body stream out of her and evaporate into the air. It was a nice way to cleanse herself, and to expunge any negativity that she had subsumed during the day. After class was over, Helen remained on her mat for an extra ten minutes, not yet willing to give up her relaxation pose. This was the state in which she was most content. If she could always be half asleep in a deep meditation, life would be so much easier.

"You okay?" asked Lisa, her teacher. She was a young blond woman with a boy's body who was prone to deep, penetrating looks.

Helen opened her eyes. "Yes."

"I hate to interrupt you, but we've got to lock up now. I think you fell asleep there."

"Really?" asked Helen, sitting up. The room was empty, and Lisa had already blown out her candles and extinguished the incense.

"Yeah, class ended about twenty minutes ago, but I could tell you were really in a space so I didn't want to disturb you," said Lisa.

"Sorry about that," said Helen, rising and rolling up her mat.

"No prob. I love it when people really feel the energy. I could tell you were totally vibing tonight."

"Yeah, I guess I was."

Helen put on her sweatshirt and hooked her mat under her arm, then walked over to open up the door. Lisa followed and turned out the lights behind them. They walked outside and said good-bye, and Helen felt the warm July air caress her body. Yoga made her feel so much more in touch with everything around her. And yet . . . it also made her feel as if she was so far apart from everything that was really close to her.

Helen turned her Lincoln Navigator onto Sunset and confidently guided it toward her house, which was located on one of the prime streets in the poshest section of the Palisades, known as The Riviera. When she had met Wesley, Helen was living in a small, run-down Hacienda apartment in Hollywood and could never have imagined that one day she'd reside in an enormous, modern white structure with walls of glass that showcased stunning 360-degree views of the city and the ocean. The onetime apprentice of an exceedingly famous architect, who unlike his mentor never achieved fame, had designed the house. Perhaps because of his inability to master scale, the public rooms were enormous but the sleeping rooms were as small as jewelry boxes. And the house itself, like most Los Angeles residences, took up the majority of the property, aggressively cannibalizing the lawn with purely decorative white walls that abruptly dead-ended. On the east side there was a sliver of space just big enough for a small lap pool that neither Helen nor Wesley ever set foot in, and a Japanese garden replete with a koi pond and a statue of Buddha that was meticulously maintained by three Guatemalan gardeners.

When Helen pulled into her driveway she saw a Jeep Wrangler parked next to her husband's car and knew that Andy was over. Andy was a recent friend of Wesley's, someone Wesley had met and quickly bonded with on a hiking trail. Hiking was Wesley's obsession, one that had progressed from a once-a-month activity into a daily adventure. The first few times Helen had gone with Wesley but had quickly grown tired of it. Sure, it was nice to look around at the beautiful scenery and digest nature, but it felt ultimately pointless to Helen. You go up, then you come down. There was something futile about that. But Wesley was a totally committed enthusiast—in part, Helen believed, to avoid dealing with his career. But then again, he had so much money, he didn't really have to. Maybe that was the problem.

When Helen entered her Asian-meets-Palm-Springs-in-the-1950s-inspired living room, she was confronted by a powerful smell of what are sometimes called "funny-smelling cigarettes."

Wesley was seated on the shag rug, leaning against the slate gray Dunbar sofa. Helen glanced down from the back of his bald head and saw that he was wearing an untucked button-down shirt, khakis that were shredded at the bottom, and no shoes. Andy sat across from him, also on the floor. Even though it was a warm night, the fire was going.

"Hey, Helen," said Andy, popping up off the Moroccan throw pillow and coming over to give her a big kiss. He always kissed her, she had noticed. If she left the room even for a few minutes, he found some excuse to come over and re-greet her and plant another wet one on her. Wesley didn't seem to observe or care, so she didn't make a big deal of it, but it was sort of weird. Not that Wesley would ever suspect that she was interested in Andy, and she wasn't really. She usually liked very lean men with small features, and mostly blonds, which was funny, considering Wesley was neither. Andy was about ten years younger than Wesley and was a big guy in shape, but with a slight belly that could easily be eliminated if he didn't eat or drink so much. And he had longish floppy brown hair and big bushy eyebrows. He looked kind of like a giant puppy that jumps up and slobbers all over you when you walk in the door.

"Hey, Andy," said Helen. She glanced over at Wesley, whose lips were parted as he took a huge drag of marijuana, and saw the bags of Veggie Booty and realized that Andy had been there for a while. Although a film editor by trade, Andy was a pothead by vocation. He didn't deal, but he didn't turn down money for his "fine Colombian friend" when Wesley offered it to him. And it seemed as though lately they had been doing a lot of smoking.

"How was yoga?" asked Wesley, taking a deep breath.

"It was great," said Helen. "I think I'll go shower."

"Want some?" asked Andy, holding the joint out to Helen.

She paused. She wasn't against the occasional toke but she was really enjoying the ride her endorphins were giving her after yoga and hated to compromise that sensation.

"No thanks," she said finally.

In the shower, Helen thought about her plans for the next week. She wanted to do yoga every day, and her friend Amy had said that there was a really good core fusion teacher coming to town from Seattle and she'd host a workshop at her house, so she was definitely on board for that. She also wanted to go to Manhattan Beach and photograph the smokestacks, because she really sensed a place for them in her new photo collage. She was compiling pictures of things that were so ugly that they were pretty, a project her photo teacher had suggested and that really excited her. But as she progressed, she realized that everything in L.A. was so ugly it was pretty. It was like examining a bruise. At first you shudder, but then you see the purple, blue, and red colors under the flesh and find beauty in it. But only if you look really hard. At quick glance, it's hideous. Same with L.A. In fact, it kind of made her eyes sore to think how ugly this town was.

Helen's mind briefly flickered on her daughter, Lauren, and then immediately moved on. Lauren, age seven, was a beautiful, sweet, and precocious child. But it was clear from the start that she was a daddy's girl. Helen didn't even try to compete. She knew Wesley was a better parent. She had not had a good example in that department so was ill equipped. Better to let Wesley take care of her.

"Sorry," said Andy.

Helen spun around. She had gotten out of the shower and was drying herself off, and didn't hear the door open. She immediately held the towel over her body.

"It's okay," she said. She waited for Andy to leave. But he

didn't. He stood there staring at her through the steam, his eyes watering slightly, his face unreadable.

"You're beautiful, you know that?" he asked. His tone was neutral, not accusatory, not scandalous, just sort of factual. Helen didn't know how to respond.

"Thank you," she managed.

She should probably be freaking out and demand that he leave the bathroom. The situation was all so weird: her husband was in the next room and was Andy coming on to her? But somehow she felt weighted down and didn't want anything to happen. There was no sense of urgency, no sense of fear, just a desire to play out the scene but allow someone else to be the director.

"I guess I'll go," said Andy finally, but remaining motionless.

"Okay," said Helen.

He paused another second and cocked his head to the side as if he were going to say something else, but then he stepped back and closed the door, leaving Helen alone. Helen turned and wiped off the steamed mirror with her hand until she could see her face. She didn't feel beautiful. And she wasn't really attracted to Andy. But it was exciting to her that he had said that. Something inside her started to flutter, a sensation she hadn't felt in a long time. And she suddenly felt as if she were coming alive.

When she'd finally dressed she decided not to return to the living room, instead reading her book and waiting until she heard the front door close and Andy's car drive away. Before Wesley entered the bedroom, Helen had turned off the lights and closed her eyes.

"**So how much** can we put you down for, Leelee?"

Ashley Windham cocked her perfect oval face to the side and gazed at Leelee with her bright blue long-lashed eyes. Leelee stared at Ashley's hand, in which she held a solid gold Tiffany pen that was poised and ready to take down a notation in her pink leather Kate Spade notebook, and blinked. Leelee wanted to say three thousand like Emily, or five thousand like Meredith or even a thousand like Brooke, but she couldn't. She was maxed out. There was no way she could buy more than two tickets for the ovarian cancer lunch. Just no way.

"I'll take two tickets," said Leelee finally. Three hundred and fifty dollars. That's still a lot, Leelee wanted to scream as she watched Ashley write down the number in her bubble handwriting. Three hundred and fifty dollars for a plate of leaves, a small piece of grilled chicken breast, and a scoop of sorbet that no one would touch even if she wanted to. She knew it was going to a good cause, but Leelee could really use that money. She could pay her cell phone, TiVo, and dry cleaning bills for a month with that money. Or she could sign Charlotte up for baby cooking classes for an entire session. Or she could get one Jimmy Choo shoe and not have to buy the rip-off Banana Republic version. It was so demoralizing.

"Great, so now let's go over items for the silent auction," said Ashley, wiping a wisp of her white blond hair out of her eyes.

Leelee felt herself panic. The silent auction. More money to cough up. She was in over her head. The problem was that everyone *assumed* Leelee had a lot more money than she did, because she was a Swift. Leelee Swift Adams. She never failed to mention her maiden name. *"Yes, that's Swift, like the toaster."* Her great-grandfather, Branson R. Swift, had been the founder of Swift Industries, the man who revolutionized the method of attaining hot bread as we know it. Leelee was in the *Social Register.* She was a Daughter of the American Revolution. She grew up in a rambling town house in Boston, summered in "the Vineyard," attended a preppy boarding school and college, and took a semester in Australia. Her family kept up all appearances, but the fact was, they had no connection to the mammoth conglomerate that Swift Industries had become, and no money to speak of. Her father had been a spoiled dilettante whose less than prudent business decisions and general distaste for scheduled labor had rendered the family virtually penniless. Houses were mortgaged, club dues paid out of a minimal trust fund that her mother had received from a benevolent aunt, and costs kept to a minimum. No, there was no extra money to be thrown around at a charity lunch.

"Before we do that, y'all, I have some great news," said Brooke in her enthusiastic Charleston, South Carolina, accent. Brooke moved her eyes across every committee member's face, making sure that she had everyone's complete attention. "My super-duper hubby has gotten his dear friend and motorcycle buddy Jay Leno to agree to be the auctioneer for the live auction part of our event. Can y'all deal? How great is that?"

It was *great,* everyone agreed. It was so fantastic that it unleashed ten solid minutes of superlatives and praise directed toward Brooke, her husband, Trip, and his dear friend Jay Leno. Take that, breast cancer benefit committee members! The ovarian cancer benefit would kick your benefit's butt! The conversation then digressed into what should be the live auction item. Ashley said her husband could probably secure a golf game with Michael Douglas and Catherine Zeta-Jones. "They owe him a favor" is how she phrased it. Meredith chipped in a round-trip flight to New York aboard her private jet. Other women added jewelry from Harry Winston, a weekend at the Four Seasons Punta Mita, and season tickets to the Hollywood Bowl. Then it was Leelee's turn.

"Gosh, I'll have to brainstorm," said Leelee. She had been planning on asking Burke Williams to donate a massage gift certificate, but now that seemed so lame.

"Maybe Brad can get something from work?" asked Ashley, a perfectly groomed eyebrow raised.

"Maybe," said Leelee softly. "I'll definitely ask him."

But she would not ask him. It would be a waste of time. She already knew the answer: he had nothing to offer. He had no connections, no access to anything remotely glamorous, and nothing that anyone would bid on at a charity auction emceed by the king of nighttime.

"Hey, aren't you friends with the Porters? Maybe you could ask Senator Porter for tickets to the Democratic Convention?" asked Meredith suddenly.

Yes! The Porters! Why hadn't she thought of that? "Of course, I could. The Porters are dear, dear family friends. Jack and I are like . . . brother and sister. We e-mail *every single day.*"

Jack Porter, son of Senator and Mrs. Ward Porter (D, Rhode Island). The man Leelee was supposed to have married. Her mother had wanted it, his mother had wanted it, and Leelee had wanted it. The only person who hadn't wanted it was Jack.

"I'll ask Jack today," said Leelee with a smile. And it was the first time all day that she felt good about herself.

That night, after distractedly feeding her daughters, Charlotte and Violet, chicken nuggets (organic), tater tots, and lima beans, Leelee planted them in the living room, flipped on *Dora the Explorer,* and wheeled out their enormous Barbie camper so that she would have time to clean the kitchen in peace. She set up her little iPod speakers in the kitchen and turned on her eighties beach party mix, then hummed along to the songs that had carried her through her angst-filled teenage years while washing the dishes. They had a dishwasher, but sometimes Leelee liked to spend the extra time soaking her hands in the warm, soapy water and washing the delicate Tiffany plates that she'd gotten for her wedding and insisted on using even when they didn't have company. Because the fact was, on their budget, they couldn't really afford to have company, not to mention that they didn't have the space. Their house was cute but tiny (the Realtor had called it "charming"), and rather than opting for a dining room Brad had insisted that they use the extra space for a TV and play area for the kids. It made more sense, but it still frustrated Leelee that she had to live in a compromised state.

Brad was working late, as usual, and it didn't even bother Leelee anymore. It meant that she could put the girls to bed, chat on the phone, eat dinner on a tray in the family room, and watch all the reality shows that her husband loathed. She didn't even miss his presence, especially lately, when his moods were increasingly gloomy. Brad now was not the man she married. She had met him at a graduation party. She had just majored in political science at Trinity and Brad was a friend of the hostess's older brother. She would never have given Brad the time of day if Jack had not just shown up at her graduation and whispered in her ear that he had just eloped with his anorexic, silly blond socialite girlfriend, Tierney Harris, subsequently smashing Leelee's heart into a million pieces. But then there was Brad. Standing by the keg in a white button-down shirt and a blue Patagonia vest, smiling his genuine white-toothed grin at Leelee. She was intrigued, and became even more so when she learned that he had quit his job at Morgan Stanley and founded an Internet company, Birthday Reminder1.com, which was now worth an estimated five hundred million dollars. That night they had sex in a broom closet with sound effects so loud that a small group gathered outside the door and applauded them when they finally emerged. They were married six months later in a lavish wedding on the Vineyard replete with fireworks and a cameo appearance by Aerosmith. When Brad carried Leelee over the threshold of their new 7,000-square-foot loft in Tribeca, she thought she was the happiest woman on earth.

And then it happened. The dot bomb. Leelee had literally been shopping for private jets when Brad called her and told her to come home, and when she did, he told her that he had lost everything. *Everything.* He was mortgaged and leveraged and everything else, and was not actually really rich but something she learned was a "paper millionaire," which meant he had nothing. Brad collapsed in tears on the floor of their indoor basketball court and begged for Leelee's forgiveness but she could not help him. She was furious. If she had not been eight months pregnant with Charlotte, she would have left him. She had always sworn to herself that she would never be like her parents. She never wanted to be one of the have-nots, one of the people constantly "keeping up with the Joneses." She had seen how her mother regarded her father with disgust; she had been subjected to years of her mother's disparaging comments and petty remarks about her dad, or the neighbors, or anyone who had money or who had somehow wronged her mother in reality or her imagination, and she swore she wouldn't do that. But when it took Brad a year and a half to find a job, and it turned out that it was in *Los Angeles,* a place where they had no connections and no friends, and they had to move into a rental on an Alphabet Street north of Sunset in the Palisades, Leelee couldn't help herself.

She felt wronged. She felt as if Brad were no longer a man. And he knew it, and she knew he knew it. And all she could do was try to build a life for them so that they wouldn't appear so desperate. Leelee asked her mother to ship her whatever antiques were in her parents' attic, and then took her small decorating budget and painted her walls in citrus colors courtesy of Ralph Lauren paint and invested in some well-upholstered furniture, and ultimately just made sure everyone knew that the rental was temporary until they decided what part of town they really wanted to live in, because not being native Angelinos they had no idea where they would end up. Leelee hosted trunk shows for baby clothes to make extra money, and Brad toiled away at some low-level banking job in equity sales or something boring like that—Leelee didn't even know or understand—and they lived their facade. And in the land where everyone was friends with movie stars and had estates in Hawaii, all that remained to separate Leelee from her pals was her friendship with the Porters. That was her claim to fame. And Jack Porter, who had always captured Leelee's heart and imagination, became her *everything*.

·· 7 ··

"Eliza Ryan."

Eliza felt a hand on the back of her arm and heard a somewhat familiar man's voice call her by her maiden name. When she turned around to see who it was, she was unprepared to see Greg Matthews, her high school English teacher. She finally knew what the phrase "blast from the past" meant, because she felt as if she had been hit by a large gust of wind and she wasn't sure if she would be able to remain standing.

"Mr. Matthews," she said. It was the first thing out of her mouth, and she kind of sputtered. She was always disconcerted when she ran into past lovers.

"Greg," he said with a smile. It had been fifteen years, but he had barely changed. The only difference was that his full head of dark hair, which was still a little too long around the ears and the back, just as it had been then, was now flecked with gray. His eyes, those brilliant eyes, were the same. They were large and blue and full of humor, the type of eyes that you could see across the room and that would stand out in a group photo.

"Greg, how are you? What are you doing here? Do you live in L.A.?" asked Eliza, the words all stumbling out at once. Greg Matthews. She had always wondered what happened to him. And now here he was, standing by the bathrooms on a Thursday night at the Brentwood, a darkly lit, noisy restaurant off Sunset Boulevard. She was glad she had worn her black skirt. It showed off her legs. She'd almost worn pants, but luckily she'd changed her mind.

Greg smiled. He still had a sheepish grin, which was even sexier now that his face had some age. "No, I don't live here, I'm just here for a conference at UCLA. I'm staying with friends," he said, his eyes locked on Eliza's. He was always able to do that, keep his eyes on a person until they felt embarrassed, as if he had penetrated their soul. "My wife and I are staying," he added.

Maybe she was reading into it, but he seemed a little embarrassed, or uncomfortable, maybe, mentioning his wife. And even though Declan was sitting at a table ten feet away with their friends Marshall and Stephanie, Eliza felt a pang when he said it. *His wife.* Mr. Matthews had married.

"A conference?" she asked, recovering. "What kind . . . ?" she trailed off. She didn't want to appear too eager to know the details of his life, but she was eager.

"I'm an English professor now, at Williams, in Massachusetts," he said.

"I know where Williams is," she said, and immediately wished she hadn't. She sounded so childlike. *Call on me, me, Mr. Matthews! I know the answer.*

He smiled. "Yes, well, it's a teachers' conference, actually, on Faulkner."

"That's great. And is your wife a teacher also?" she asked. He looked like a New England professor, but he had always dressed that way. Eliza took a closer look at his tweed blazer and wondered if it was the same one he had worn all those years ago. Even the blue checked button-down looked familiar. God, how she had analyzed his clothes. He'd seemed so grown up and cool when he stood in front of the class and talked about poetry.

"No, she's a stay-at-home mom," he said. Was he embarrassed about that? wondered Eliza. He'd said it kind of quickly.

"How many kids do you have?" asked Eliza, reddening. Why did she feel weird that he had kids?

"Two boys. Eight and six," he said. "But what about you? Do you live here?"

She filled him in on her life, how she wrote for magazines, had two kids, lived in L.A. ("You can't beat the weather"), and then they fell silent.

"Well, are you going in?" she said finally, motioning toward the men's room.

"No, no, heading back to the table."

"Okay, 'cause I'm gonna pop in here," she said, motioning

toward the women's room. "But stop by on your way out. I'd love to meet your wife."

"Sure, will do," he said, his eyes remaining on Eliza. The music seemed to get louder and the lights darker, and Eliza was suddenly seized with the most incredible urge to turn back the clock and be back in high school, when you were allowed to have crushes and had no responsibility. But that was impossible.

"And Eliza, you look great. Exactly the same," he said, before he turned and walked back toward his wife.

When Eliza returned to her table, Declan was in the middle of a story, so she sat quietly and let her thoughts travel. She was so curious about Mrs. Matthews. She couldn't wait to see her. Was she blond? Probably. What if she was young and gorgeous? That would really be a bummer. She needed a visual. Who was the woman who captured the heart of Eliza's first real love? The last time she had seen Greg, well, she couldn't even remember what happened, really. But it had all ended terribly. Eliza's boyfriend at the time, Danny, had found out that Eliza and Mr. Matthews were having an affair. In retribution for being cuckolded, he threatened exposure. So Mr. Matthews turned himself in and left the school, ending his relationship with Eliza. And now here he was.

She remembered the first time she knew that he liked her in a romantic way. It was subtle, but so exciting! Why couldn't those beginning moments remain in relationships? She longed for the fluttering stomach, the heart leaping when the man comes into view. It was like that then. It had been a chilly fall night, typical weather in suburban Chicago, and she found herself leaving the library at the same time as Mr. Matthews. She sensed somehow that it wasn't an accident. They were walking along, hands stuffed in their pockets, trying not to slide on the icy sidewalk, when he brought up something she had said in class:

"Why do you like T. S. Eliot?" he asked suddenly, looking at her with his head cocked to the side.

"T. S. Eliot? Oh, well, I don't really like everything he wrote, but I like a lot. My favorite is 'The Love Song of J. Alfred Prufrock.' "

"What do you like about it?" he asked.

Eliza was about to give one of her pat answers, but then she stopped and thought before she spoke. He wasn't the type of person you gave a standard answer to. He would understand. "I like that one part, just that one part, where he says, 'I'm no prophet and here's no great matter, but I have seen the moment of my greatness flicker, and I have seen the eternal footman hold my coat and snicker, and in short I was afraid.' "

Mr. Matthews stopped and looked at Eliza carefully. The wind blew a few wisps of her shoulder-length hair into her left eye, which she distractedly pushed back and hooked behind her ear. He gazed up at the sky, as if he was thinking about something hard, and then looked back at Eliza again.

"What is it about that part that you like, Eliza?" he asked finally.

It seemed as though he was asking a different question from the one he was actually asking. Eliza felt as if she had just revealed something so intimate to him, something that she never had told her family, her friends, or even Danny. Especially Danny. She somehow felt more exposed and naked than she had when she lost her virginity, and yet it was so much more exhilarating.

"It's just a perfect way to say that we are all vulnerable . . . that life is ephemeral . . . that death is scary, and we are small," she said, pulling up her collar around her neck. She suddenly felt chilled. "I like that when I read it, I feel like I want to do something different

*and special, and not live my life out in a generic suburb of a Mid-
western city. There's so much motion in that poem, 'through the rooms
the women come and go, talking of Michelangelo'... I mean, I
know people ascribe all that latent homosexuality to parts and make
a big deal about the peach, but I just like that it takes its time, and
people are going somewhere."*

*Eliza rambled, but she didn't think she'd sounded dumb. She
felt honest, and happy that she was finally able to speak her mind in
front of Mr. Matthews. And there was something about the way he
asked her what she was thinking or what she thought that was so different from the way Danny asked her. It was so much more mature
and intelligent.*

*Mr. Matthews closed his eyes tightly and then opened them. His
eyelashes seemed endless. "You're right, Eliza."*

*Before they could say anything else, they heard the cracking of
leaves, and a large panting yellow Lab came up to them, followed by
an elderly man holding its leash.*

"Eliza," she heard him say.

"Eliza?" asked Mr. Matthews again, and suddenly she was
back in Brentwood, and married to Declan, and Mr. Matthews
was at her table, standing next to a very thin, mousy, brown-
haired woman who wore unfashionable glasses and had bad pos-
ture. Thank God—she was ugly! Was that so mean? Maybe, but
if he had shown up with a fox she would have been tortured.

"This is Linda," he said. "Linda, Eliza was my student."

They made their introductions, and she was pleased to discover that Linda had a limp handshake, another mark against her.
But why did she care? Eliza watched carefully as Greg leaned
across the table to shake hands with Declan. She didn't know
what she was expecting, but she sort of wanted Greg to pull
Declan up and punch him out, to grab Eliza and say, "This is *my*

woman!" and carry her off, but he did nothing, obviously. And with a blink, he had once again left Eliza's life.

Declan returned to conversation with their friends, and Eliza was astounded that he didn't even comprehend the gravity of the moment. She had never told him of her affair and was always secretly mortified by it. She'd slept with a teacher! She was supposed to be a good girl! But she realized with horror that she was now older than Mr. Matthews had been when they had an affair. God, time goes quickly! And it was disconcerting to see her old lover, because she didn't especially feel anything for him—just for herself and all the years that had disappeared. The fact that most of life's questions were answered for her made her sad. She knew who she'd be married to, what her kids' names would be, where she'd live. Was that it? Was she never to experience love pangs again? And then she thought of the words of T. S. Eliot's poem: *I have seen the moment of my greatness flicker, and I have seen the eternal footman hold my coat and snicker, and in short, I was afraid.* And she was. She was very afraid.

·· *8* ··

The second Girls' Night Out that Victoria organized took place at Giorgio Baldi, a dimly lit celebrity-laden Italian restaurant right off the Pacific Coast Highway but with no view of the ocean. The food was delicious and the movie star spottings even more remarkable, which made it the perfect choice for a night away from husbands who always admonished their wives for gawking. (All except Justin, who actually stared at celebs even more than Victoria, who couldn't care less about famous people the more she met them.) Since the restaurant was technically in

Santa Monica, just down the hill from the Palisades, they decided to carpool, and Helen picked everyone up on her way.

They were shown to a table in the back corner, where Eliza and Leelee seated themselves on the banquette and Helen and Victoria took the chairs opposite. One quick scan of the room found Pierce Brosnan in the front, seated right next to the Spielbergs. The ladies discreetly noticed them but pretended not to, since being obvious would be tacky. They were now Angelinos, no need for ogling. Hell, their kids went to school with celebrities' kids and they saw Golden Globe winners in the grocery store. Except, no matter how cool and casual they should be about their sightings, they were excited nonetheless. Fame was such a drug nowadays that every little hit made a difference.

All four of the ladies looked their best tonight, freshly showered and a bit sunburned even though they were vigilant with the SPF 15. Eliza had her hair back in a sleek ponytail and wore a seafoam-colored short-sleeved cashmere sweater over a white eyelet skirt. Helen wore a diaphanous emerald top with light sequins over low-rise white jeans and had on dazzling hanging colored stone earrings. Leelee was wearing one of her ubiquitous tunics, this one a Tory Burch, in dark purple and black, over black Capri pants. And Victoria had on a royal blue sweater and low-rise jeans. After they had placed their orders and each had a glass of wine, Victoria got down to business.

"Okay, ladies, I have a plan," began Victoria, watching with disapproval as Leelee broke off a piece of bread. She would never say anything, but she really believed Leelee needed to watch what she ate. She wasn't fat, exactly, but she definitely had some extra pounds poking through that could so easily be shed if she would just take her up on her offer and come to kickboxing with her in Venice.

"We're ready," said Eliza, dusting some breadstick crumbs off the paper tablecloth in front of her.

"Hey, nice nails," said Helen, grabbing Eliza's hand. "Mademoiselle?"

"Fed Up, actually," Eliza said with a smile, referring to her choice of nail color. "I finally had a chance to hit the nail salon."

"Oh my God, I so need a manicure," said Leelee, holding up her bitten-down nails. "But who has the time?"

"I ruin them the second I'm out the door of the nail place," said Helen.

"That's why I don't do red anymore. Fed Up is natural," said Eliza.

"I just remember when I was pregnant the first time, I'd get mani-pedis every week. I had, like, nothing else to do. And now it's like a chore," said Leelee. She always talked about how busy she was, how she was *so* overwhelmed and crazed, yet none of her friends could figure out what was so taxing. Sure, she had two kids, but they all had two kids (except Helen, who had one). But Leelee somehow seemed to have a harder time balancing—at least, that was the only thing they could come up with.

Victoria waited patiently while they all discussed their nails. She picked up the wine and started to refill glasses, until the waiter rushed over and took the bottle out of her hands to finish the job. The ladies stopped their discussion until he was done, then remembered that Victoria had gathered them there for a reason.

"Sorry, Vic, what did you have to tell us?" asked Eliza.

Victoria put her fingers on the edge of the table and pressed down lightly. Her bangles came clanging down her toned and tanned arm and stopped at her Cartier watch. "Okay, before I begin, I want to make sure that what I am about to say will be met with utter and complete open-mindedness and that you promise to hear me out," she said sternly.

The rest of the ladies looked at one another and nodded. Victoria noticed Leelee suppress a slight giggle and felt her blood boil. Of all of her friends, Victoria was most worried about Leelee in terms of foiling her plan. Eliza was the hurdle, but once she was on board, she would be serious. Leelee, on the other hand, could be a problem. Leelee hid behind her humor, or maybe she was just incapable of anything more than topical conversation. It wasn't that Leelee was always goofy and silly; it was that she wasn't deep. Or at least she didn't allow herself to be deep.

"Are you gonna tell us or what?" said Helen impatiently.

"Okay, but drink more," said Victoria, filling their glasses up to the rim.

"Whoa, Nelly, I'm driving," said Helen.

"I'll drive," insisted Victoria.

"Victoria, are you trying to get us wasted so that you can have your way with us?" joked Leelee.

"Sort of," admitted Victoria.

"She wants to take us to bed!" Helen burst with a laugh.

"I knew it," said Leelee.

"Come on, I need you to be serious, people," said Victoria.

The waiter came over with a large plate of fried shiitake mushrooms with truffle-infused pecorino cheese, and the ladies paused to sample the fare.

"Oh my God, this is orgasmic," said Helen.

"Amazing," agreed Eliza.

Victoria watched as they oohed and aahed over the food and waited until they would return their attention to her. Finally, after several bites and moans of pleasure, they turned to Victoria.

"So what is this all about, Victoria?" asked Leelee. "Just spit it out."

"All right, I will. Look, the other night we were talking about how unhappy we are. Don't make that face, Eliza—we are . . ."

"I'm not unhappy," protested Eliza.

"Look, I don't mean we're all suicidal, but I think there is a deep sadness going on with all of us. There's an undercurrent of it. We are quote-unquote happy in our day-to-day lives, we have great, healthy kids, we have nice husbands—well, yours are—and we live a privileged existence where we can take nice vacations and go out to fancy restaurants. But the fact is, there is an unhappiness on another level—an existential level, if you will." The last point was for Helen's benefit, because that was the way to hook her. "We are closer to death. We know it. Didn't we all discuss how after the birth of each of our children we had panic attacks at night about death? And we consoled each other by saying it's the hormones, and we talked each other down, but the fear was very real."

All of the women stopped eating and stared at Victoria. They remembered those attacks. They had all suffered from them. It was a combination of new motherhood, sleep deprivation, exhaustion, and hormones. Whatever the cause, they had all spent several nights alone feeding a newborn or two newborns, seized by the terror of how short life is. Eliza said that it was the horror of the realization that her brand-new infant would one day die that disturbed her the most. Victoria remembered waking up after she had the twins and realizing that all the frivolity of her life had ebbed away and now she was chained to other human beings. Leelee still felt like a young girl, and after the birth of each of her daughters it dawned on her that she had said "till death do us part" in her vows. Lauren's birth had been traumatic for Helen. Her daughter was born with the umbilical cord around her neck, in a breech position, and it was touch and go for several hours. In fact, a resident was foolish enough to tell Helen not to get attached to the baby. Luckily Lauren had survived and was now a healthy young girl. But the resident's words never left Helen, and she was somehow unable to bond with her only child.

"Okay, Victoria, you're being really depressing," said Eliza.

"I don't want to be depressing. This is what I want to say. The other night when we were all complaining about being old and gray, I thought about how we are all in the throes of a midlife crisis. Don't look at me like I'm crazy, Leelee," snapped Victoria.

"Midlife crisis? Isn't that for forty-year-old men who run out and buy Maseratis?" asked Leelee, plucking a piece of bread from the basket and dipping it in olive oil.

"No, it isn't. Because what is the average life expectancy? Isn't it like seventy-something? So half that, and you get our age, early to midthirties. That is midlife. We're halfway done," said Victoria smugly.

"Okay, I thought we were going to have a nice, fun dinner, and now I need a razor to slash my wrists. Victoria!" wailed Eliza, taking a gulp of her wine.

Leelee patted Eliza on the hand. "Keep on drinking, honey."

"I think it's fascinating," said Helen, who was still deep in thought, processing. "It's true, we're halfway done."

"You see," said Victoria, nodding. "I'm right."

"So was this your big plan? To depress us?" asked Eliza.

"No, it's not."

The busboy came and took away the empty mushroom plate as the waiter placed each woman's appetizer in front of her. Eliza had cannelloni beans with lobster, Helen had a mixed green salad, Leelee had the langoustines, and Victoria had beef carpaccio with Parmesan shavings.

"Another bottle?" asked the waiter, holding up the empty wine bottle in his hands.

"Please." Victoria nodded.

"Yes, we're really going to need it," sighed Eliza.

When the waiter left, Victoria looked at her friends. The mood had changed. They were no longer festive but pensive. Good. They were ready. "So here's what I want to say," she began.

"Pray tell," said Leelee.

"Actually, for all of our morose whining about the state of our bodies and sexuality, we actually look really good. We're still young, we're fit"—she didn't look at Leelee when she said the last part—"and we're smart, sophisticated ladies. Yes, we have some cellulite and some grays, but in twenty years we'll look back and kick ourselves because we never realized how good we had it."

"All right, so you want us to be positive?" asked Helen. "This was just a little pep talk?"

"No," said Victoria. She glanced at all of them and leaned in. "I think we each should have an affair."

Leelee started to laugh, but when she saw that Victoria was serious she immediately stopped. Victoria hated to be laughed at. Eliza furrowed her brow in confusion, but only Helen took the news calmly.

"You're joking," said Eliza.

"I'm not," said Victoria. And for the first time that evening, she took a bite of food. She savored the raw meat in her mouth as she watched her friends digest her suggestion.

"Okay, so many levels going on here," said Eliza, smoothing

the placemat in front of her. "Not sure I follow you. You're saying we're about to die, but we're actually still young, or at least we look good, and we should cheat because we're old?"

"First of all, I hate the word *cheat*. I mean, really, who invented that? I prefer the term 'taking a lover.' It's very French. Look at Mitterand."

"We're not French," said Eliza.

Victoria rolled her eyes. Eliza was such a goody-goody. "That's irrelevant. The point I'm making is that marriage, as well as the laws of civilization, religion, and all of those ephemeral societal rules, are all relative. Things are in and then they are out. Like fashion. Every hundred years or so, it's a new thing. Remember, Henry the eighth really modernized divorce."

"By chopping off his wives' heads," said Eliza.

"Listen before speaking," said Victoria, exasperated. "I'm saying that it's unfortunate that we're living at a time when having sex with someone who is not your husband is frowned upon. It's not natural, if you think about it. If it was, we'd marry our spouse and never have any feelings for another man again."

"Just think, no one would go see Brad Pitt movies anymore," said Leelee.

"The box office would be dead," agreed Helen.

"Human nature cannot be made to constrict to the rules of fashion. Emotions can be constrained, but they really can't be controlled. Attraction is a chemical reaction. Hence love at first sight . . ." said Victoria. She knew it existed, and although she had never felt it, she was sure that the example would appeal to her target audience.

"We're married, we're not dead," said Helen.

"Excellent point," said Victoria, turning to Helen. "We're not dead. We have emotions. We have needs. And life is so fucking short, we need to fulfill these needs. It doesn't make us bad people. We deserve this."

"Do our husbands deserve this?" asked Eliza.

"They don't have to know," interjected Helen, before Victoria could answer.

"Yes, they deserve this," said Victoria. "Most of them take us for granted. They think it's just dandy that we have to opt out of the workforce, put our brain on hold, and raise their little rugrats. I mean, don't get me wrong, I love my boys, but I wonder why it was that *I* had to be the one to quit my job and take care of them. I would probably have made more money than Justin. Hell, I mean, I went to better schools. But no, he gets to go off and schmooze and wine and dine and make deals while I hold down the fort."

"Maybe you should just go back to work," suggested Eliza softly.

"Come on, you know that is not possible. Having it all is a lie. A lie! So if I can't have it all, and I'm not really having anything that is for me, why is it wrong to change that?" said Victoria heatedly.

"I definitely don't want to go back to work," said Leelee, trying to lighten the mood.

"Maybe not, but aren't you in a rut? Don't you see yourself in a holding pattern? Is there anything that really excites you anymore?" asked Victoria with hostility.

"My new headboard should be ready next week," offered Leelee lamely.

"See," said Victoria, pointing at Leelee. "How pathetic is that? A new fucking headboard. I mean, really. Has life come to this? There's nothing else to get us jazzed up but a stupid Ballard Designs headboard. We know it, our husbands know it. But we can do something about it. We can spice it all up. If we go out, get some action, feel good about ourselves, then when we come back to our marriage, it will be so much better."

"Yes, but then we will be racked with guilt, everyone will know, our husbands will be cuckolded . . ." said Eliza, shaking her head.

"Can you imagine those bitchy gossips at the club?" asked Leelee, nodding.

"Here's my plan," began Victoria with a commanding voice while flicking her flaxen hair behind her ear. When Victoria was *on*, she was *on*. She could be the most magnetic person in the room. There was a reason that women got nervous when their husbands were seated next to her at dinner parties. (Women at luncheons also got jealous when they *weren't* seated next to her.) "One of the biggest problems, the biggest, with having extramarital relations—I refuse to call it cheating, Eliza—is that someone always finds out. The reason is that the philanderer—usually the woman, because surprisingly men can be more discreet—has to tell someone. It makes the affair more titillating, and that's actually a third of the reason that we tell. The other part is guilt; it's the nature of the beast. And only our friends can assuage our fears. But if we are having affairs to feel coveted—as Eliza said the other night—well, you can't truly feel coveted unless you tell your best friend you were. It's human nature. So my proposal is that we all have affairs and we tell each other only."

"An infidelity pact?" asked Eliza, incredulous. But no one else appeared as fazed as she did.

"So, you mean like we cheat, with ground rules?" asked Helen.

"Not cheat, *have affairs*. Make ourselves happy. We have one year to do it. Relationship—or relationships, depending on what you want—have to be started and finished in one year. We don't sleep with each other's husbands—"

"Thank you," said Eliza, sarcastically.

"And we try to avoid psychos. But the most important thing is, we tell only each other."

"But—"

"Think about it as you would a spa treatment. You get your nails done, your bikini line waxed, your eyebrows plucked, your hair colored—all of that stuff to look good. When all you really need is a good fuck. You get that, your husband will be happy as a clam."

"You're insane . . ." interrupted Eliza.

"Shhh . . . I want you all to think about it for one minute. Literally one minute. I'll time you. Enjoy your appetizers," said Victoria, taking a bite of her carpaccio.

Helen had been thinking about having an affair for a while. In fact, Victoria knew this because one night after they'd had too many drinks at the Fourth of July party at the beach club, they had wandered down to the edge of the ocean, slipped off their shoes, dipped their feet in, and confessed how miserable they were to each other. Helen couldn't even attempt to comprehend the depths of her misery with Wesley. There was no rancor or nasty fights (unlike with Victoria and Justin), and no obvious sources of pain such as money problems or infidelity; there was just . . . indifference. When Helen married Wesley she knew what she was getting into: he was much older, and a repressed, conservative, somewhat uptight upper-class British lord. Those types are hardly renowned for their openness or effusiveness. But she thought she could handle his personality and what she perceived as shortcomings precisely because she was the opposite. Whereas Wesley would choose not to discuss something, avoiding testy topics and jokingly moving on when discussions turned contentious or revelatory, Helen dove in completely. She felt that her life journey—which is how she referred to it—was a personal quest for information, understanding, and, most of all, connection. But the more she pressed Wesley, the further he retreated. She knew he was frustrated with his career, and yet he wouldn't talk about it. She knew that his parents, who were now in their seventies, still irritated him immensely, and she suspected that one of the reasons was their opinion about his marrying her, a Korean American, but he wouldn't talk about them. She knew he must have dreams and goals, but he wouldn't talk about those either. The more she pushed, the more distant he became. Every conversation was topical, with doses of humor to lighten up a touchy subject. If she freaked out about something, he immediately did whatever he could to placate her. Maybe it was a British thing. But whatever the source, they were left living like formal acquaintances in their stark modern home, and Helen felt as if she was re-creating the childhood that she had loathed.

When a minute was up, Victoria raised her finger. "Okay."

"You are more outrageous than I thought," said Leelee, teasingly wagging her finger at Victoria. The question was, could *she* be that outrageous? Infidelity had never occurred to Leelee, but then, why not? But for her it wouldn't be with just anyone. It would have to be with Jack. It was Jack or nothing.

"The consequences would be too devastating. Someone would find out, and too many people would be hurt," said Eliza, looking at her friends, who, she was sure, would agree with her. She would never go there. It was fun to think about for a second, but that was it. And yes, she had thought about it when she saw Greg Matthews, but that had been in her mind. You can entertain a lot of possibilities in your mind—it's your actions that matter.

"I don't know. If we really agree not to tell anyone else . . ." said Helen, sliding her finger around the edge of her wineglass. "I mean, maybe it would make us happier and no one would get hurt in the long run."

"We'd have to be strategic about who we picked," said Leelee, excitement in her voice. "It can't just be Joe Schmo."

"It can be whomever we want," said Victoria. "We shouldn't make rules other than silence."

"And it can be more than one person," said Helen. "Like, maybe that way we don't make a real connection, one that would ruin our marriages."

"You guys, are you serious?" asked Eliza. She couldn't believe that her friends were actually entertaining the thought of committing infidelity. "This will never work. First of all, didn't we promise to love, honor, and cherish? We all took our vows."

"The divorce rate is more than fifty percent," said Victoria, matter of fact.

"Okay, well, look . . . yes, in theory this is an amazing idea. We all get our kicks and walk away unscathed. But that will never happen. Someone will get hurt," said Eliza.

"But maybe we're just hurting ourselves by not taking a chance. Do you want to be half dead?" asked Victoria.

"I don't feel half dead," protested Eliza.

"Listen, Eliza. Remember you had a crush on that actor you interviewed, Tyler Trask?" asked Helen, leaning in.

Tyler Trask. Eliza could barely hear his name without blushing. When she'd see his face plastered on the cover of some tabloid, she had to do everything in her power to avert her eyes. She just couldn't go there.

"What if you could get together with him?" continued Helen. "You said you had a connection."

"Oh, that was years ago," said Eliza. "I'm sure he's forgotten who I am. And maybe I was making it up. It was probably nothing."

But she knew she wasn't making it up. Tyler still invited her to his premieres and even left a message or two when he was in from Australia. Now that he had a baby with his girlfriend, she'd thought he would forget her, but he had sent her a postcard as recently as Christmas. It was a picture of San Fernando Valley in all its glory, a reference to a joke they'd had between them about the outer parts of L.A. He had written only *Wish you were here*.

"You know that's not true," said Helen.

"Yeah, remember the postcard?" asked Leelee.

Eliza never should have told them about the postcard. "Whatever. Okay, say I do go with Tyler and have this stormy affair. Then what? Am I really going to leave my husband for some movie star who has women at every port?"

"It's not about leaving our husbands," said Victoria. "It's about one year; it's about taking necessary, emergency steps to make ourselves feel like viable, attractive human beings. And the fact that we are all in it together, that we are making this pact to have relations with men other than our spouses, means that we will all look out for each other. If someone gets in too deep or someone needs advice or help or whatever, we are all there for each other," said Victoria with precision.

"Have some more wine," she then instructed, motioning to their glasses. "And take another moment to fantasize. Think about a life other than the one you have now. One that is less predictable, where you have some sense of excitement, one where you feel as though it *matters* if you look good, that you worked out." She said the last part for Eliza's benefit.

For a few minutes no one spoke; each was lost in her reverie.

The alcohol that Victoria was plying them with had the desired effect. It was a great equalizer, allowing desires and fears to coexist. And in the darkened romantic restaurant (a prescient choice by Victoria) it made all the women, even reluctant Eliza, feel dreamy. In their now hazy minds they had visions of themselves with other men. How nice it had been for Helen when the handsome new pottery teacher at the art center had wrapped his hands around hers to show her how to make an urn. She felt like Demi Moore in *Ghost*. She had wanted him to take that clay and spread it all over her body, to get down and dirty with him but in the most sensual and organic way, to coat each other with clay from the earth . . . Eliza thought about Tyler. He was the person who would be able to conjure up those emotions that she had suppressed for so long . . . Leelee thought of the man of her dreams, the one who had betrayed her terribly, and with the alcohol enhancing her imagination, she dreamed of a different outcome to her life.

Victoria knew what she was doing.

The busboy took away their appetizers and all the women kept their eyes on Eliza.

"I think it's our only chance, Eliza," said Helen.

"So you're in?" asked Victoria, turning to Helen for confirmation.

"Absolutely. I need to rejoin the world of the living," sighed Helen.

"What about you, Leelee?" asked Victoria.

Leelee glanced at all of them coyly. "Sure," she said, giggling. For tonight, anyway. This way she could dream about Jack with a little more hope than she usually did.

"What about you, Eliza?" asked Victoria.

"Guys, sorry, but no."

"Eliza, one day you'll realize that life is so short. We have only tiny moments cobbled together and then we are gone. You should enjoy it. If you want to feel coveted, then you *need* to feel coveted. Maybe what you need is not a physical affair but an emotional one. Maybe you just need a connection with another male," said Helen. She brought up life and death often, having learned early how inexorably linked they were.

"Don't make Eliza decide now. Let's talk about it tomorrow, after she's had a day of carpooling and grocery shopping," said Victoria.

Before Eliza could reply, Anson Larrabee, an acquaintance who lived in the Palisades, interrupted them. He was exactly the type of person who would be a great danger to the girls if he had heard any of their conversation from the past thirty minutes. Anson was a larger-than-life character in every sense. He stood six feet, four inches tall and had an enormous belly and a mop of blond hair on his head that was still thick even in his forty-seventh year of life. His voice was just as grand and booming as his body, and had a southern lilt to it. He was the town gossip, who reigned over the society column in the *Palisades Press* with his poison pen, and enjoyed lunching with ladies to find out the comings and goings of everyone in the neighborhood. Although his sexuality was dubious, he referred to the recent divorcées that he squired around town in his convertible Mercedes as his "lady friends," and he showered them with gifts until they moved on to someone else, no hard feelings. He was currently "dating" Imelda Rosenberg, Eurasian former restaurant hostess who had just left her husband, a high-ranking executive at Paramount. Actually, he had left her; when he found out she was sleeping with the tennis pro he threw all of her clothes out the front window of their house, which was right on Alma Real, where everyone could see. A minor scandal to say the least.

"Now this looks like a *fuuuun* dinner," said Anson with his Alabama accent. "I bet half of the ladies in the Palisades have ringing ears—no doubt you all are havin' one of your good old-fashion' bitchfests."

If it was meant to be funny, it fell flat. Eliza and Victoria exchanged an eye roll, and Leelee gave Anson her iciest smile. None of them liked him. Had he been merely a harmless wit, they would have given him a pass. But they had all been subjected to his vitriolic tongue and had quickly and rightly discerned that it was best to stay away from him.

"Oh, Anson, you know we never talk about other people," said Helen with a cold laugh. "We leave that to you."

Anson smiled at what he probably took to be a compliment. "Well, if you can think of anything interesting for my column, let me know—my deadline's tomorrow. So far the only thing I have is that Imelda and I ate dinner next to Tyler Trask and he had not one, not two, but *three* bottles of wine. Probably needs that much alcohol to get through dinner with his girlfriend . . . I hear she is a total *bo-ore*. A darling figure but air running through the head."

The ladies all turned and looked at Eliza. Tyler Trask? Eliza's crush? Eating dinner at the same restaurant as them? Surely this was a sign.

"Tyler's here now?" asked Leelee, her head bobbing over the others to scan the restaurant.

"He just left," said Anson. "Probably outside beating up paparazzi. Why can't these actors act like gentlemen? Do they think it's sexy to punch people out?"

"I thought Tyler lived in Australia," said Helen. She was asking Anson but staring at Eliza, who was feigning nonchalance by swirling her bread in her tomato sauce.

"In town, making a movie. Don't you gals read *Variety?*" asked Anson.

Before they could answer, Imelda emerged from the bathroom and wrapped her arm around Anson. They were an odd pair. She was tiny, but had overdone everything about herself so that she appeared out of scale. Her eyes were over-shadowed, her cheeks over-rouged, her raccoon-streaked hair overly teased into large Farrah Fawcett clumps that cast a shadow across her face. And her outfits were always tight and flashy. Tonight she was clad in pencil-thin, skintight black leather pants and an ostentatious leopard-print tank top. Anson, on the other hand, wore his requisite pastels; tonight it was a bright pink button-down shirt with apple green pants, held up with a peppermint whale-print belt. He called his look "Palm Beach chic," which it probably was at one time, but he hadn't been there since the seventies.

The women all greeted each other before Imelda gave Anson a look, and he took his leave.

"Toot-a-loo, gals," he said, waving as he walked away.

The ladies waited a beat to make extra sure he was out of earshot before turning to Eliza in astonishment.

"Okay, how random is it that the man of your dreams was *in this very restaurant* tonight, when you were talking about having an affair with him?" asked Leelee, excited.

"I wasn't talking about having an affair with him," insisted Eliza.

"This is cosmic, sweetie. This is the gods talking and telling you it's okay. You have to believe in signs," said Helen, dreamy-eyed.

"You guys, come off it," protested Eliza.

"Seriously, Eliza, you know I'm not as out there as Helen," began Victoria. "But this is odd. How can this be a coincidence? If ever there was something telling you to go for it, this is it."

Eliza gave them all a skeptical look. But inside she was exploding. Although she wasn't as New Agey as Helen, she did think that it was somehow a sign. And she knew that no matter how much she loved her husband, Tyler Trask was the one man on earth who could steal her heart. But it was dangerous, and he was dangerous. Was it worth the risk?

"I'm not agreeing, but I wouldn't mind seeing him again," she finally sighed. "Now that I look semidecent, it would be nice to have someone appreciate it. But I'm not promising anything, and you have to help me track him down."

The ladies squealed in delight.

"You won't regret it," said Victoria.

"I don't think I have any more room for regrets," said Leelee.

"Guys, I want to make it clear: I'm not agreeing, I'm just saying I'll see Tyler, which means nothing, and only if you guys help me arrange it," said Eliza.

"We know, we know, but you'll come around," said Victoria with certainty. She would do everything in her power to make sure Eliza agreed. Eliza was the one she needed to help her most of all.

"Don't forget, we only live once. We've got to live each day as our last," said Helen. She leaned across the table and put out her hand. Eliza, Victoria, and Leelee put their hands on top of hers, and they all squeezed.

On the day Victoria first met Wayne, the weather was overcast and everything that had transpired earlier had put her in a lousy mood. She couldn't find a parking space outside her kickboxing class, so she was late and therefore relegated to the worst bag in the gym. Then she had sat through an endless Lilly Pulitzer Advisory Board lunch meeting where the spring collection was brought out on a large rack and select invited women analyzed each outfit down to the very last accessory and gave their assessment as to whether or not their friends would wear it. She had never seen so much effort put into dissecting a mock turtleneck and she could not, *could not,* believe that grown women, with college educations—some even with master's degrees!—could debate the size of the blue turtles on the pink Capris for forty minutes. *Forty minutes!* Didn't these women have to *be* anywhere? Get a life. She could not fathom how she had ended up in this suburban hell. She had gone to Harvard. She had an MBA from Stanford. She had been the youngest VP *ever* at Twentieth Century Fox, and now she was talking about *stitched turtles*? It was insane. Just bury me now, she thought.

And after that it only got worse. Because of the endless lunch from Hades, she ended up being last in the carpool lane to pick up the twins from school, and after ditching them with Marguerita, her Spanish nanny who spoke no English, so she could make her hair appointment with Khao at Fred Segal, she found that she had raced down the hill at top speed just to sit in the goddamn waiting room for forty minutes with two-month-old

*Vogue*s because some young starlet on the WB Network was late to get her roots covered. And as she sat there steaming, Victoria saw nymphet after nymphet, in their midriff-baring Britney Spears–wannabe outfits, pass her by without so much as a glance, because to them she was just another middle-aged studio exec wife. Okay, agent wife, but may as well be studio exec for all they care, but of course they don't! And what were these women thinking wearing those outfits? Granted, it was California, but it was April—save it for the beach! When she got home, her hair finally done and her outfit for the evening ready because she had managed to beg the man in the dry cleaner's to reopen the door and let her get her new Chloe cling dress, her husband from hell called to tell her that he was skipping the premiere and was instead going to dinner with Tad Baxter, because he was officially Tad Baxter's bitch. All that running around, getting her hair blown out, letting the woman at the makeup counter "sample" makeup on her so she could get a free makeover, and spending a stupid hour getting a mani-pedi and a lip wax, and for naught.

Victoria was about to crumple in a ball, throw off her clothes, curl up in front of the TV with a bowl of microwave popcorn and the latest episode of *Grey's Anatomy* from her TiVo list, when she stopped herself. She didn't have to do that anymore. Why the hell did she have to wait for Justin to come home from sucking his client's dick (not really, but for all she knew, really) when she had just spent her whole day and millions of hours to look amazing? She was going to that premiere.

It was too last-minute to enlist any of her posse to accompany her, but with her newfound attitude, she couldn't care less. She would stroll down that red carpet alone, watch that movie alone—the new Drew Barrymore/Vince Vaughn, which was supposed to be cute, and she was actually psyched to see it—and then go to the after party by herself. The fact was, going it alone wasn't all that ballsy, because whenever she was there with Justin he always ditched her anyway and went to lick his clients' and potential clients' balls. She would inevitably link up with the other ditched wives and commiserate over how seldom they saw their husbands and then how awful their husbands were when they actually did see them. She used to just listen, never bash, just take it all in and hold her cards close. But lately she didn't care and would openly bash Justin. He was just too much of an asshole to her publicly to try to pretend that she was a happy, dutiful wife.

In the end she was glad she went; the film was humorous and helped put her in a better mood. As expected, she sat with other wives while their husbands "watched" the movie (that is, scanned the room for clients or potential clients) and had a huge bag of popcorn to herself. It was nice not to share it with Justin, who usually scarfed down the entire thing himself, licking his buttery fingers and dipping them back in, slobber still on them. God, he was repulsive. The premiere had been in Westwood, by UCLA, a frequent locale for premieres for reasons she didn't understand but was grateful for; it was much easier going there from the Palisades than, say, Hollywood. The after party was being held at the Buffalo Club, a dark-paneled, overpriced restaurant with a large garden in back, located on an innocuous strip of Olympic Boulevard in Santa Monica.

With new determination, Victoria sped across the city in her black Mercedes SUV with the identical Britax baby seats in the back and Eminem blaring on the stereo. Eminem was a secret crush. She loved the contradiction of his take-no-prisoners attitude and his obsession with his daughter and inability to get over Kim. That was one thing she liked about strong men. Strong women brought them to their knees. They could be such tough assholes and yet they were able to be tortured and manipulated by a certain woman who knew just how to do that to them. In fact, any woman could do that to them; she just had to have the recipe for that particular man. Kim sure had Marshall's number. She wished she had it also; he was a hottie. She'd seen *Eight Mile* something like ten times. Victoria didn't feel as though she really had Justin's number, when she thought about it. She used to, when she had been pursuing/ignoring him. But then when she got him . . . she wasn't sure how it happened, but she couldn't get his attention anymore. Probably they were too much alike, both just in it for the kill. And probably because there wasn't any sort of true love there. There had been sex and passion and now there was just mutual torture. Pathetic.

Victoria strode into the party, head held high, and actually felt as if her new kick-ass attitude was getting her a lot more looks than her old confident-wife attitude. The club was packed— people were mingling, gripping drinks, starting from the bar inside all the way to the bar outside, and every seat was taken. Whenever anyone came through the door to the garden, every head turned to see if Drew or Vince or any other celeb had dared to make a cameo, and when they realized it was just another studio exec, they all just turned back to the person they were talking to and fake-listened to the conversation again. Victoria went to the bar and waited patiently for the bartender to serve twenty men and thirty nymphets who had all cut in front of her, and when she finally got her dirty martini she turned around to find her friends. In her haste she practically knocked into the man in front of her, the alcohol in her glass dipping perilously close to the edge, and she was cursing out loud before she looked up to see that it was Wayne Mercer, the self-proclaimed "über agent" at ACM (Artists' Creative Management) and the man her husband hated most.

"Sorry, did I get you?" he asked, unnecessarily clasping his arm around her wrist and squeezing it. She felt like she had just dipped herself into a wave of Calvin Klein cologne.

Wayne looked like every other agent, gelled dark hair, bonded teeth, Zegna suit, everything a little too slimy, a little too slick. She had no idea who had started it, but Wayne and Justin were constantly engaged in battle for each other's clients. The war was probably launched by Wayne, who stole Dominique Swain from Justin, and then Justin in turn stole Leelee Sobiesky from Wayne. (Hard to say who actually won that fracas, considering the careers of the ladies in question.) Victoria just knew that Wayne Mercer's name was dirt in their house, and if she was ever to see him at a party or anywhere else, she was ordered to run for the hills.

"Almost, but I'm okay," said Victoria, literally batting her eyes and placing her hand on his shoulder and rubbing it.

Wayne looked at Victoria and smiled. "Wayne Mercer," he said, still holding on to her wrist.

"Victoria Rand." She had kept her maiden name—Coleman was just so pedestrian to her—but for a fleeting second she wished she hadn't. How fun to see if Wayne could make the connection.

"You look familiar. Are you with the studio? Drew? Vince?" he asked, still holding on to her wrist but letting his eyes wander up and down her body. She was glad she had worn the dress, which had a slit up the side to show off her toned legs and somehow managed to cling and fold into every desirable nook and cranny of her body. Glad that she had picked it up from the dry cleaner's, glad that she had gotten her hair and makeup done, and glad that she had worked out that morning.

"I'm with me," she said, swirling the olive in her drink and taking a sip. Then she licked her lips seductively. She couldn't believe she was actually doing it, but what the hell. With these monkeys, you had to lay it all out.

Wayne was intrigued. "Ha ha," he chuckled. "Haven't heard that one before." She knew he was dying for her to ask him who he was with, she also knew he was "with Vince" because his agency repped him—so not actually *with* him, but he would spin it that way. She knew that he wanted to brag and that associating yourself with a celeb was the only way to win brownie points in this town, but she didn't want to give him the satisfaction yet. The conversation would too quickly go to industry talk, too quickly get to who her husband was, and ultimately too quickly end. She wanted to play this one out, so she said nothing.

Wayne raised his eyebrows, as if intrigued that she didn't ask him the question, and then started to say something. He stopped, obviously changing his mind, and leaned in instead. "What do you say I grab a drink, we go inside and sit in one of those booths and have a real dinner, and a real conversation?" He said the last part proudly, as if she had *never* had a real conversation.

Victoria cocked her head and examined her prey. Yes, he had that oily agent look, but he did have thick eyelashes and nice blue eyes, and his skin was smooth and soft-looking. He obviously worked out. He wasn't gorgeous, but hey, he was her husband's enemy. That was enough.

"Sounds great," she said with a smile.

·· *10* ··

After dinner at Giorgio Baldi, Victoria, it seemed, was the only one of the group who believed that the pact had been agreed upon. Within a week, Victoria was cajoling her friends to get started on their extramarital activities. Leelee had readily agreed to cheat, but only because she thought that it was a fun conversation they were all having and it would lead nowhere. She wasn't morally disgusted the way Eliza was, but uncertain. Could she really do this? Helen was on board, and the only reason she had not made headway was because it always took her a long time to do anything. She had to analyze, consider, reconsider, hesitate, dissect, and brood before she could make a move. Eliza remained unconvinced. She had a wonderful husband who appreciated her. Why would she mess that up?

But over the next few days, things started to change. The fantasy started to overwhelm the reality and become much more desirable. Because what was their reality after all? Shopping? Working out? Carpooling?

On Monday morning Eliza was getting ready to go out. She was in fact admiring herself in the mirror and had a vivid flashback to a Thanksgiving long ago when she was in high school and she realized her body had undergone a metamorphosis and she was now a full-fledged woman. Even though she hadn't gained very much during her pregnancy, she had never felt this fit. The bread belt that had nestled around the middle of her body like a life preserver had disappeared. She actually had a six-pack!

Declan came out of the bathroom and smiled at her. "Admiring your body again?"

"No—well, yes. I'm just psyched this trainer paid off!"

"Me too, at eighty bucks a pop," he said. He started to button his shirt and put his tie on.

"Worth every penny," said Eliza, putting on her shoes.

"Maybe I should work out," said Declan. "But who has the time?"

Eliza looked over at her husband and stared at his protruding stomach. He was a large man, so he never really would be fat, but he definitely had a belly, and his arms were in no way toned.

"You should work out. You should find the time," said Eliza.

"Come on, then I'd never see you," he said, putting on his pants. "Besides, you don't care what I look like. We have each other."

"Do you mean you don't care what I look like?" asked Eliza.

"I do, and you look great. But, you know, you're in your midthirties, you're a mom—you look great for that."

Eliza was instantly pissed. "What are you saying, no one else would find me hot?"

"What do you care what anyone else thinks? You're married," said Declan, putting on his blazer.

"Then why did I kill myself in the gym? If you don't care how I look and no one else is looking at me, what's the point?" asked Eliza, her voice rising.

"Well, for one, it's better for you to be fit. And two, you know the ladies in your social group. They all talk behind one another's back. God forbid someone weigh an extra fifteen pounds. Look how Victoria talks about Leelee."

Eliza slumped down on the bed. "You just made me feel really bad. I was feeling so good, and now you made me feel old and ugly."

Declan came over and put his arm around her. "I didn't mean to do that, sweetie. You're gorgeous to me, and you always will be."

"Right."

"What, you want other men to want you? Isn't that a little strange, considering we're married?"

"No. Don't you want other men to think I'm attractive?" asked Eliza.

"Sure, but I don't want you working out so that other men will. There's something a little distorted about it."

"Whatever."

Declan rose. "Look, honey, you look great. But we live in Los Angeles. There's an Angelina Jolie on every corner. Don't try to compare yourself with them."

"Right," said Eliza.

Declan went downstairs and Eliza sat, steaming, on the edge of the bed. She picked up one of her small flowered boudoir pillows and fondled the scalloped edge with her fingers. Why did her husband always have to be a pragmatist? Why did he never indulge in any of her stupid fantasies that maybe she was now the sexiest mom in the 'hood? She had sweated and toiled to get this body. It would be nice to have more appreciation. Tyler Trask would appreciate her. He'd liked her when she still had an extra fifteen pounds on her!

Eliza lay down on the bed and thought back to when she'd first met Tyler. Things were so different then. She and Declan were living in New York, and she was still working full-time writing for *Chat*. She had just had Donovan and was dying to get back into the land of the living when her editor called and begged her to do an interview with "the incorrigible Tyler Trask." *It would be a huge favor to me,* he said. It's a huge favor for *me,* Eliza had thought. She loved her new baby but was feeling overwhelmed by waking up all hours of the night and experiencing hormone malfunctions and everything else that went with new motherhood. Going back to work was like coming up for air after almost drowning. And her encounter with Tyler did stop her from drowning. She closed her eyes and tried to remember how it felt, and why it was so good.

She had arranged to meet him at his hotel room at the Mark. She arrived early, nervous and wishing she wasn't. He's just a human being, she thought. Why get nervous? Hollywood actors were granted too much credit. She was sure he would be just like the rest of them. He was on the phone when she got there, and his publicist let her in and offered her bottled water. While she made polite chitchat with the publicist, she watched Tyler out of the corner of her eye. He was much handsomer in person, which was unusual, because she found that typically actors were less attractive in person—generally much shorter than they appeared on-screen, and they either had delicate fey features or really extreme features from the front but looked flat-headed from the side. Actresses were the opposite: they were far more attractive in person, and they were all emaciated. Tyler was an anomaly. He was about six feet tall, with a big, buff body and masculine, rugged features. He was all man.

He brought her water. He smiled. He asked his publicist to leave, which he did, reluctantly. They talked about small things, his latest film role, where he got his clothes, then big things, such as why he had such a terrible reputation for fighting, his alcohol benders, for which he had great remorse but refused to become a teetotaler, how his mother died of cancer, and the nature of fame. It got darker outside, then started to rain, and Eliza called her babysitter and told her she'd be late. Tyler told her she looked great for someone who'd just had a baby. They ordered room service. Then the interview took a strange turn.

Tyler was lying back on the couch, shoes flipped off, legs on the arm, popping peanuts into his mouth. She in turn was sitting Indian-style on the floor, swirling the red wine in her glass.

"Why do you think people are obsessed with famous people?" asked Eliza. "I mean, why do you think they want your autograph or a picture with you? What do you think it is?"

"Oh, I know what I think it is. I believe that people are not really so excited to see me; I think they're more excited for me to see them. It's like this: if someone famous, someone who everyone knows, sees you, an average Joe, then it validates you in a way. It's mad, but people think that if I see them, acknowledge them, have a smoke or a pint with them, then they exist."

Eliza thought about that for a moment. She supposed it was true. So many people wanted to be recognized, noticed.

"You're right. And I'm sure that everyone wants a little bit of your luster to rub off on them."

Tyler sat up and smiled. "I don't know if I have luster . . . just lust. Hey, you want a beer?"

"No thanks," she said, watching him walk over to the minibar. It was now almost five o'clock. She was drunk and had a baby to go home to. "I should go . . ."

Tyler turned around in surprise. "Why? I thought we were just getting started."

He stared at her for a long time, and she saw an intensity in his eyes. She'd seen it on-screen, but it was overwhelming in reality, and especially now that it was directed at her.

"The babysitter . . ." she said lamely.

He looked at her again and saw she was conflicted. "You haven't even asked me about my next role," he said, marching back to the couch and plopping down. He took a swig of his beer.

Eliza turned and faced him. "Oh yeah—what is it?"

"I'm going to play Mr. Darcy. They're doing another remake of Pride and Prejudice."

Eliza groaned. "Not again! We don't need another. No offense, but the BBC version with Colin Firth was amazing! Why did you agree to do it?"

"Relax, it's on stage in London. And why not? I want to play a lovable character. Everyone loves Mr. Darcy. Why is that, anyway?"

"First off, he's not exactly lovable. Although every woman does love Darcy. I cannot deny that I'm also in that fan club," she said, smiling.

"I only just read the book, and he seems like a nasty bloke. Until the end. I thought the ladies would like the gentle rich guy—you know, Bingley. He's all sweet and sensitive, caring and generous. That's what women want, at least according to women's magazines."

"No, no. Women want two things: they want the guy to be a total rogue initially, but then they want him to change for them. There's nothing sexier than a guy who will change for you."

Tyler nodded. "Okay then."

"And the thing about Darcy," began Eliza, the wine controlling her thoughts, "is almost like what you said about famous people. Elizabeth Bennett, Jane Austen makes clear, is not the prettiest girl in the room or the town, but she is the cleverest, the most desirable if you really get to know her, and certainly the most accessible to the readers. Because that's how every woman views herself: as the most special once you get to know her. That's why we love Darcy. He can have any girl he wants in London or Hertfordshire, but he picks the one with the brain and the wit . . ."

Eliza's voice trailed off, and she became embarrassed. She looked at Tyler, who was sitting up on the couch, watching her keenly. The room was dark now, and the rain had started to come down again outside.

"That sounds like you," he said. Before she could answer, Tyler stood up and walked over to Eliza. He cupped her face with his hands *and leaned in and kissed her. Eliza was stunned. At first she didn't kiss back, and then she did, but then she pulled away.*

"Tyler . . ." she said, putting her head down so she wouldn't have eye contact with him.

"I know you feel it too," he said, rubbing his hands up and down her arms.

"I'm married," she said lamely. She was, but it sounded so stupid. She felt immature. Immature for not wanting to cheat? she asked herself. Yes.

"Is that the only reason?" asked Tyler, raising her chin up to face him.

She stared into his eyes. She felt as though she were in a movie. If only she was an actress and could make out with him and then head home to Declan and tell him, Yeah, honey, made out with Tyler Trask today, all in a day's work. But this was real life.

"It would be just . . . wrong," she said, her voice a whisper. She could feel his breath on her face, and his hands were still running up and down her arms. It would be so easy to collapse into him, feel his hard chest press against her. He seemed so big and strong, and she liked that she felt little and weak next to him. It made her feel safe and protected. But she was no longer safe.

"It's not wrong," said Tyler, staring at her. "You're only human. You don't need to be the good girl, Eliza. You just have to do what your heart wants."

It was the phrase "good girl" that jolted Eliza back to reality. She pulled away.

"I have to go," she said, walking over to the chair and grabbing her bag and coat. Tyler watched her gather her belongings in silence.

"Sorry," she said softly. She was embarrassed, but now determined to get out of there. It made her feel weird that Tyler wasn't saying anything, just watching her curiously. When she got to the door,

she turned and faced him. "In another life . . ." she said. It sounded dumb, but it was true. She would be his if things were different.

"I know I'll see you again, Eliza. In this life. I know this was meant to happen. I will be waiting for your call," he said, with such force that Eliza was convinced that they would meet again. He leaned forward and pecked her on the cheek, and then she opened the door and was gone.

Suddenly Eliza was back in her bed in the Palisades and late to drop Donovan off at preschool. What *was* the point of being a good girl? Why not live her life?

·· *11* ··

At ten o'clock Helen finally got out of bed, threw on her army pants and a small black James Perse T-shirt and made herself a pot of herbal tea. She cupped the mug in her hands, letting the steam give her a mini facial, and opened the screen door. After plopping herself on her favorite chair on the deck, which afforded a pristine view of the ocean, she took a sip of the Red Zinger and thought about what she would do that day. Suddenly, she was interrupted by the phone. She wasn't going to answer it, but Wesley always reprimanded her when she didn't. *What if something happened to Lauren?* he'd say. She didn't want to get into a "row" about it, so she reluctantly made her way inside and picked up the cordless.

"Oh, hello, Helen, it's Margaret," said her mother-in-law on the other end of the phone. Although she was well on in years, her clipped British voice always remained energetic and chipper, although void of friendliness.

"Hello, Margaret. You're up late. What time is it in England?" asked Helen, looking at her watch.

"Oh, we're not in England. We're still in New York," said Margaret.

"New York? I didn't know you were in New York. Are you coming to L.A.?" asked Helen, hoping the answer was no.

"No, that's why we saw Wesley here this weekend. Such fun . . . anyhow, we're sorry not to see you and Lauren, but we are doing a bit of a shop tomorrow and I need her size. I want to buy her some proper dresses. Wesley showed me some pictures of her and she seems a little . . . casual. Like a hippie. I found a store called Bonpoint that is just charming and lovely . . ."

As she continued her rambling, Helen zoned out. Wesley had gone to visit his parents in New York? She knew he had gone to New York, but she thought it was just to meet with a screenwriter about some movie. He had never mentioned that his parents were there. Why didn't he tell her? Why didn't he want her to go? She loved New York. It would be fun to take Lauren, she hadn't been since she was very little. They could go to Serendipity, and maybe a Broadway show . . . Why hadn't Wesley invited her?

All of Helen's deepest and darkest insecurities seized her. Was Wesley with someone else? Was he ashamed of her? Why did they never tell each other anything? She got off the phone with Margaret quickly and walked back into Wesley's office, where he sat on the tufted leather couch, reading a script.

She leaned against the doorway and watched him. His features had thickened over the years, and there were more lines cutting through the skin on his forehead. That, coupled with the hair loss, actually gave a more distinguished impression. He seemed like someone who had made it. He had that wonderfully posh British accent, that confident Oxford gait, and those smooth Sloane manners. And yet . . . he hadn't made it. His great-grandparents had made it.

"You didn't tell me you saw your parents in New York," Helen said, her arms folded.

Wesley looked up in surprise. "I didn't? Sorry, love."

"Why didn't you want me to come?" she asked, her voice wounded.

"I didn't think you would have wanted to come. You don't like my parents," he said, his voice even, but filled more with surprise than recrimination.

"I like your parents," she said lamely. She didn't, really. "I'm just really stunned you wouldn't have asked me."

"Sorry, love. I will next time."

Helen stared at Wesley, who stared back at her. She didn't even feel anger. Just . . . emptiness. It was more of a facade, as if she was supposed to care that he didn't ask her. She also felt that it was not right that he didn't even tell her. But then, they really didn't talk anymore. And she remembered that when he told her he was going to New York she had taken a phone call from her pottery teacher in the middle of the conversation. So maybe he would have if she had given him the opportunity.

"Well, I'm off," she said.

"Have fun," he said, already looking down at his script.

Helen walked out, her bare feet tingling from the cold concrete floor as she made her way back to the patio. Had she and Wesley ever had anything to talk about? She couldn't remember. They had cultivated a level of aloofness that shielded the bubbling layer of hostility laying beneath it. But now that apathy was so normal that it would have been odd to exist without it. The only thing they ever quarreled about was Lauren, and on her Helen had ceded to him years ago. He was right; he *was* a better parent. He had never said it, but she felt it. And anyway, what would she know about parenting? She had been adopted from a Korean orphanage, disposed of by her own flesh and blood, only to be "saved" and transported to Orange County by religious zealots with whom she never bonded. Okay, Wesley, chalk up a point for your team. She felt anger stir within her. She blamed Wesley for every unpleasantness and inconvenience in her life. She knew it was wrong, but he was around, he was there, so who else could she blame?

Why had they married? There must have been something that brought her to marry him. He was older, and wiser, and made her feel safe. Suddenly she shuddered. Was it only because . . . ? No, it couldn't be. And yet the only memory she had of truly loving Wesley and knowing with certainty that he would be the right person for her was that night. Oh, God, she hated to think about that night.

She leaned her head back in her chair and closed her eyes, trying to think of something else, but her mind kept drifting back to the defining moment for her and Wesley. She was young then. She'd just majored in communications at Boston University and headed back west to Los Angeles to try her luck in the film world. She was unable to land a coveted spot in the CAA training program, so she took a position as a "D girl," or development assistant, in a small production company owned by Dirk Hastings, a big shot director whose last few action movies had made more than a billion dollars combined. It was in theory a glamorous job; she'd meet with writers and wannabe directors all day and listen to pitches and then read scripts all night in an effort to find the next directing vehicle for Dirk. Problem was, Dirk already had his next five films lined up and little to no interest in producing one with a novice director (even though he claimed in every interview that he wanted to "cultivate talent") so the whole thing was a sham vanity project. He had cool offices in a loftlike space on Sunset, but as one of only three other people working there, Helen was bored out of her mind.

Those were the days, thought Helen. All the possibilities in the world, no obligations. She'd spend her evenings with friends from BU, attending industry parties that their bosses had been invited to but sent them instead, or at crappy "women drink free" happy hours, where they would fill up on two-dollar jalapeño poppers and buffalo wings in an effort to save money on dinner. It was all very carefree, until that one night. That one fatal night. Helen was at a bar on Melrose with a girlfriend—she couldn't even remember her name years later—letting a rowdy group of Australian guys buy them woo-woo shots, when she felt a tap on her shoulder. She turned around to see an older man, well dressed and with a receding hairline but youthful eyes.

"Hi, Helen," he said in a British accent.

She had no idea who he was. "Hey, how are you?"

He smiled. "I'm well." He stared at her and smiled. "Wesley Fairbanks. I met with you last week about possibly directing Fireworks.*"*

"Of course!" said Helen, still not remembering him at all. He was so nondescript. Had she really had a meeting with him? She would have remembered the accent, wouldn't she have?

"Well, cheerio," he said.

"Wait," she said, feeling bad. "Have a shot with us!"

He was nice. They talked all evening. She wasn't at all attracted to him, but she was impressed by how articulate and intelligent he was. He was not at all like anyone she'd met in Hollywood. He was totally unpretentious, embarrassed a bit to be pounding the pavement

looking for work, and he was reserved and well mannered. She knew
they were having a pleasant time, but she felt the age abyss between
them, and several times during the conversation she felt young and
silly. It would never have occurred to her that he looked at her in a
romantic sense, and she was surprised when he asked her out.

"Oh! Okay," she said. She didn't want to be mean, but she
wasn't really that interested. He was old! She only dated younger
guys—really hot guys who looked like Brad Pitt.

"Morton's? Friday at nine?" he asked.

She had always wanted to go to Morton's. That sounded so
grown up. Enough with going out with friends and taking advantage
of the free hors d'oeuvres at happy hour. Hell, yes, she'd go with this
guy for a good free meal.

"Sure. But make it ten," she added. She didn't want to flush the
entire night down the toilet, so she thought she might want to get in
some drinks at Trader Vic's beforehand.

"Okay, well done then," he said cheerfully.

She wrote it down in her date book and didn't think about it for
the rest of the week.

On Friday, Dirk made one of his rare appearances in the office.
He was tall and thin, with bushy dark hair, and had a loud voice
that could be heard across any room. Helen was a little intimidated
by him. She had heard that he was really mean to the women in his
movies, even the famous actresses, always telling them how fat they
were and calling their agents to complain that they were ruining the
movie due to their obesity, when the truth was they were almost
anorexic. It was some sort of a disorder. She had heard he was a
woman hater, and it was believable. But he was brilliant, and that
was a turn-on. Brilliant and difficult, a little bit crazy but passion-
ate, so of course any woman he came into contact with left him feel-
ing a little bit in love, and Helen was no different. Dirk had never

seemed to notice Helen; even though it was such a small office and they had been in several meetings together, she firmly believed that if she ran into him out of context he wouldn't know who the hell she was. And yet on this particular Friday, Dirk came storming into the office, ranting about the evils of the studio, and stopped short at Helen's desk.

"What do you think, Helen? Do you think I should tell the folks at Paramount to go fuck themselves?"

Helen was so surprised that he knew her name that she didn't even think before she answered the question. "Yes," she said, nodding.

"That's what I thought! FUCK MY AGENT! FUCK MY LAWYER! They just want my FUCKING money!" he yelled, stomping into his office. He entered the room and then popped his head out a second later.

"You're having dinner with me tonight. You probably like sushi, right? Just like mom used to make?"

"I'm Korean, not Japanese, and my mother is a blue-eyed blonde from Orange County who only knew how to pop a TV dinner into the microwave," said Helen tartly. "But yes, I like sushi."

He was totally nonplussed. "Great. We'll leave as soon as we're done."

Helen was speechless. She wasn't sure if she should be offended or unfazed, so she chose to ignore it.

But by the end of the day, when everyone else in the company had left and Dirk still had not emerged from his office, Helen thought that maybe she had misheard him. Had he invited her to dinner? She could see him through the glass door in his office, chatting on the phone, his legs up on his desk, his hand going in and out of a bag of Fritos. The clock ticked past departure hour, and Helen lingered. Finally, she decided to knock on his office door to see if he was ready. He looked up at her and motioned her in, still on the phone.

"Fuck that shithead. Fuck it," he said into the receiver.

Helen stood at the door, her back pressed against it, and waited. He talked on and on for almost ten minutes, and she started to leave, but then he put his finger up for her to wait. Finally he got off the phone.

"What do you want?" he asked roughly.

"Um, you asked me to dinner," she said weakly.

"I did?" he said, looking at her up and down. She was mortified. "Okay."

He opened his top drawer and took out a small bag of white powder and a mirror and began to make lines with a rolled-up twenty dollar bill. He took a large sniff of the first and then the second, then looked up at Helen.

"Want some?"

She wasn't sure. She'd tried coke once before and she was not crazy about it, preferring instead pot or mushrooms—but what the hell. She leaned down and snorted a line.

"Let's go," he said, shoving all the drug paraphernalia into his drawer and slamming it shut.

They went to a small nondescript Japanese restaurant in a strip mall, where the waiters placed sashimi in front of them without even asking what they wanted. Helen and Dirk didn't really speak that much, and she started to wonder what she was doing there. Arm candy? Did he just not want to be alone? Did he realize he'd made a mistake but didn't know how to get out of it?

After dinner, Dirk invited her to his house. She didn't really want to go, but something about Dirk scared her. He was so volatile—he was just the type to make a scene if she said no. So she agreed. Since they both had their own cars at work, she had to follow behind him in her little Honda. He was driving a new souped-up Porsche, and was obviously a glutton for speed. With no consideration for the fact that she was trying to keep up with him and had no idea where his house was, he took off, higher and higher up into the Hollywood Hills, whipping around the corners of those streets so narrow that only one car could pass through at a time.

His house was an ugly modern structure teetering on the edge of a ravine, with no yard in the front or back, and giant metal gates that looked foreboding. Of course Dirk didn't even wait for her to get out of her car, marching instead into his house and leaving her to fend off the two slobbering and barking pit bulls that were less than thrilled to see her. When she entered the living room, it was dark, but she could see an enormous television, and an entire wall covered in stereo system equipment, with giant speakers and several shelves of CDs. There were black leather couches and a shag rug, and a disco ball hanging from the ceiling.

"Dirk?" she asked.

"In here," came his voice from another room. Helen walked through the living room and turned a corner into a dark foyer. She turned again into what must be Dirk's bedroom, and he was sitting on a king-size bed with black sheets, snorting more coke.

"Sit down," he said, not looking up.

Helen was feeling less and less enthused about this whole adventure. She'd been flattered that Dirk asked her to dinner, but now he repulsed her. He was just an asshole with a drug problem. They had no connection whatsoever.

Dirk looked up and offered her some coke. "No thanks," she said.

He shrugged and put the coke down on the side of the bed. Before she knew it, he had pulled her into his arms and had his hands down her shirt and was kneading her breasts.

"Uh, Dirk . . ."

"Shhh," he commanded. He leaned back and pulled down his

pants, and then yanked Helen's arm so that she fell to her knees. "Give me a blow job," he ordered.

Helen felt herself being both repelled and attracted to him. She had never been with someone who was so bossy, and frankly it was kind of kinky. She did as she was ordered. After he came, he leaned back on his bed. She wiped her mouth and stood up. Was there to be no tit for tat?

"Hey, dude, are you going to pleasure me, or what?" asked Helen boldly.

Dirk closed his eyes and crossed his arms behind his head. "No thanks."

Helen felt the blood rush to her face. "Not cool," she said.

Dirk opened his eyes and gave her a surprised look. Then he leaned over and snorted another two lines of coke without saying a word.

"I'm gonna go," she said finally.

"Don't go—I want you to watch that French movie with me," he said, picking up the remote and turning on the large-screen television on the wall. But then he stood up and started pacing. "Or maybe we should go dancing? You want to go dancing?"

"Um, no thanks," she said. She could see that the drugs were hitting him. He was now entering that frantic mode that she had seen too often in Hollywood.

"Let's go listen to music, then," he said, walking into the living room. She followed him and he turned on some sort of techno music extremely loud.

"Wait, I want you to hear this," he said, and started searching through his CDs maniacally.

"I'm gonna split," she said, walking to the door. The dogs came out of their beds and started barking, and just as she was about to leave, Dirk put his hand on the door and slammed it shut.

"You're not leaving," he said evenly. He was glaring at her so intensely that she immediately became fearful.

"Dirk . . ."

Then his mood changed and the severity lifted. "Stay, please," he whined. "One more song."

She stood where she was, frozen, and watched him. He was flipping through the CDs, discarding them everywhere, and then he jerked up and walked over to the bar. He opened a drawer and pulled out more cocaine and did another line.

"This feels so good . . ." he said, and thrust his head back.

All of the sudden, he fell backwards. The dogs started barking and went up and licked his face, but he remained motionless.

"Dirk?" asked Helen.

He didn't respond. She waited and then said his name again. "Dirk?"

The dogs were still licking his face, and Helen went over to get a closer look. He had foam coming out of his mouth. "Dirk!" she screamed frantically, feeling for his heart. It wasn't beating.

"Oh, God!"

She pounded on his chest. Nothing happened. She didn't know CPR, but she attempted to blow in his mouth, like she had seen TV doctors do. No response. He seemed . . . dead.

She didn't know what to do. Call 911? But would she get caught up in some drug and sex scandal? Call a friend? But who? She ran to her bag and pulled out her Filofax. It opened to her date book and she looked down and was horrified to see that she was supposed to have a date with that guy Wesley tonight. At Morton's. Oh, shit. She looked at her watch. It was 10:13. He was probably there waiting already. For some reason, she became convinced that she had to get in touch with Wesley. He was older, seemed mature, he'd know *what to do. She dialed Morton's and explained to the guy that she had to speak to Wesley Fairbanks. She waited until he came to the phone.*

"You have to come here, to meet me," she said, and Wesley agreed. She rummaged through Dirk's wallet to find out his exact address on the license, and then told Wesley. She hung up after telling him to rush.

What seemed like an eternity passed, and Helen paced around the room. The dogs were still barking but had calmed down considerably and ultimately went back to their beds. It was odd to see Dirk dead. She was scared to be in the same room with him, so she sat in the bedroom. Suddenly the doorbell rang and the dogs started barking again. Helen went to get it, and Wesley entered. He looked adorable in a tweed blazer and a tie, even. She pointed at Dirk. "My boss . . ." she said.

Wesley, to his credit, remained completely calm, as if he saw dead people all the time. He checked his pulse and confirmed he was dead. "What do you want to do?" he asked, composed.

"I want to get the hell out of here. I want to have never been here," she said. She knew she should call the police or an ambulance, but what help could they be? He was dead.

"Okay," said Wesley, as if leaving the scene of a crime, or a death, were totally normal. "Tell me everything you touched."

Helen watched as Wesley washed off imaginary fingerprints, cleaned up the walls that Helen might have brushed against, and erased traces of her. Helen was touched by how in control and strong Wesley seemed. He hadn't asked her any embarrassing questions, like did they have sex or anything—he just went about cleaning up her mess.

"Wow, it seems like you've done this before," said Helen, lamely

attempting a joke to break the ice. Wesley looked up at her but didn't say anything. Then he returned to his cleanup. When they decided they were done, Wesley turned to her.

"You must never tell anyone you were here. For all you know, this never happened," he ordered, gently but firmly.

"I promise," Helen said, nodding.

Helen glanced over at Dirk's dead body with a wave of disgust. He was a jerk. He deserved to die. Just because someone is dead doesn't mean he was a good person. Good people die, but bad people die too. You can only hope that bad people die earlier than good people.

Wesley got up and put his arms around Helen. "You'll be okay. I've taken care of it," he said.

She turned and looked at Wesley, who had rescued her. It was that moment that Helen knew she would marry him. He had saved her. This was fate. They should be together.

On Monday, Helen returned to work. When her boss told her that Dirk had been found dead of a drug overdose over the weekend, she channeled Meryl Streep and acted shocked and depressed. She was even able to muster up some tears to cap off her performance. No one suspected a thing.

That was years ago. They'd married, had a daughter and . . . and, what? Helen couldn't think of anything else. Wesley had come for her, taken care of things, and she had married him. Classic damsel in distress. She'd thought he would save her forever, but she found herself still in distress. Perhaps he wasn't her knight in shining armor. And what if the man she was *supposed* to be with was still out there? What if that person would be the one to make her feel whole?

Leelee was anxiously waiting for Brad to get home. Today was an important day, because he was meeting with his boss to ask for the promotion that the boss had been dangling in front of him for weeks. This promotion would mean more money, which could mean a new house. Leelee had already secretly met with a Realtor and looked at a few houses on the sly. She knew Brad would get angry and feel pressed, but she really wanted out of the tiny jewelry box that they called home.

Another thing that would come out of this promotion was the possible return of Brad. With his work pressure, he had become morose and testy, and was completely withdrawn. They had their good moments, but she couldn't get over her feeling of disappointment with him, and he sensed it. She was obsessed with everything she couldn't afford, and the fact that she was already in her thirties and her friends were so much better off than she was. She wished it didn't matter, but it did! Brad had let her down. And now everything was suffering. They had virtually no sex life. At first she wasn't interested, and then he couldn't get aroused. She knew it was because he didn't feel like a man, and she also knew she could do nothing about it. To hell with him. She was the one who was trying to make the most out of their situation. She had done up the house really nicely, had gotten them into the right clubs and made sure their kids went to the right schools and they socialized with the right people. All he had to do was bring home the bacon. But he failed. It would be one thing if he would put on a happy face, but it was getting impossible to live with such a depressed person.

Jack would never do this to her, Leelee thought. She was increasingly comparing her life to his. If she were Jack's wife, everything would be great. But he had chosen Tierney, a shallow, silly girl who liked to go out every night. Maybe he regretted it. Maybe she really should follow Victoria's advice and go after Jack. Why not?

Brad walked into the house and put his briefcase in the corner as Leelee leapt up from the sofa where she had been reading *Eloise in Moscow* to the girls.

"So?" she asked eagerly. She noticed he was wearing his good suit, and the monogrammed gold cuff links that she had given him as a wedding present.

Brad shook his head and went into the kitchen.

"What do you mean?" asked Leelee, the blood draining from her face.

"He said no," snapped Brad, opening the refrigerator.

"That's it? Did you ask . . ."

"He said I need to bring in more clients and all this stuff, just making up excuses."

"Do you think he wants you out?" said Leelee, a tremor in her voice.

"I don't want to talk about it," he said, interrupting her. He walked over to the stove and lifted the lid on a pot. Seeing that it was soba noodles with tofu and bean sprouts, he scrunched up his nose in disgust and returned the lid.

"Brad," she began.

"I don't want to talk about it," he snapped.

"But we have to . . ."

"No, we don't. Because it's just going to be the same: how

this affects *you,* how *you* can't have the life you want, et cetera, et cetera. What about me? This is devastating for *me.*"

Leelee stared at Brad, whose eyes were gleaming. He walked back to the refrigerator and reopened the door as if something new would have sprouted there in the ten seconds between the last time he looked.

"I'm sorry you feel that way, Brad," she said. "I just want what is best for *us* and for our girls."

"Well, it didn't happen. There's nothing I can do about it!" he said, slamming the refrigerator door.

She felt like screaming, but instead she calmly went upstairs to their bathroom and closed the door. She got undressed, carefully folding her clothes and placing them on the hamper, took the bath mat off the side of the tub and aligned it on the floor, and got into the shower. As she let the hot water run over her body, she thought about Jack.

It wasn't hard to love Jack Porter. As charismatic and brilliant as his father, he was even handsomer, and he possessed that insouciant confidence that comes with both privilege and good looks. He was brave but not dangerous, mischievous but not inappropriate. He had exquisite manners and was a comfortable public speaker, and his only fault was that he sometimes came off as a little too suave—not slick, in a cheesy way, but just a little too self-assured and cocky. But that didn't bother Leelee. Her mother's constant promotion of the divine Jack Porter coupled with the shiny radiance of the boy himself always made him the most mythical, magnetic, fantastic creature in Leelee's eyes. There was no question that her heart belonged to him. There had been no question in her mind that they would be together. There was one time in Martha's Vineyard when it almost happened. It was August, the summer after Leelee's junior year of high school and

Jack's senior year. She could remember the events as if they were yesterday.

Leelee was in her bedroom getting dressed for a beach party. When a breeze came through the window she knew she'd have to wear something warmer than the usual shapeless white Hanes V-neck T-shirts she favored. Since she'd left all her fall and winter clothes in Brookline, she rummaged through her mother's drawer to borrow something and could come up with only a tight black ribbed turtle-neck sweater that fit very snugly on her ample bust. She was still a little sensitive about her breasts, annoyed that they had recently come in, and that they had come in so large. It hindered her field hockey game, made running a real drag, and also made her the recipient of unwanted older male attention. It really grossed her out when some guy her dad's age leered at her. In efforts to avoid that, she always put on the baggy T-shirts, but unfortunately tonight she would have no choice.

When she went downstairs Jack was already waiting and talk-ing to her father. Although in essence he was acting only as a desig-nated driver, in Leelee's mind he was always her date picking her up. He was laughing at something her father said when he turned and watched Leelee enter the room. "Heeey, Swifty," he said—he always called her Swifty, his pet name for her. (Jack gave everyone nick-names. It was his thing. She, in turn, called him Porty.) But after greeting her warmly, something in his dark eyes changed and he gave her a surprised look.

"What?" asked Leelee, walking over to her dad and Jack.

"Nothing," said Jack.

"You look nice, sweetie," said her father. "Where are you kids off to?"

"I'm having a beach party. Gonna get your little girl all liquored up," said Jack, slapping Leelee's dad on the back. Her father laughed

and wished them a good night. Only Jack Porter could get away with something like that, thought Leelee.

As soon as she was in the car, Leelee immediately started reprogramming the radio stations. "You cannot listen to these terrible grunge bands, Jack!" scolded Leelee. She adored being maternal with him and was often reprimanding him for this or that. They were their roles: Jack was the naughty child and she was the mother. She thought it was an indication of their closeness that Jack would confess bad things he had done and she would scold him, and she was quite territorial if any other girl tried to assume that role.

After fiddling with the dials on the radio, she suddenly realized that Jack hadn't pulled out of the driveway and was instead staring at her. She looked up at him.

"What?" she asked. He was giving her a curious look, one she hadn't seen before, as if he was deciding something, or confused by something.

"You look different," he finally said.

Leelee immediately blushed, and unfortunately with her fair, freckled skin there was no way to conceal it. "What do you mean?" she asked defensively.

"I'm not sure yet. Did you get your hair cut?" asked Jack.

Leelee brought her hand to her strawberry blond hair and played with the ends. "No."

Jack squinted his eyes a little as if thinking. "There's something . . . I can't quite pinpoint it."

For the first time Leelee felt that Jack was actually looking at her as a girl and not as the family best friend that she had been for so many years. She had been waiting for this moment, but she was totally unprepared.

"Well, is it good or bad, Porty?" she finally sputtered.

"Good, good," he murmured, still looking at her intently. Jack

had the ability to eat you up with his eyes. "I'm gonna think of it, Swifty. I'll let you know," he said, starting up the car and backing out of the driveway.

When they got to Katama Beach and unloaded the keg by the bonfire that some of Jack's friends had already started, Leelee made a beeline over to her friend Hilary, who like all of Leelee's friends knew everything about Leelee's love and complete devotion to Jack, and all of her plans to marry him. Even though she and Jack had never been romantic, Leelee had staked him out as her own and would have been completely traumatized if any of her friends had ever attempted to make a move on her man. After she told Hilary about the conversation in the car, Hilary looked at Leelee from head to toe.

"It's because you're finally showing off your boobs," she said, taking a sip from the blue plastic beer cup she held.

Leelee immediately hunched over and dropped to the sand, and pulled Hilary down with her. "What are you talking about?" she whispered, embarrassed. God, she was so self-conscious now in this sweater!

"You know, you always wear those loose T-shirts, no one can tell that you've got a wicked rack under there."

"Easy for you to say! You're like a board!" snapped Leelee. She was mortified. Had Jack noticed her breasts?

"Hey, don't get defensive, loser—it's a good thing! I don't know why you hide those puppies," said Hilary.

Leelee glanced across the bonfire and watched Jack manning the keg. He was bending over, filling up two plastic cups with the hose, when he looked up and caught Leelee's glance. Through the flames she could see his face brighten, and he gave her a big wide grin. Leelee's heart melted.

"Really? Do you think that's why?" asked Leelee.

"Yes. You look awesome tonight. You really should wear tighter-fitting clothes. You gotta flaunt what you got," advised Hilary.

"Okay," said Leelee, taking a gulp of her beer. It felt strange, almost pornographic, to suddenly be showing off her boobs, but if that's what it took to get Jack to sit up and notice, that's what she would do. And Hilary was right: she should flaunt what she had. She was aware that she didn't have very good legs, and cursed her mother, whose sturdy, muscular trunks she had inherited. Unfortunately, legs were something you could do nothing about, no matter how much you exercised, and Leelee did an awful lot of exercising, being a star member of the Varsity field hockey, ice hockey, and lacrosse teams. Better to hide her legs under pants and long skirts and show off those newfound knockers that just might be her ticket to love.

The rest of the night took on a long-awaited surreal tone. Hilary got word from one of Jack's best friends that he was digging Leelee tonight and even considering fooling around with her. Leelee couldn't believe it. The moment she was waiting for had arrived. It was so odd, because they had been together day in and day out all summer. Leelee was so nervous with anticipation and euphoric that this instant had finally arrived that she found herself drinking more than usual, which was a lot. She refilled her cup every half hour and gulped down the ice-cold brew (that tasted like cat piss) as if it were water. She hadn't really interacted with Jack at the beginning of the night, but by the end he was putting his arm around her and rubbing her back, acting very flirty.

Some couples had disappeared off into the dunes, while others were making out in their cars in the parking lot. Leelee wondered if Jack would suggest that they do the same. And how would he suggest it? Would he grab her hand and lead her off into darkness? Most of the stars were covered by a dense layer of haze, so the only light came from the bonfire. She imagined herself tucked away in a dune or under the empty lifeguard's chair, nestled in Jack's arms . . . it was too sweet to think about.

"Can you believe that you and Jack will finally get together tonight? It's so awesome!" said Hilary.

"I know, I know," said Leelee, holding her skewered marshmallow over the flame. It was getting brown, just toasty enough to smush it between two graham crackers and a piece of Hershey's chocolate bar to make the most delicious s'more. "I just feel . . . well, I feel so calm now, knowing everything's going to happen. Usually I just plant myself by Jack, but tonight, now that it's a done deal, I can relax and hang around and let him mingle, and just enjoy myself."

"You guys make a great couple," said Hilary, rising. "Want another beer?"

"Sure," said Leelee. Why not? She had everything to celebrate.

Finally, after almost everyone had taken off, Jack came up behind her and put his hands on her shoulders. Hilary, who she had been talking with, gave her a big supportive grin, and Leelee leaned back into Jack's chest.

"Shall we take off?" he asked.

"Sure," she said. "See ya," she said to Hilary.

"Be good, you two!" said Hilary, wagging her finger at them in a motherly way.

Jack took Leelee by the hand and started leading her up the dune to the parking lot. "We will," he shouted over his shoulder.

"Promise," Leelee said, laughing.

Jack was moving quickly, and it wasn't until she was trudging through the sand that she realized just how drunk she was. Wow, she had head spins. If only she could have something to eat, to sober her up a little. But what did it matter? She was going to finally kiss Jack!

Jack opened the door for her and she immediately turned on the radio. "I love this song!" she yelled, when Yas's "Mr. Blue" came on. She began to sing along. She looked over at Jack, who gave her a small smile.

"Leelee," he began. He called her Leelee, not Swifty! This was major.

"Oh my God, I left my shoes!" she said, interrupting him and slapping her forehead. "They're by the fire!"

"Do you want me to go get them?" he asked.

Yes, they were her new Jack Rogers sandals. But no, then he would leave. She wasn't sure. "It's okay," she said, finally. She felt strange. She was excited that she knew that tonight would end differently. All those nights of Jack dropping her off, and her thanking him and shutting the door and going into her house and up the stairs and into her room and going to sleep alone, with sand in her bed from her feet and the smell of fire still in her hair and beer on her breath and no one to cuddle with . . . That was done! She would get a good night kiss!

"Are you sure?"

"Yes. I mean no. I mean yes." She giggled. It was too much! Jack and Leelee sitting in a tree, K-I-S-S-I-N-G, she sang in her head.

"Are you okay?" asked Jack, concerned.

"What do you mean? I'm okay, you're okay," she said, bursting out laughing. She couldn't stop. It was all too funny.

Jack stared at her, and then started the car. "You've had a lot to drink. I should get you home," he said, backing up.

So he would kiss her at her house, not here. Fine! Leelee rolled down the window all the way and let the breeze blow in her face. It felt good. Suddenly, Jack jerked to a stop at a stop sign.

"Sorry, I didn't see that," said Jack.

"It's all right," said Leelee, who had been propelled forward. Luckily she was wearing her seat belt. But unluckily, the jerk had *made her feel sick. Really sick. She now fully comprehended how much alcohol she had digested. Too much. She put her head back against the seat.*

"Are you okay?" asked Jack.

"My head is spinning . . ." she said. Oh God, she felt so sick. "I'm going to hurl . . ." she said finally, lurching forward.

Jack swerved the car to the shoulder and Leelee got out. She ran into the bushes, and just as Jack made it over to her, she began barfing. Over and over again.

"Shh, it's okay," said Jack, rubbing her back.

She couldn't speak. She was too sick to be embarrassed. She tasted vomit in her mouth, in her nose, everywhere. She had never felt so sick. After she lost her entire dinner, Jack helped her back into the car.

"Don't worry," he said soothingly.

She was so dizzy and ill that all she could do was nod. She started to doze off, and later she remembered only Jack helping her to the door and up the stairs before she collapsed in her bed.

The next day she woke up mortified and furious at herself, with a large hangover to boot. Jack called to check up on her, and laughed when she told him how embarrassed she was.

"Don't worry, Swifty," he said.

"Okay, but can I make it up to you? Let's go out tonight and get some fried shrimp and I promise not to vomit," she said.

Jack laughed his adorable laugh. "I'd love to, but I'm leaving tonight. It's Henry Walsh's birthday bash in the Hamptons and I'm heading out there before I go back to D.C."

What? He was going? Summer was over? What about their kiss? "I didn't know you were leaving," accused Leelee.

"I thought I told you. Sorry."

No matter what kind of teasing or cajoling Leelee tried on Jack for the next twenty minutes, he still insisted that he was going. And so when Leelee hung up the phone, she realized that that was it: she had missed her chance. She was tortured over the next few months, especially when she had to return to school and hear about everyone else's hookups. How could she have gotten so drunk?

But then one night, after too much eggnog at Christmas break, Leelee confessed everything to her mother, who in turn gave her the best possible advice.

"Honey, you don't want to play around with Jack Porter now! He's marriage material. Let him have his fun and you have yours, and then one day he'll be ready to get married and he'll look over and realize it's you he's wanted all along," advised her mom.

"You think so?" she asked, hopeful.

"Sure. Why buy the cow when you can get the milk for free?" asked her mother.

And Leelee felt her mother was right. Let Jack have all his wild adventures, foolish hookups, and irrelevant dalliances. When the time was right, she would make her move. Because the only thing she wanted in life was to be Mrs. Jack Porter. Actually, make that First Lady Leslie Porter.

But that wasn't what happened. There had been a terrible error. But errors could be fixed, couldn't they? Leelee got out of the shower and dried herself off with a fluffy monogrammed towel. Yes, her life was all wrong. It had to be fixed. Now was the time.

·· *13* ··

Victoria had come home late from tennis clinic and was rushing to shower and change before she had to meet some of the mothers from the boys' school at Terry's to have a "working

lunch" coordinating the silent auction items for the winter benefit. When the phone rang she forgot to let voice mail pick it up,
and, not thinking, she threw her sneaker across the room and
leapt toward the extension next to her bed.

"Hello?" she asked.

"You little sneak—you didn't tell me you were Justin Coleman's *wife,*" said the voice on the other end.

Victoria felt the sweat beads from her scalp drip onto her
forehead. It was Wayne Mercer. She'd know that slick voice anywhere.

"You didn't ask," she said calmly. So he had tracked her
down. Impressive. She had only ever given him her first and
maiden names and vague details, but he had made the effort to
find her. Why was she surprised? He was cunning.

"I knew I recognized you. I told you all along," he said,
boastful.

"Yes, you did."

"But do you know who I am?" he asked.

"Yes," she said.

"No, I mean, do you know *who I am*?" he asked.

"You're my husband's nemesis," she replied calmly. This was
her favorite part of the game: the cat and mouse. It couldn't be
called a courtship because she never liked the fairy-tale endings.
She was all about the pursuit.

Wayne started laughing. She didn't like his laugh—it was too
smirky, oily. "You are one cold bitch, you know that? What kind
of woman would go to bed with the man her husband most
wanted to be like?"

For some reason she felt protective of Justin. "He doesn't
want to *be* like you, Wayne. He loathes you."

"Come on, he wants my life. He wants my clients, my job,

everything. And even his bitch wants me, so you can't blame him," he said, laughing again.

Wayne was cruel. Victoria had wanted to keep him out of everything and had erroneously thought she could handle him. "You're evil," she said.

"Not as evil as you," he said, almost languidly. Then his tone changed. "Meet me tomorrow at our place and wear what I like."

"I can't tomorrow," Victoria began to protest.

"You can and you will," he said, and hung up the phone.

Why did she always go for jerks? Her friends had always been confounded by her choice of men. They insisted she could have *anyone* but she always went for the ones that treated her horribly, the druggies or the assholes. What kind of sickness did she have? But she knew the truth: somehow, deep down, being a victim in a relationship was a cozy place for her. Because for all of Victoria's success, there weren't many other cozy places in her inner life. She glanced across the room at the framed photograph of her and Justin on their wedding day and sighed. Her friends had told her not to marry him. So had her father, but he was an asshole who cheated on her mother, so she didn't listen to him. His advice had maybe even sealed the deal. It was a great big fuck-you to Daddy. And now she was stuck with this nightmare. She had wanted Justin so badly, she thought, shuddering slightly at the memory. He was a god to her. What had she been thinking?

It was because he hadn't wanted her. On the first day of her summer internship at International Artists Association, Justin Coleman was the only agent who hadn't given Victoria a second look. He shook her hand, curtly said "Nice to meet you," and was immediately distracted by something else. That had never happened to Victoria before, and certainly not in Hollywood. Everyone, without fail, had given her the once-over, or done a double take when they saw her walk down the hall. Her hair was blown dry stick straight to perfection. She was wearing a new Prada suit that was short enough to show off her tanned legs. She had on her two-inch Jimmy Choos. She knew she looked amazing. If Justin were gay, he would have looked at her appraisingly, for every inch of her was accessorized and decked out with precision and class. She couldn't figure out why he had blown her off, but she was determined to get to the bottom of it.

It didn't take long to get the scoop on Justin. He was engaged to Marcy Ostroff, the daughter of legendary producer Arthur Ostroff, who for the past three decades had twelve hit shows on television and who was also one of IAA's biggest clients, natch. It was clearly a career move, Victoria decided. Justin wasn't drop-dead gorgeous, but he was handsome, with dark hair, eyes, and eyebrows. He wasn't very tall or muscular, but he exuded confidence and attitude, and it was his cockiness that made him more magnetic. Marcy, on the other hand, was nothing to write home about. Sure, she was skinny with pert breasts (probably not real, but done by a very good plastic surgeon) and wavy, honey-colored hair. But she'd had a bad nose job (probably done by a different plastic surgeon), her eyes were very far apart, and, frankly, there was nothing special or interesting about her appearance. Had she not been Arthur Ostroff's daughter, she would have been answering phones in a dental office. Instead, she was his right hand, "associate producing" her way through all of his projects, much to the ire of the legitimate professionals who had toiled for him for years. The wedding was in August, two months away, and set to be the wedding of the summer, maybe even the year. Victoria vowed to herself that there would be no wedding.

Much to Victoria's surprise, Justin was immune to her overtures. She'd attempted to make casual conversation with him, never alone, but when there were several people in an elevator or in the kitchen, asking for restaurant advice or where to play tennis, always reminding everyone that she was new in town. But Justin never offered up anything. Instead, she had about thirteen other colleagues calling her and offering to take her to Spago or for a round at the Bel Air Golf Club. Justin stubbornly refused to take the bait. And to make matters worse, because she was an intern and lower than he was on the food chain, he made a point of dumping all sorts of work on her. He'd even gone so far as to make her run out and get McDonald's for a young up-and-coming movie star client who had a hankering for McNuggets. It was demeaning. Here Victoria was getting her MBA at Stanford, and she was on fast food runs for an idiot who'd dropped out of high school. But she didn't complain; she just bided her time. She wore her short skirts and flirted with all of Justin's friends, and she waited for him to notice her.

Victoria laughed bitterly now at the thought. If only she had let it go, just forgotten Justin. But no, she'd had to be headstrong. She'd plotted and planned and then finally her moment came. She was at Fred Segal on Melrose, trying on outfits for a friend's wedding in the dressing room, when all of a sudden she heard the unmistakable nasal, whiny voice with the sibilant *s*'s come drifting out of the dressing room next to hers, ordering the salesperson to get more jeans for her to try on. She had heard that voice before. In Justin's office, when she had to cover Justin's phone, and even once on *Entertainment Tonight*. It was Marcy Ostroff's. Victoria waited a minute and then went out of her dressing room. Marcy was standing in front of the full-length mirror, twisting a lock of hair with her finger and turning backward and forward to check out her appearance. She was wearing the tightest jeans Victoria had ever seen, and a shimmery sequined tank top. She looked repulsive.

"*That looks so cute on you,*" lied Victoria.

"*You think so?*" said Marcy, twirling around in front of the mirror.

"*Darling. You have a great figure.*"

"*Thanks,*" said Marcy, in a tone that indicated she agreed. Then she turned and looked at Victoria, who was positively glowing in a white eyelet dress. "*You look cute also!*" she said, as if surprised.

"*You think so?*" said Victoria with false modesty. "*I have to go to a wedding . . .*"

"*Oh my God—I'm getting married!*"

"*You are?*"

"*Yes, August thirty-first at the Hotel Bel Air.*"

"*That's bizarre,*" said Victoria. "*I think a guy I work with is getting married that day . . .*"

"*Who?*" asked Marcy, annoyed.

"*Justin Coleman?*" fake-asked Victoria.

"*That's my sweetie!*" said Marcy, shrieking with joy. "*You work at IAA?*"

"*Yes,*" said Victoria. "*You must be Marcy! I've talked to you on the phone! Let me tell you, Justin's a great guy. And he is madly in love with you!*"

"*Awwwww, he's so cute,*" said Marcy. She got lost in her thoughts and then she turned back to Victoria.

"*What's your name?*"

"*Victoria Rand.*"

"*I'm Marcy Ostroff.*" She said the last name clearly, making sure Victoria heard it. "*You want to grab some lunch?*"

"Sure," said Victoria. *If she had to get to Justin through his lady, so be it.*

"Don't stop, fucking me," chanted Victoria. "Give it to me—harder, harder," she repeated.

Justin had her pinned against the door to his office. He had ripped open her shirt, popping off all the buttons, and had yanked down her panties. Now he had one leg up, and the other clasped around her. With his pants around his ankles, he was pumping Victoria with a ferocity that she had never experienced before.

"Harder, harder," Victoria begged.

"You slut!" said Justin, and he slapped her around the face. She liked it rough. It was always the best sex.

Seconds later, Justin's body shook and he came into her. He immediately pulled back and yanked up his pants, buckling them before Victoria had a chance to take a breath. She could feel his cum start to drip down her leg, and the sweat under her armpits. Breathing heavily, she pulled down her skirt and collapsed on the couch in his office.

"Hey, watch the sofa. I just had it upholstered," said Justin. He was looking at himself in the mirror that he kept in his top drawer, running his hands through his hair to straighten out the cowlicks.

Victoria flung her legs down on the floor and sat up. "Wanna go to dinner?"

"Can't," said Justin, still looking in the mirror.

"Marcy?"

"Just can't," said Justin.

It had been three weeks since she had become Marcy's best friend and one week since Justin had finally succumbed to her advances. She had organized her seduction the way she organized her projects from business school. *Marcy's continuous gushing about Justin had helped Victoria fill in the flash cards. And luckily Marcy was vain and indiscreet, so she confessed even the most intimate details, like how Justin liked it rough, how nothing turned him on more than anal sex, and how his biggest fantasy was getting a blow job under the table at a restaurant. Piece of cake.*

At first Justin seemed irked that Victoria had struck up a friendship with Marcy. He ignored her, but when he couldn't, he gave her every indication that her presence was not welcome. But then one night the three of them went out to a Polish restaurant in the valley. Victoria had picked the place when she heard from her hairdresser (whom she normally ignored) that not only was the food good (which it wasn't) but the dimly lit restaurant had dark leather booths with thick red tablecloths that swept the floor. He told her that he and his lover had gotten busy under the table one night, and that was all she needed to know. Getting Justin to come along was a challenge, but when she told him it was supposedly George Clooney's favorite restaurant, he agreed (always the star fucker). And when Marcy went to the bathroom and Victoria slipped under the table and pulled down Justin's zipper, he was glad he'd agreed. Marcy returned and asked where Victoria was, and in his compromised position Justin was able to motion outside and mumble that Marcy should go check on her, and by the time she returned, confused, Victoria was sitting back at her seat, pretending all was normal. They laughed over the confusion, and Justin became very animated the rest of the night. From then on, it was a sexfest.

But even though Victoria was having sex with Justin, she still couldn't get him to cancel the wedding or dump Marcy. He was determined to marry her. And when he did, Victoria returned to her last year of business school furious. She had always gotten what she wanted when it came to men, and she certainly would with Justin. The more unattainable he was, the more she desired him. In her mind, he had become her greatest challenge, and that somehow elevated her opinion of him in general. She knew he would be successful because he could push people's buttons. His success would be her success. He was a competitive guy; she just had to figure out what he really wanted, or what made him want something. It took some research, but she eventually learned what he wanted. He wanted to screw over his enemies at any cost. And his biggest enemies were the rival agents who stole his clients.

Upon graduation from business school, Victoria returned to L.A. and went to work at Fox. One day, she "accidentally" bumped into Justin at lunch at the Ivy. She asked after Marcy, and he was vague. He asked her what she was up to, and she was vague. But later that week she went to lunch with Marcy, and told her that she was seeing Wayne Mercer, Justin's biggest enemy. At the time, it was a lie, but it certainly got Justin's attention. That night there was a knock at her door. Justin was there, flowers in hand. She wouldn't let him in, telling him she had company. For three months she held out, blowing him off, and he wooed her as if she were the biggest celebrity on the planet and he was dying to represent her. The perks were amazing: new clothes, use of private jets, a BMW made available to her (all courtesy of IAA). In the end, it was the smallest thing that got her. Sure, the buckets of roses were amazing, but it was the single daisy that he placed on her doormat one morning next to the small handwritten note that got her. Please say yes. *She would finally say yes. The divorce was done in record speed, and Victoria and Justin eloped in Vegas.*

Happily ever after, laughed Victoria. Not. A marriage built on a sham always remains a sham. Justin didn't care about her, and she didn't really care about him. But right now, Wayne was more of a problem. He was dangerous, unlike anyone she had dealt with. It was time to pull the plug.

·· *14* ··

"**When all of** a sudden you have been given permission to reenter the world of the swinging singles, every member of the opposite sex somehow seems amazingly attractive—you know what I mean?" Helen asked Eliza during the break in their YAS class. YAS, or Yoga and Spinning, was located in Venice, and Helen had insisted that Eliza come along and check it out. The first thirty minutes were spent spinning on bicycles, trying to get cardio out of the way, and the second thirty minutes were spent stretching out in yoga. A perfect combination.

"I guess," answered Eliza.

"No more sublimating every sexual yearning I feel. I mean, look at that guy over there," whispered Helen, motioning toward a slight man with longish blond hair unrolling his yoga mat. "He's hot. Starving actor probably. Me likey," she said with a smile. That was exactly Helen's type: slender, fair-haired, and creative. At least that's what Helen always said, even though her husband was clearly not slender or fair-haired. Creative, yes.

Eliza looked over at the guy. He was cute but he definitely wasn't her thing. "He looks about twelve," she said.

"No way," said Helen, shaking her head. "You think?"

"Fetus," Eliza confirmed.

The teacher came in and the members of the class went to their mats and started their sun salutations. Downward facing dog here, upward facing dog there. Everyone was rhythmically contorting his or her body into pretzel positions, attempting to gain serenity and drop some pounds at the same time.

Helen had come to terms with the idea first and now fully embraced the decision to be unfaithful. It wasn't that she took her marriage vows lightly. But she felt that over the past two weeks she had done a three-dimensional analysis of her marriage and her relationship with Wesley and realized that nothing would suffer if she were to sleep with another man. First of all, was it really natural for human beings to be monogamous? Or was it just a myth that society created to keep people in check? They weren't totally monogamous in ancient Rome, and that was a flourishing civilization—some might even say the benchmark. True, it collapsed, but at the rate the U.S. government was racking up enemies, who knew how long our society would exist?

Secondly, she and Wesley rarely had sex. And that certainly was not natural. Before marriage, she had been extremely sexually active, some might even say promiscuous. Okay, a little slutty, in retrospect, but she'd been finding herself. There were just so many men that she found attractive, why not check them all out? She wanted to have a real connection, to allow someone to see deep into her soul and make her heart beat again. And that might even *help* her marriage.

"I don't think he was that young, Eliza, really. I think he was about twenty-four," said Helen after class was over and they were walking to Jin Patisserie to get some tea and sandwiches. She had been watching the hot blond from the corner of her eye for the entire class.

Eliza rolled her eyes at Helen. "Delusional. He was young. But hey, that doesn't mean he wouldn't go for it."

"You think?" asked Helen, her eyes brightening. "I mean, yes, here he sees me all sweaty and gross, but the other day we had a very long conversation about the yoga retreat that he went on in Fiji. He said the nature there is astonishing, and he felt like he had been rebirthed."

"Rebirthed? Okay, he sounds a little pretentious," said Eliza. Helen always seemed to buy into those conversations. Could she really take someone like that seriously?

"I've read a little about it. I think it's fascinating. If you want, there's a lecture next month at UCLA," said Helen.

Eliza stopped and turned to face her friend. "Helen, are you seriously thinking about doing this?" she asked.

"The lecture?"

"No, sleeping with this guy," said Eliza.

"You know, I really think I am, Eliza," said Helen. "I need to be defibrillated. I need to become whole again."

"And having sex with this dude from YAS will do all that?"

"Maybe not him, but I have to try. I have to begin my journey."

"I don't know, Helen."

"And I think you should, too. But only with Tyler. Because you definitely have something out there with him, something cosmic, and I think you need to get it out of your system or it will haunt you. You'll be on your deathbed and thinking about him. Even if you've had a great life with Declan and maybe you, like, won a Pulitzer Prize for your writing, you will still want to recapture that beat of your life. So, carpe diem."

Eliza was about to protest and then stopped and shook her head. Helen was right, she hated to admit. In fact, she knew deep down that she was doing all this protesting just to get it on record. The truth was, she wanted Tyler. And now he was in town.

At ten o'clock at night, Leelee was home in front of her computer. It was her absolute favorite time of the day. The girls had gone down easily, bath time, story time, bedtime, it all ran like clockwork. She loved the ritual and so did Charlotte and Violet. Leelee knew she was lucky: she had the sweetest, most beautiful flaxen-haired girls in town. They were only two and four, but people had already told her they should model or act. She would never do that—that was beyond cheesy—but she did relish the compliments and believe that if they were really put to the test they would put Dakota and Elle Fanning to shame.

Brad was watching some game on TV, always some seasonal sports thing: baseball, football, hockey, basketball . . . she couldn't keep track. He liked all of those American sports that every guy did. She went in more for reality television shows, *The Bachelor* and *The Apprentice* (especially the Martha Stewart one), but she was of course addicted to *Desperate Housewives*. Although, if she could pick only one show in the world to watch, it would be *Oprah*. She worshipped that lady.

But television was far from Leelee's mind as she sat at her Pottery Barn "Bedford" desk in front of her baby blue Macintosh in the small office off the kitchen that she had claimed as her own. This was her tiny retreat. She'd had the walls painted a light pink and kept the trim white, putting white and pink gingham curtains on the narrow window. On one wall was a framed Mary Cassatt print of a mother and a baby, and on the other wall was a white bulletin board covered with forms from the girls' schools and playgroups, as well as a pink and white ribbon board that held pictures and recent baby announcements. She had drawers full of stationery in her name, Leslie Swift Adams, in her and Brad's name, Bradley and Leslie Adams, and in the girls' names, Charlotte Swift Adams and Violet Belle Adams, each color-coded and meticulously arranged. Everything from the Post-its on her desk to the slipcover on the chair that she sat on was monogrammed. Leelee loved monogramming. In fact, the house held countless articles that were monogrammed: the doormat, the bath towels, the hand towels, the dish towels, the bedspreads, the notepads, the glasses, the silverware, the toothbrush holders, the picture frames, the photo albums, and on and on. She was always awaiting delivery of this or that from some catalog, and whatever arrived inevitably bore a giant *A* nestled between a smaller *B* and *L*.

Leelee was online, instant-messaging with Jack Porter. She never kept a diary, but everything she would have written in it was instead downloaded to Jack. Well, not everything. She didn't really get into Brad or her girls, and besides, what would she say about her husband? She preferred instead to exchange meretricious gossip, current events round-ups, and everyday advice with the guy who had been her confidant since she was two. Jack didn't mention his wife often and would instead talk about his work and his father's, or engage in some sort of political discussion. But his favorite thing to do was to "press Leelee's buttons," and for that effect, he would send her the raunchiest, most explicit jokes he could find. Usually Leelee would laugh to herself and reply "Naughty boy" or just ignore them, but tonight she felt different.

When the girls all agreed to be unfaithful to their husbands, Leelee immediately pronounced herself on board because she would never allow herself to be the naysayer in a crowd. She considered herself a team player, and her group of girlfriends was extremely important to her, so she'd "take one for the team," as they say, if she had to. In the back of her mind, she was sure it wouldn't come down to cheating, because first of all, Eliza and Declan had a pretty good marriage, and even though Eliza had a crush on a movie star, no matter what connection she claimed to have had with him five years ago, there was no chance she was getting in his pants. Eliza was a reasonable person; she wouldn't mess up her life for an *Us Weekly* fantasy. Probably Victoria would cheat, but Leelee had a suspicion she may have already. Her marriage to Justin was all messed up anyway, and Leelee had no doubt that it would end in divorce. Brad had once gone to the Peninsula late at night to meet clients from Switzerland, and he saw Justin there with two girls, doing shots at the bar. Granted, they may have been clients, but come on. He has a wife and family sitting at home. What's he doing at a hotel with two girls? Helen was less easy to gauge, but she was so out there that you never knew. She might have a "spiritual connection" with someone from another dimension and consider that cheating. Leelee was sure in a few weeks this whole idea would be null and void.

But as she sat there going back and forth with Jack as he sent her joke after joke, each one dirtier than the next, she paused before sending back her usual reprimanding reply. What if she stopped playing the role of disapproving mommy to Jack and called him on his little flirtations? They *were* flirtations, weren't they? Why else would he use the language he did and make the implications that he did with her? He had plenty of guy friends. Suddenly excited, Leelee reread the latest entry that Jack had sent:

What's grosser than gross? Finding dandruff in your pubic hair.

Typical Jack. A little immature, a little random. Leelee took a deep breath and began to type:

I don't have dandruff in mine. But you're too pussy to know if I'm telling the truth. Aren't you?

She gritted her teeth and pressed Send. It felt like four hours before Jack replied, and every emotion from exultation to panic flashed through her body while she waited. Finally a message popped up.

Am intrigued. Is that an invitation?

·· 16 ··

Two weeks into the infidelity pact, the ladies were already at various stages in their pursuit of other men. Victoria was being cryptic to her friends, but they surmised that something was up. Helen had introduced herself to the hot young guy from YAS and asked him to coffee, which had turned into a four-hour discourse about the teachings of Deepak Chopra. Leelee and Jack were exchanging racy jokes full of heated innuendo but had not yet made the leap into cybersex, and Leelee was still uncertain if that would happen at all. Only Eliza had done nothing to contact Tyler Trask and was still wishy-washy about the entire experiment.

On that Friday night, Helen and Wesley had a dinner party to introduce their local friends to one of Wesley's oldest pals, Harry Sutherland (a.k.a. the Duke of Locksdowne), and his new bride, Tessa, a former model who was a good two decades his junior. Helen and Wesley entertained often, whether it be dinner parties, cocktail parties, Oscar parties, brunches, Boxing Day lunch—no occasion was too small. Helen liked to entertain by theme, and because she knew that Wesley and Harry had once spent a month lounging at La Mamounia in Marrakesh, she decided to "do Moroccan" for the evening. That meant that everyone would sit on plush satin pillows (purchased specifically for this event) at a low table and feast on traditional dishes like chicken and meat kabobs, lamb tagines, and vegetable-flecked couscous followed by mint tea and baklava, all served by a waiter clad in an authentic Moroccan outfit. Helen enjoyed taking advantage of any opportunity to spice up her parties, and she had a particular interest in impressing Harry's new bride after she'd heard how "brilliant" she was from Wesley's usually reticent parents. If this chick had dazzled her hard-to-please in-laws, then Helen wanted to make sure that Tessa had only good things to say about her when she went back over the pond. Helen always felt that her in-laws disapproved of her, and although she usually didn't care much ("Out of sight, out of mind," she would say), when there was any chance that they might hear something about her, she wanted the information to be delivered with superlatives.

Declan was distraught by the seating situation. As soon as he and Eliza arrived and noticed that Helen was doing one of her ethnic dinners, he already felt the soreness in his legs. How was six-four Declan supposed to eat dinner sitting on a smushy pillow with his legs crammed under a table that was only four inches from the ground? It was going to be agony! Eliza knew at once that Declan was perturbed, and she wrapped her arm around him and gave him a commiserating look.

"I already know what you're thinking," she said with a smile.

"Is she crazy?" he asked. "This setup should be for a kids' party, not for grown-ups."

"I'm sorry," said Eliza.

"I'll need a few drinks to be able to sit down. What can I get you?" he asked.

"White wine," she said.

"Be right back."

Eliza watched Declan as he walked over to the bar. She tried to look at him objectively, but it was impossible. They had been together so long—almost ten years—that she sometimes forgot that he was not an extension of herself. He was definitely handsome. She loved his height, and that he still had a thick head of dark hair. He was smart and witty and got along with almost everyone. It was nice to know she could just chuck him into any social setting and he would do well. And he was successful; he'd worked for the same bank for years and just kept moving up the ladder. No, she didn't have any problem with Declan. That's why the whole cheating thing was hard. It would be purely for selfish, hedonistic reasons, purely an effort to feed her vanity. She really did miss those moments when a look from someone special made her stomach leap. It was so unfair that once you signed on for marriage, you had to shut down that emotion. Sometimes she still had it with Declan, usually when they were at a party and she saw him talking to someone who was impressed by him. That was when he was his most gorgeous to her. That was sick, she realized. She most wanted her husband when someone else did. No, it wasn't that. It was that sometimes it takes someone else appreciating what you have in order for you to appreciate it.

It was funny: Eliza remembered that she never liked the "getting to know you" phase of dating. Sure, there were the moments of her heart doing flip-flops, but she always craved nestling into the comfort zone, where she was totally relaxed with a person, so she didn't mind if he saw her in baggy underwear or with a chipped manicure. But now, all she wanted was another shot at the "getting to know you" phase. Of course, the grass is always greener.

"You're deep in thought," said Victoria, who had come up beside Eliza without her even noticing.

"Yeah—hey. Sorry," said Eliza.

Victoria, who was clad in a white tailored Stella McCartney suit, with her hair back in a sleek ponytail, gave Eliza a sly smile. "I can imagine what, or, let me say *who*, you are thinking about."

Eliza laughed. Victoria looked good. She always dressed well. Eliza had thought her own silky black Jil Sander pants and tunic looked great, until she saw her friend. Victoria just had innate style.

"So, what's up?" asked Eliza.

"Nothing much," said Victoria. "Well, that's not true. A little, but I'll update you later. Here comes your hubby."

Declan approached and the conversation shifted. Victoria had wanted to talk about Wayne, who had been texting her for weeks, but she didn't want to get into anything when her husband was ten feet away. God, Justin. He repulsed her so much. How the hell could she have married that greaseball? In theory it would be so much easier to just pull the plug now on her marriage and avoid any further pain. But she couldn't. First of all, there were her boys. They adored Justin. Even though they cringed when she and Justin bickered—which was now an hourly occurrence—they would be devastated if his presence in their lives were relegated to weekend visits. He was barely ever home, but when he was, they were thrilled. But on the other hand, she thought that if there was so much tension in the house, they might turn into serial killers when they grew up. Shit. What should she do?

There were other reasons she knew she wouldn't leave Justin. She didn't want to admit she had failed. It wasn't that she wanted to impress everyone—at this point, she really didn't care what people thought. There was only one person whose opinion she cared about. Well, she didn't *care* about his opinion, but she didn't want him to be right. And that was her "beloved" father. She had seen him once in fifteen years, and that was when she was walking down the street in New York with Justin. They were newly engaged and had just had lunch on Madison Avenue. When they got out of the restaurant, who did they bump right into but dear old Daddy. Daddy, pushing a stroller with his new wife, Tracy, a blond bimbo with a bad nose job and fake boobs, who was the same age as Victoria. She had cut him out of her life when she found out he was a serial philanderer who had cheated on her mother from the start. After years of throwing out her father's letters and slamming the phone down on him when he called, she was now face-to-face with him. She was too shocked to flee, so after initial introductions, she watched with peculiar detachment as her father talked to the man who would be her husband. She thought Justin came across well, and she was proud, and in some ways she felt a little more at peace with her dad. That's why she took his call the next day. And when he warned Victoria that she was making a huge mistake if she married Justin, that he was all wrong for her and "had shifty eyes," she slammed the phone down on him again and wiped him out of her life forever. If she divorced Justin, her dad would be proven right. And she couldn't have that. No way. Not after all the pain he had caused her.

"Dinner," said Helen, ushering her guests into the dining room. She flicked off her shoes in the foyer and encouraged others to follow suit before strolling to the head of the table and plopping herself down.

"This is a feast," said Harry appreciatively.

"You sit next to me," Helen said, yanking Harry down. It was the first time since he and Tessa had arrived that they were not holding hands, making out, feeling each other up, or exhibiting any other forms of PDA, and Helen wanted to seize the moment. Helen had always been the trophy wife in her husband's circle of friends, and had liked that role. But now here was Tessa, a younger, thinner, and prettier trophy wife, and Helen felt as if her role was usurped.

"Okay, and Tessa can sit on my other side when she gets back from the loo," said Harry.

"Right," said Helen. For a grown man, he was acting like a baby. Yes, Tessa was beautiful. She had no body fat, shiny blond hair, and legs as long as palm trees, but come on! She had never seen Harry so gaga. And he was an attractive man, in that tall, thin, shaggy-haired British way. He'd definitely had his share of the ladies. Gosh, new love. Helen couldn't remember what that felt like. She glanced down the table to where Wesley had perched himself next to Eliza and Leelee. Sometimes she couldn't believe this guy was her husband. She hated to admit it, but sometimes he felt like a perfect stranger.

Helen had seen pictures of Wesley as a child, and he was gorgeous, with an ethereal beauty that proper English children often have. But now that he had grown up, his serene features had washed out a bit, making him entirely forgettable. It was almost as if he were slipping away, which is how Helen felt about their marriage. There was no rancor, no drama, no tension. They both led separate lives. Wesley was obsessed with movies and went practically every day or night, and when he wasn't doing that he was taking Lauren to school or classes and tweaking a script that he had been working on for several years. Helen was busy with her photo projects, going on yoga retreats and New Age seminars, and generally trying to heal the spiritual side of her that she felt was wounded. Their life was a little too sleepy when they were alone, so that's why they liked having parties.

"Helen, this is amazing!" shouted Leelee from her end of the table. "I can't believe you did all of this! Bravo!"

Everyone held up a glass and toasted the hostess. Leelee was genuinely impressed, and definitely a little jealous. See, *this* is how her life was supposed to be. She was supposed to be throwing these amazing parties, living in a huge mansion with an around-the-clock staff to tend to her every need. That's what she thought when she'd married Brad. She glanced over at her husband, who looked positively beefy squeezed between Victoria and Tessa. Tessa was laughing at something Brad was saying, and Leelee wondered what he could possibly say that was so funny. Tessa probably wouldn't think it was so funny if she knew what a loser Brad was. It was so hard being around people who were more successful than Brad, and that was usually the case these days. She had married middle management. And now he was going gray, getting fatter, and had generally nothing to talk about because his job selling equities or whatever the hell he did in that bank was so boring. He was no Jack Porter, that was for sure.

"Ladies and gentlemen, I want to thank you all for coming," said Wesley, rising with his glass in hand. "I'd like to toast first my dearest friend in the world, Harry. And say that I still think he's taking the piss out of me, because I can't believe such a gorgeous creature would marry this old cad . . ."

"I bribed her!" shouted Harry.

"But seriously, welcome to our home. Tessa, you are so charming, and it's lovely to meet you. I hope you will come more often and visit us—without Harry, if possible. And I want to thank my lovely wife for such a fantastic dinner. Thank you!" Wesley raised his glass while Helen nodded.

Eliza thought Wesley had given such a cute toast that she couldn't understand why Helen thought he was so dull. Victoria thought Wesley was so physically unattractive that she couldn't imagine sleeping with him. Leelee wondered who was richer,

Wesley or Harry? And Helen didn't even listen to what her husband said. She was thinking about that hot guy from YAS class.

"I have a surprise, everyone!" said Helen. She rang a bell, and seconds later three belly dancers as well as several men toting musical instruments entered the room.

"You didn't!" screamed Leelee.

"Let's boogie, people!" shouted Helen. She stood up and lowered the lights.

The musicians started playing and the belly dancers started shaking their tambourines and strutting their stuff. Throughout the evening the waiters had constantly refilled glasses and everyone was more or less inebriated, so with the entrance of the dancers the atmosphere positively ignited. Soon many of the guests had risen and were joining the dancers. As the drums thumped, the candles flickered and the people dancing cast dramatic shadows across the walls.

Leelee and Helen were mock–belly dancing with each other, laughing and throwing their hands in the air. Harry and Tessa were practically having sex on the dance floor, so immersed in their own little newlywed world that they couldn't have cared less what people thought. Wesley, Eliza, and Declan were avowed nondancers—all had on many occasions claimed that they were rhythmically impaired and incapable—so they sat there and drank and watched their friends. They didn't say a word; the music was too loud and they were immersed in their thoughts. Tonight Eliza secretly wished she had rhythm or grace so that she could get up there and just let loose. But more than that, she wished that Declan would grab her by the hand and stand her up and dance with her. She wanted him to do something different, display a spontaneous impulse and just go with it. She wanted to be wooed.

Most surprising of all were Justin and Victoria, who were passionately dancing in a provocative manner. It was a moment when the line between love and hate is blurred and emotion just takes control. The dancing got more and more frantic, and Victoria and Justin kept giving each other strange looks as they danced closer and closer, until Justin turned away and started dancing in the same manner with the belly dancer. Not missing a beat, Victoria danced over to Helen and Leelee and spun around furiously. Sweaty and excited, all three ripped off their jackets and danced in their bras or camisoles.

The alcohol, the music, the richness of the food, the darkness of the night, all culminated to give the room added intensity. Perhaps watching people newly in love when others felt at the end of love made everything more poignant. But whatever it was, that was the moment when all four women truly realized that they were going to change their lives. There would be no going back. They wanted every night to be like this. They wanted to hear the thumping of the drums, the ringing of the tambourines, the pulsing of their hearts.

·· *17* ··

Declan was so proud of Eliza for continuing to work after the birth of their children. He couldn't stand the hypocrisy of American women who were so concerned with equal rights and feminism and then chucked their entire careers as soon as they had children and expected the men to bring home the paycheck and be equal partners with dealing with the kids and household problems. How does that mesh with the whole emancipation thing? he would ask, adding that then the whole responsibility of making a living is put on the husband, while the woman gets a full-time nanny and demands to be taken seriously. Eliza half agreed with him, but half disagreed, too, so it was always a debate. She said that a lot of these women who had intense careers like investment banking or the law didn't anticipate how hard it would be to leave their children at home, and they had unfortunately chosen careers that didn't accommodate part-time.

Eliza was also proud that she worked. Sure, she could mostly do it from home and it was on her terms, but it was still employment, she still made money. She would have liked it if Declan appreciated the fact that she worked a little more, and, you know, didn't take it for granted just because his mother worked his entire childhood, but he never gave her extra kudos. Sometimes she just wished that he wouldn't be so hard on her. It was always write more, exercise more, clean the house more, play with the kids more. She often craved softness, a husband who would say, *Everything is amazing no matter how you do it.* But that was a fairy tale. And he was right, she supposed, to kick her ass. She received her accolades from her friends, who were very impressed that she could juggle motherhood and writing. The truth was, writing came easily to Eliza, and so she couldn't really congratulate herself. In fact, she knew that she should push herself a little bit harder and try to write a book. Doing articles is one thing, but anyone can do them. It was all about a book.

But for now, Eliza was a contributing editor of *Chat* magazine and wrote almost every celebrity interview, as well as a small column titled "What's Happening in L.A.?" that covered openings of stores, restaurants, and art exhibitions. She had considerable leeway in choosing who or what to cover, so no one would think it odd that she had selected Tyler Trask for her next cover story. After all, he was a major movie star who had a major movie coming out in a few months, and as luck would have it, he was in L.A. filming another picture, so it would be easy to coordinate a photo shoot. And the initial phone calls with his publicist had gone extremely well; they were excited to get him on a cover— after his incident in the bar he was considered somewhat controversial and therefore not easy to place. A date and time for Eliza to meet him had been set up quickly, and when Eliza mentioned that she had covered him for *Chat* a few years earlier, the publicist had pretended to remember her fondly. It was set that Eliza would meet Tyler at two o'clock on Friday at his trailer on the Sony lot, and they would take it from there. When Eliza hung up the phone in her office, her hand was shaking. She was going to do it.

"That was great," said Mark as he rolled off Helen. He reached over to the side of his bed and grabbed his bottle of Aquafina and guzzled it down. Helen distractedly watched his Adam's apple bob up and down with each glug and wished she had a cigarette. Or, better yet, some pot.

"Do you have any pot?" she asked.

"I'm not into that," said Mark, running a hand through his long greasy hair. "I like to keep my body healthy."

It was a good body to keep healthy, thought Helen. Mark from YAS had tight muscles, not a glimmer of fat on him, and a perfect suntan. A real California surfer boy.

"Shall we try it again?" said Helen, flipping over on top of him.

"Lady, you're crazy!"

"What? You don't have the stamina?" asked Helen, disappointed. She'd had an orgasm, but the effects of it seemed to dissipate quickly, and now something seemed to be missing. Mark was cute, and their lunch had been very interesting; he told her of his acting ambitions and mentioned that he worked at a Montessori nursery school to support himself, and they even discussed his newfound Buddhism. Everything was promising, and Helen had been so excited that she suggested moving on to his small apartment in Venice.

This is it! thought Helen. I'm finally about to come alive!

Pretty much as soon as they walked in the door of his shabby rental, they pulled off their clothes and landed with a thump on his unmade bed (really just a mattress on the floor), entwined in each other's arms. Probably because he was an actor, Mark took the act of fornication very seriously and dramatically; there were long, drawn-out passionate kisses, lots of nipple nuzzling and cunnilingus. It was all well and good, except that Helen sensed they had no bond. It just felt so empty. She thought of sex with Wesley, which was now a rare occurrence, and wondered if it was better than this. It was odd, but she couldn't remember. Maybe because she wasn't usually sober when they did it.

"I have the stamina . . . um, but you have to get me excited," he said, pushing her head down between his legs.

It was the first time Helen got a close look at his penis, and she wasn't impressed. She took it into her mouth disinterestedly and started to suck on it. But after a while, his flaccid little man meat remained limp, so she stopped.

"What's up?" she asked.

"Sorry," he said, rising. He seemed embarrassed, and quickly picked up his boxers off the floor and put them on. "I guess I need some wheatgrass juice or something. That wine at lunch did me in. Wanna go get a Jamba Juice and come back and try this again?"

Helen stared at Mark with a discriminating eye. Sure, he was cute and young. But damn, she thought she'd feel more fulfilled from an extramarital liaison. Instead, she felt nothing. He was a little dorky, actually, the more she looked at him.

"Sorry, gotta pick up my daughter at school," she said, standing up and getting her clothes.

"Your daughter?" he asked, surprised.

"Yeah," she said, pulling on her underwear. She felt very liberated standing naked in front of a guy. Granted, she'd just had sex with him, but she remembered the time when she was embarrassed to be naked in front of anyone. And her body then had been so much better! No cellulite, no stretch marks, no inches that you can pinch. God, if she could have the confidence she had now, with that bod . . . watch out!

"How old is she?" he asked, still surprised.

"Seven," said Helen.

"Um, do you want to talk about this?" asked Mark. He looked worried. What did he think? that she was planning on marrying him?

"No," she said, looking at her watch. Shoot, she wouldn't make it to Lauren's school on time. She'd have to call Wesley again to pick her up. "Gotta fly."

As she drove back to her house, she thought about her virgin voyage into philandering. It wasn't so hard. In fact, she felt fine about it. The trick would be to find someone she was really into. Maybe someone she'd already slept with. Because it didn't count if she had slept with him before marriage—it was, like, null and void. She'd have to check out her old address book. Mark was just a warm-up. She was now ready for a good roll in the hay.

Leelee had spent the morning at the beach club with Violet and the afternoon with Charlotte at ballet class, followed by an early dinner with another mother and daughter at the Cheesecake Factory, and after picking up takeout for Brad at Terry's and getting the girls bathed and into bed, she ran to her computer. Brad was working late, thank God, and she finally had her moment to e-mail with Jack. Her favorite part of day used to be her morning vanilla mocha latte from the Coffee Bean & Tea Leaf, but now it was definitely when she was instant messaging with her old friend.

She had been angry with Jack for so many years, but he had totally come through for her when times were tough with Brad financially. She couldn't really explain it to anyone, but Jack was the only sparkle in her life, the only thing that separated her from her situation and made her feel special, unique. It was as if the fact that Jack Porter, the gorgeous son of the next president of the United States, probably, had chosen *her* as his best friend and confidante gave her a validity that nothing else in her life did. And that's why she was so protective of him and cherished the friendship. If she had Jack picking her out of the suburban mom line-up, then she was as special as she'd always thought she was. That's what she hated about her stupid financial situation—that she was just a number. How could she have gotten herself into this? How could Brad have done this to her? How could Jack have run off with that stupid size-zero airhead Tierney Harris? Whatever. She didn't want to think about it now. She wanted to get online and hear what was happening on the other side of the country. She was excited to see her AOL sign bopping up and down. A message!

Hi, sexy! I had to go to the Vineyard today to check on the pipes in the house, and I thought of you, kiddo. It's freezing there now. Remember when our stupid families decided to celebrate Christmas there one year? Disaster.

Leelee remembered that. It was fun to spend Christmas with Jack. He made everything better.

I was thinking about the Vineyard also. Remember those parties on Katama Beach? Those were the days. I can still smell the bonfires and feel the sand under my feet.

She waited for his reply.

You live in California. You can have a beach party every day! I'm the one freezing my balls off.

It wasn't the response she wanted. Leelee took a sip of the pinot noir that she had cracked open and poured into the Tiffany crystal wineglass that was a wedding present. It was cold tonight, and she was feeling romantic.

Yeah, but you don't live here.

She debated sending that, as it could be construed in so many ways. Normally she would preface it and say, *You don't live here, and we're not young, and I miss all our friends and the East Coast,* but tonight she wanted to take her chances.

Remember that one summer . . . Wait, I shouldn't bring this up.

What did that mean? She was intrigued. Would it be embarrassing?

What summer? What shouldn't you bring up?

She waited nervously. She felt queasy. It was a long time before Jack responded.

That one summer where you and I almost hooked up. But then you booted and it was over . . . Ha ha—have you learned how to hold your liquor yet, Swifty?

So she hadn't dreamt it. He knew it almost happened also. But why didn't it happen another night? Why had she had only one chance?

I've learned how to control my liquor, thank you. I've learned a lot of things. But I've never quite learned why you were too pussy to make a move on me all those years ago. Surely you didn't let a little vomit get in your way? Were you just shy?

She was going for it. They had not talked in such a serious tone in years. It was surreal.

I guess I was a pussy. Didn't want to mess up our great friendship. I do regret it.

Wow, the great Jack Porter admitting error! She was excited.

You can fix it. No need for regrets. It's never too late.

The cursor flashed on the screen for what seemed like an eternity. Had she gone too far? She looked at the clock on the screen as the minutes flicked by. It was three whole minutes before a message appeared.

Meet me at the Ritz in Boston the weekend after Labor Day. I just made a rez under the name Porty Swifty. I'll book an e-ticket for you at AA. I'll be waiting.

Leelee reread it three times before breathing. Holy moly. This was happening. Before she could fully digest the information, she heard the front door slam. Brad was home. When they went to bed, Leelee was feeling both excited and benevolent, so she pulled out her secret cache of sex toys and seduced her husband. It was the best sex they'd had in years.

After his orgasm, he rolled over. She knew he would be asleep in two minutes, so she had to make her move.

"I forgot to tell you. I need to go to Boston next month. It's an event for Senator Porter and my parents want me to go. They're paying."

"Fine," said Brad, who was half asleep.

"Thanks. It's just for a weekend."

"Great," said Brad, and before she knew it, he was snoring.

It was several hours before Leelee could fall asleep.

Victoria had wanted to have another Girls' Night Out, but scheduling around everyone's lives proved tricky, as it was the end of the summer. Eliza and crew went to visit her family in Chicago for a week, and then Helen and Wesley were going to Hawaii next week, so there was really only one afternoon when they all could converge. Everyone met for a girls' tea/catch-up on Tuesday at four. Victoria lived in a Spanish-style abode on Toyopa Road in the Huntington Palisades, equidistant to Helen's and Eliza's houses. When she married Justin she'd made a strong point of telling him she didn't "do houses," so the decorating of the residence was turned over to Marcus Harrington, a well-known L.A. designer with an affinity for Eastern art and furnishings. Victoria had never wanted to be one of those women who spent hours contemplating tassels and fringe and couldn't be bothered dissecting the pros and cons of brushed nickel versus stainless steel hardware in the kitchen and bathrooms, so Marcus was given pretty much free rein to do as he pleased. The result was a very nice, sophisticated Asian-inspired home with mostly modern furnishings, little artwork on the walls, and even fewer objects that reflected the true personality of the denizens. That was fine with Victoria, who viewed homes as functional places for eating and sleeping, and little else. Her one caveat was that it be kept immaculate.

"Oh my God, where did you get these little pies? They're delicious!" said Leelee, cutting another piece of the apple and sliding it onto her plate. On a black lacquer tray on top of the

Chinese rattan coffee table, there was a meticulously arranged spread of small apple, peach, and pecan pies on red flowered plates, next to the sliced lemon and honey sticks for the tea. When Victoria invited someone over for tea, she took it seriously. But she herself would never indulge in sweets.

Victoria looked at Leelee with revulsion. "Marguerita picked them up at Urth Caffe."

"Love!" said Leelee. She knew that Victoria was giving her that look because she thought she was fat, but she didn't really care. Victoria was a skeleton, and although that was trendy, it was not attractive. No guy she knew ever went for that anorexic Nicole Kidman look. They liked women with knockers and curves and it was only the gay fashion designers who wanted women to look like little boys and decided to make it fashionable to be Karen Carpenter. Well, folks, news flash: Karen Carpenter died of anorexia, and Kate Moss has a drug problem, so those 'rexi broads are not paradigms.

"So, who goes first?" asked Helen, leaning back on the sleek armless sofa and taking a sip of her chamomile tea. She was psyched to dish about her young buck, but she didn't want to monopolize.

"Well, who has something to report?" asked Victoria, glancing at all of them.

Before anyone could answer, the sounds of a vacuum came floating in from the family room.

"Ugh, excuse me," said Victoria, standing up and marching across the stripped redwood floors of the living room and turning left into the next room to have a word with her nanny.

"This pie *is* good," said Eliza, taking a bite. She didn't like to eat in front of Victoria, who was very competitive about food, so she often sneaked a bite when she wasn't there. Pathetic.

"I know. I could Hoover it, but Vicki would have a conniption," said Leelee mischievously.

Victoria came striding back in, the heels of her metallic Jack Rogers shoes clicking along the way, and stood over them.

"Austin threw up in the family room, and Marguerita has to clean it up. I can't deal with this commotion, so why don't we all go up to my bedroom? Then I can get you that dress you want to borrow, Helen, and we can have some privacy sans noise."

It was more of an order than a suggestion.

"Is Austin okay?" asked Eliza.

"He'll be fine," said Victoria, picking up the tea tray. "Does anyone want more pie, or shall I leave it and just take the tea?" She looked at Leelee when she said this.

Leelee wanted more pie but now she couldn't be the only one to say it. Victoria could be such a bitch. She'd hate to be married to her.

"I'm done," said Leelee.

"Good," said Victoria, clacking her heels on the wood floors and making her way upstairs.

Victoria's beige bedroom was capacious; one end held an austere wrought-iron bed adorned in Moroccan pillows and Afghani throws, bookended by teak side tables holding blood red reading lamps. On the other side was a sitting room with a crisp beige couch, two stuffed armchairs in a Ralph Lauren beige and red paisley fabric, and a low ebony coffee table. The ladies all plopped down on that end as the ocean breeze filtered in through the window.

Victoria went out of the room and returned a second later with her baby monitor, which she plugged in to the outlet next to the couch.

"I'm using two different monitors these days. I have them all over the house. I want to hear what Marguerita is saying to the boys. I asked her to speak *only Spanish,* but I've heard from another mother in the park that she speaks to the boys in her pidgin English!" explained Victoria. "I mean, why have a Spanish nanny if she's not going to speak Spanish, right?"

"Maybe you need a nanny cam," said Helen, jokingly.

"I just ordered one," said Victoria. "Now, where were we? Why don't you start, Helen?"

Helen put down her teacup and smiled at her friends. "So, I did the hottie from YAS. It was good, not great. I think I need someone older. We're just at different stages of life . . ."

Eliza and Leelee were surprised. Helen had already done it? And she was ready for number two? But Victoria received the information clinically, in the same manner as a doctor would listen to a patient's symptoms.

"And how do you feel?" asked Victoria.

Helen nodded. "I feel good. I feel much better, actually."

"Okay, *whoaaaaaa* . . . we need more details, please," said Eliza.

"Yeah, like, big dick, tiny dick?" asked Leelee.

"Medium," said Helen. And then she conveyed in minute detail every kiss, touch, grope, as well as a full anatomical description, to her rapt audience. When she was done, she leaned back in her chair.

"Wow," said Eliza.

"You go, girl!" said Leelee.

"You know what's funny?" asked Helen rhetorically. "When you get married, suddenly you become this vestal virgin. It's like people—guys, I mean—place you in the off-limits category; they don't look at you or give you any sense that you're a sexual being. And then when you're a few years into your marriage, after you've had a kid or two, they look at you differently. It's like you reenter the game. Is it because we are more confident? Is it because we have some sort of spiritual fulfillment that makes us whole, fulfillment that comes from marriage? I don't know . . . But you can either pick up on it or not. And since we've made this pact, I've noticed it. I've noticed that I am a viable sexual person again and men perceive me as such. It's exciting. It's titillating."

The ladies all digested what she had said. Eliza didn't yet feel that way, although she yearned to. She wasn't sure that any guy saw her as sexual. Leelee knew what Helen meant. It was all of a sudden going to happen with Jack, and it hadn't been that way before, ever. Victoria knew about what Helen was saying all along, and she felt that she was always perceived that way. You just had to avoid thinking of yourself as the vestal virgin when you get married and no one else will.

"What about you guys?" asked Helen, finally.

"I'm meeting Tyler Trask on Friday, and we'll see," said Eliza. Her news was met by hoots and hollers and a few off-color remarks. Eliza tried to turn the conversation away from herself as quickly as possible, so she asked Leelee what her status was.

"You guys have to promise you won't tell anyone, because we're talking major national secret here," said Leelee.

All of the women promised.

"Okay. I'm going to Boston to rendezvous with Jack Porter. We've been exchanging e-mails like every second. He's fed up with his marriage. He has feelings for me . . ." Leelee's cheeks glowed when she said this. The other women were aghast.

"This is unbelievable!" said Eliza.

"This is what you've always wanted!" said Helen.

It felt like high school again. That feeling when your friend, who is popular but not the most popular, somehow lands the most popular guy, who she has been in love with forever. Despite whatever reservations they all had, they were giddy with excitement. It was romantic in that teenage way. They felt young.

Finally the attention turned to Victoria. She leaned back in her seat and looked at her friends carefully.

"I had sex with Wayne Mercer last night," she said finally. "He's my husband's archenemy. We did it on the kitchen floor of his house, in the bathroom, in the living room. He was magnificent. It was dirty, and raunchy. He's a naughty boy."

They all looked at Victoria's smug face with astonishment.

"Wow, that's a real jab at Justin," said Eliza.

"Yeah," said Victoria. "The funny part was, I made him put that movie *Seersuckers* on in the background, muted, of course. It's the one that stars Tad Baxter, that loser that Justin represents. Wayne told me that he's going to poach him from Justin."

"You're crazy!" said Helen.

"No. I just want my revenge," said Victoria.

Before anyone else could say anything, there was a loud fuzzy sound. They looked around. It was coming from the baby monitor. Victoria leaned down and adjusted it with her finger.

"Interference," said Victoria.

"That's one thing we don't need," said Leelee.

Later, when they were leaving and saying good-bye to Victoria, they noticed Anson Larrabee standing on the edge of Victoria's lawn, holding the leash of his Corgi, Samantha, who was taking a piss.

"Hi, Anson," the ladies all chanted in singsong voices. None of them liked this enormous buffoon, who was wearing belted green Capri pants and a pink Oxford.

"Hello, ladies," said Anson. He gave them a strange look.

None of them thought anything of it at the time. But later, they wished they had.

·· *19* ··

The pedicurist gently loofahed the heel of Anson's foot with soapy lather, taking extra care in scraping the dead skin off the big toe, just as he had specified. It was "beauty day" for Anson and Imelda, and they were at Aggie's getting their highlights done, followed by their fingers polished, their corns softened, and a quick neck massage to loosen those knots.

"This is the life," said Anson in his southern drawl, keeping a careful eye on the manicurist's emory board.

"I know. Who said maintenance has to be hard work?" asked Imelda, increasing the vibrations of her spa chair with the remote.

Imelda and Anson had been "dating" for several months now, and the relationship was beneficial to both. Imelda enjoyed going out to dinner and the movies, and Anson was a good companion. Anson, in turn, liked to be seen in the company of attractive women, and usually dated divorcées before they found their next husbands. In fact, Imelda had been introduced to Anson by her friend Rebecca, who dated him between her second and third husbands. When they split, there'd been no acrimony or tears, just fond farewells. Imelda easily slipped in where Rebecca had been, and she would be helpful in finding Anson a replacement when she left him for someone else.

"I have that guy coming tomorrow to give me a massage—you know, Enrique?" said Anson.

"Right," said Imelda, not really listening. She had no problem zoning out when Anson talked. He talked and talked, so it was actually quite a useful skill.

"He's gay but he's very good," said Anson. "I just don't want people to talk when they see a gay guy entering my house with a massage table."

"Anson, *you* are the only one who would talk!" said Imelda, bursting into laughter.

"You're terrible!" said Anson.

In the midst of his laughter, Anson noticed Victoria Rand enter and speak to the women at the front reception desk.

"Look who's here," said Anson, under his breath.

"Bitch," whispered Imelda.

"Yoo-hoo! Victoria!" boomed Anson, waving across the salon. "How are you?"

Victoria took a deep breath. She hated Anson, so toxic and useless, one of those people you wished you had never been introduced to in the first place. But it was better not to snub him. She didn't really care, but he was a neighbor, and Justin seemed to want to kiss his ass for some reason. So she sighed and made her way over to him and Imelda. Giant, oversize Anson squished into a tiny pedicure chair was, after all, an irresistible sight.

"Hello, Anson, Imelda," said Victoria.

"We're having our beauty day!" said Anson. "Are you joining us?"

"No, making an appointment for later."

"Making sure your nails are spic and span? Justin told me that his biggest pet peeve is a woman with sloppy nails," said Anson.

"He did?" asked Victoria, surprised. Justin probably said that, but it was bizarre that Anson would remember it. But then,

Anson remembered everything, every little detail. That's why he was dangerous.

"Yes. So where are you rushing off to?" asked Anson.

"I've got to pick up a dress at Elise Walker and then take the boys to karate," said Victoria, wondering why she was telling him anything. Anson had a way of twisting any information into something sinister.

"Oh, what's the dress for? A sexy date?" asked Anson, raising his eyebrows.

Victoria was caught off-guard. "Sexy date with Justin? Hardly. Just an industry party."

"Too bad! I thought maybe you and your charmin' hubby were going out dancing or something exciting like that," said Anson.

It was odd that he said dancing, because she and Wayne had just agreed to go to a Spanish dance club in downtown L.A. But Anson would have no way of knowing that.

"No, nothing that exciting."

"Dancing is a good workout," added Imelda, in a non sequitur fashion.

"Well, I should dash," said Victoria, not wanting to waste another minute.

Anson waited until the door closed after Victoria, then turned and whispered to Imelda.

"She's a nasty girl," he said.

"Bitch," said Imelda.

"And up to no good," said Anson knowingly.

Imelda knew that that was what Anson said when he had something on someone. "What do you mean?"

Anson looked around carefully to make sure no one else was listening. "Well, you know Victoria is my neighbor. And you know I have a baby monitor," he said, raising his eyebrows up and down to make the implication.

"But you don't have a baby," said Imelda, confused.

Anson sighed. Imelda was definitely not the brightest bulb on the porch. It was often like dealing with a retarded child. "Honey-child, you don't have to have a baby to have a baby monitor."

"Why not?"

He was getting impatient. "Because you can use a monitor to listen to other things. There's interference. Victoria's house backs up to mine, and her monitor is literally only a few feet away. If she's talking in the room that the monitor is in, I can pick up everything she says or does. She's on my frequency. I can hear her having sex, I can hear her on the phone, and I can hear her and her friends discussing things they shouldn't be doing."

"Like what?"

"I will tell you in good time. Believe me, it's not a good secret to harbor. But the best part is that I have a tape recorder plugged next to my monitor, so I am certainly getting it all down and recorded and will be putting it in a place where it's safe. I plan to use it one day, when the time is right. And then those bitchy ladies will be at my mercy. They will beg to be my friend, they will know I have the upper hand, and they will be made to suffer."

"You're naughty, Anson," said Imelda with a smirk. That's what she loved about Anson, his wickedness. Her ex-husband told her she was the most evil person he had ever met, but he didn't know Anson.

20

On her way to meet Tyler Trask on the set of his movie, Eliza decided to allow herself to be convinced that she was doing the right thing, engaging in this pact. But she was conflicted. She had a lot of experience with secrets being revealed and she knew it was hard for people to keep their mouths shut. She also knew that human nature could be tricky and that there was no predicting what people would do or say, least of all yourself.

As she drove her BMW SUV up Washington Boulevard, she thought about Tyler. She couldn't believe she was going to see him again. Was she really going to cheat on Declan? She thought about Bridget and Donovan. They worshipped their father. He was everything to them, the giant teddy bear that they crawled all over, the guy who flipped pancakes for them every Saturday morning, the ghostbuster who cleared out all the demons that they believed lived in their closets. Would she really risk messing up their lives just for a hedonistic impulse? Every night her kids waited by the window at seven-thirty for when their dad pulled in the driveway, and there was euphoria when he walked through the door. Was a one-night stand really worth tearing them from that? Her parents had never cheated. They'd been married forty years. And Declan's parents were also still married. She had to remember, after all, that this scheme had been concocted by Victoria, whose parents were divorced. People with divorced parents seemed to take marriage a little more cavalierly, she thought. It was a gross generalization, but she found it to be true. Every one of her friends who had "starter marriages"—those short one-year childless flings—had parents who had been divorced. People lead by example. And what kind of example would she be living if she slept with a movie star? So pathetic.

But then there was the other side. The half-dead side that wanted to rejoin life again. She wanted to feel pretty, to feel desirable, and she knew from experience that Tyler Trask was the only human being on earth who could make her feel that way. Maybe that's why she'd spent more than an hour getting ready, discarding outfits as if they were rotten fruit until finally settling on a white oxford tucked into a sleek black skirt with a slit up the side. It was conservative, but when she left the top button of her blouse open and accessorized with black Manolo Blahniks and a turquoise Ralph Lauren necklace, she seemed more casual. After debating for twenty minutes whether or not to wear her hair in a sleek ponytail or down, she opted for the latter, spending an extra ten minutes with a hair iron. Who said being pretty wasn't work?

"It's been a long time," said Tyler when he opened the door to his trailer.

"I know," she said, blushing. She put her face down so he couldn't tell and brushed by him to enter the trailer.

It was a deluxe mobile home, with comfortable leather seats, a plasma television, a fully equipped kitchen, and, from what she could see, a bed in the back. That made her blush even more. Eliza was still too nervous to look at him, so she glanced around the place several more times, noticing that everything was fairly neat and orderly except for the marble coffee table, which was strewn with scribbled on notepads, books on F.D.R. and the New Deal, the *New York Times,* and several venti-size Starbucks cups. Although there was some sunlight coming in through the slats on the shades, the lights were not on in the trailer.

"Sit down," said Tyler, motioning toward the couch. She stole a glance at him out of the corner of her eye and saw that he was wearing a plaid shirt and cargo pants. So cool. Why couldn't Declan dress like that? He was always so preppy.

Eliza walked over and sat down, and when Tyler sat across from her, she finally turned her eyes to look at him. She'd seen his face countless times in movies or on television interview shows that she had believed she wouldn't be fazed by facing him again in the flesh. But she was wrong. Although he was hailed as one of the most expressive actors in history, celluloid had never been able to capture the depths of his eyes. There was something about them that sucked you in, made you want to search deeper and deeper into them, all the while knowing that you will never get inside. His entire countenance was so powerful, so masculine, that Eliza literally felt as if he were a magnet pulling her toward him. She felt almost queasy with desire until something caught her eye on the windowsill behind Tyler. Then her heart sank and she was snapped back to reality. It was a picture of Tyler's girlfriend, Jane, holding their one-year-old son, Christian. She wanted to barf. But instead she stood up and took the picture in her hand and said in her sweetest voice, "Oh my God, is this your son? He's so cute."

She held up the picture to Tyler, but instead of replying, in one quick, smooth move, he swung her around and took her into his arms and sat her down on his lap.

"I knew you'd come back to me," he said.

21

The phone calls were frightening.

"Now listen here, bitch, you get over here in half an hour or I'm calling your husband," he'd hiss.

Or: "You fucking slut, I'm down the street. I'm coming inside unless you get out here."

Victoria would feel her stomach drop and not know what to do. He'd phone when Justin would be lying next to her asleep, and she'd have no choice but to quickly get dressed and go outside to see him. She'd beg Wayne to stop calling, but when he persisted, she moved into a guest bedroom, claiming to Justin that she was suffering from insomnia and didn't want to rouse him, but all the while fearing that the phone would ring and she would have to plead with Wayne in hushed tones to be sensible, kind, *merciful.* But so far he refused.

She had only herself to blame for getting into this situation. Sure, it was fun at first, thrilling. She loved the whole idea of screwing her husband's enemy because it was evil. But then she learned that Wayne was evil. She thought he was playing along with *her* in the beginning, but she quickly learned she was playing along with *him.* And she didn't have a choice. The sex got rougher—painful, even. He was a sadist and liked to slap her, make marks on her body. She tried to cut it off several times, but he'd call and call. Once she told him she had to go pick up her kids and he showed up outside their school! Another time he cornered her at a party where Justin was ten feet away and pressed his groin into her and made her promise to meet him. She knew that it wasn't that she was so great but just that he adored controlling her, loved that he was socking it to his enemy. And then when one of his clients left him and switched to Justin, Wayne became a maniac. All of his rage was directed at Victoria, and he was a monster.

Last night she had tried to end it with him again, and he'd gone ballistic.

"You little slut, you can't walk away from this," he said, pinning her against the wall in his front hall. She could feel his fingers squeezing her wrist so hard that a dark red mark was already forming.

"It's over, Wayne. Accept it," she hissed.

"It's not over until I say it's over, you whore," he said, twisting her arm tighter.

He was not used to getting dumped. He was an agent, after all—he wanted to control and own people and then discard them on *his* terms.

"Let's just be two adults and get over this. It was fun, now it's done," she said, her last attempt to break it off neatly.

"No, I'm not ready for it to end," he said.

"Why, Wayne? Is it ego? 'Cause I know I'm good, but I can't believe I'm *that* good."

Wayne let her go and started pacing around the house. His eyes were wild. She had thought initially that it was just one of those crazy looks that people in Hollywood get, but then after spending a few nights with Wayne she realized it was cocaine. The guy was majorly into the drug, and it was the cause of most of his insanity.

"You're not going, you bitch! I have video of us together! I will tell Justin!"

He had threatened this before, and that's what scared her. Was he telling the truth? What video? She had heard about some of those sick people who have their bedrooms set up with hidden video cameras just for this purpose, but was Wayne one of those? He had definitely shown his true colors.

Victoria had never anticipated how cruel and insane Wayne would be, and she knew it would be impossible for her to deal with him on her own. She wished she could tell Justin, but she knew his temper. He also had the capacity to be cruel and harsh. It would ruin everything. Not that their marriage was so wonderful, but it certainly would be over if she told Justin. She worried that she'd lose the kids. The divorce would be a mess. She hadn't worked for a few years, so she needed to get everything she could out of him if they split, and her infidelity with Wayne would not work in her favor.

Victoria wasn't the type of person to take this shit from someone. She wanted to be in control. But she needed help. That's why she had to enlist her friends. She thought it was weak to rely on them, asking them for help, but the truth was, she *was* weak and did need their help. That also infuriated Victoria. She didn't want to depend on anyone or appear feeble. So she was determined that her friends not be less innocent than she, and have some understanding of everything before she could let them in on her secret. Unless you walk in someone else's shoes, you have no idea what they are going through, her father always told her. Maybe there was some truth to that.

When the time was right, a month and a half after the infidelity pact, Victoria called Helen and Eliza and asked to meet them for lunch. She didn't call Leelee, because Leelee was annoying her and she wished that she hadn't brought her into this whole agreement. On the one hand, it was working well for Leelee, and she was about to go off and meet Jack for a romantic weekend. That meant she was totally committed. But Victoria still suspected that Leelee was being immature and not entirely straightforward, so she preferred to unload her problems to Helen and Eliza, who were much more reasonable. Eliza had just had her tryst with Tyler, so she was fully on board the project, and Helen had just struck up an affair with Daniela Fox, the lipstick lesbian who was the one lady in town able to seduce straight women. Victoria couldn't wait to hear the details.

On her way out the door, the phone rang. Victoria bit her lip. Should she get it? It was probably Wayne, and she didn't want to deal with him. She ignored it.

"Oh my God, Victoria, that's horrible," said Eliza after Victoria had confided the entire awful situation to her and Helen.

"This guy is obviously disturbed," said Helen. "What's his sign?"

Victoria glared at Helen. "What?"

"Sorry, I just . . ." Helen trailed off. But if he was a Taurus or a Leo, Victoria was in for it.

"What can we do?" asked Eliza.

The waitress came and put down their entrées, grilled fish for Helen and Eliza and a hamburger for Victoria. They were at Houston's near the promenade. It was noisy and open and mostly full of tourists at lunchtime.

"He said something about videos, and I need to find out if he has them. I need to get into his bedroom when he's not around. The problem is that he has a state-of-the-art security system—this guy is paranoid, and he won't leave me alone for a second when I'm there," sighed Victoria.

"But knowing you, you have a plan," said Eliza.

Victoria turned and smiled, the first time all day. "You know me. I always have a plan."

"So what is it?" asked Eliza, waiting.

"We're going to steal the tape. You and I, Eliza, are going to Wayne's house. We're going to get it."

"I don't know . . ." began Eliza. She didn't want to get into the middle of this sordid mess. Of course she wanted to help her friend, but stealing something? Sneaking into someone's room? She was not a heroine in a detective novel. There was no way her nerves could handle that.

"What about me?" asked Helen, offended.

"Sorry, sweetie, but we all know how you panic under those stressful situations," said Victoria with a knowing look.

"You're right," said Helen, knowing it was true. She'd be useless. "So what's the plan?"

Victoria wiped away crumbs on the tablemat, took a deep breath, and detailed all of her plan to her friends. She had thought about it all morning and knew she was being thorough. Helen nodded and agreed that it was a sound plan, but of course she didn't have to do anything. It was up to Eliza. After much cajoling, Eliza relented.

It wasn't until they were walking to the parking garage that Victoria remembered to ask Eliza about her rendezvous with Tyler.

"It was . . ." began Eliza.

"Orgasmic?" asked Helen.

"How big is he?" asked Victoria. "I've always been curious."

"Please!" said Eliza. "Okay, listen. I'm not ready to talk about it yet. Give me some time."

Her friends were disappointed, but they knew it was hard to get information like that out of Eliza, so they had no choice but to wait.

"Okay, but you have to tell us soon. We're dying," said Victoria.

"I will tell you everything soon," promised Eliza.

·· 22 ··

Listening in on Victoria and her friends had become an obsession for Anson. It was better than watching *Desperate Housewives*, better than eating Teuscher's chocolate candies, and most certainly better than sex. It seemed as though every spare moment now he would plant himself in his comfy settee with his big mug of tea and listen to their innermost secrets, all their confessions, and the most graphic details of their sex life. The more he listened to their conversations on his baby monitor, as he dunked his tea bag in and out of the steaming liquid, the more he couldn't believe what they were saying.

Victoria was a tough-as-nails bitch—everyone knew that—so he wasn't surprised that she was looking for love with someone else. He'd always hated her. She seemed so haughty and barely said hello. Her husband was also an ass, cutting Anson off mid-sentence when he asked if he might take a look at his screenplay. *Every busboy this side of Nevada has a screenplay. Take a number.* He didn't have to be so nasty. Eliza's affair shocked him. Tyler Trask? He was a rogue. And Eliza didn't seem like the type to cheat. But she also wasn't as nice as she pretended to be. He had asked her on more than one occasion—not explicitly, but she knew what he was talking about—to introduce him to her magazine editor so that he might pick up some extra work. He was great at interviewing people, and he knew he would be great at doing it for a magazine. But she had shrugged him off. Since then he had put her on his list. Helen was so out there that it didn't surprise him the least. She probably had an open marriage anyway. He didn't know quite what to make of her, but he had always held a grudge against her for scheduling her art show at the library on the same day as he was reading a collection of his columns at Village Books. But the one he hated most was Leelee. That short, fat blond cheerleader. She was so fake sweet and nice, and yet she would stab you in the back with daggers. He knew that she was the one personally responsible for blackballing him from the beach club. How could she have so much power? He'd lived in town much longer.

At first Anson was merely amused to have the knowledge that his prim and proper neighbors were cheating on their spouses, but the more he thought about it, the more it dawned on him that he could use it to his advantage. He had a brilliant screenplay just sitting in his top drawer. Surely Justin could get it into the studios, or refer him to the right agent at his office. And right now the best way to get to Justin was through Victoria, and to do that, he had to make it worth her while. That's why he planted the first blind item in his column. He worked hard on it, crafting it with his usual mix of flattery and intrigue, and found himself giggling about it for the rest of the night.

Who would you rather have, Justin Coleman or Wayne Mercer? Oh, take your mind out of the gutter, ladies, I'm not speaking in amorous terms—we all know that Justin is happily married to his ever-loyal wife, Victoria. I mean, who would you rather have

represent you? The starlet Hadley Whitaker is currently deciding be-
tween the two men this very minute. Will she go with IAA or ACM?
Stay tuned. I know I will.

It would only be the beginning. Next week Anson would
write something about Helen. Her husband was a director—
perhaps he could be of some use. And who knows? If he got to
Eliza, perhaps she could get Tyler Trask to star in his movie? The
world was his oyster.

·· 23 ··

The Ritz in Boston had always been Leelee's favorite hotel. She'd
stayed at the Plaza Athénée in Paris and the Connaught in London, but nothing compared to her hometown hotel, where she
had spent so many glorious weekends escaping boarding school
and college with a bunch of friends for the Head of the Charles.
Her father's fiftieth birthday party had been there, she held a tea
party on the day of her debut there, and most special of all were
the Sunday brunches with the Porter family when they were in
town. She had not needed another reason to worship the place,
but she was given one when Jack met her on that rainy Friday
night in a suite on the sixth floor.

On her way up in the elevator she felt like Countess Olen-
ska going to meet Newland Archer. Somehow the place evoked
Edith Wharton, and she had specifically read *The Age of Innocence*
on the plane to psyche herself up. The man at reception had told
her that Jack had already checked in, or rather, "Mr. Swifty" had
checked in, and with every illuminated red button in the elevator,
Leelee knew she was one floor closer to her beloved. She had decided that she should enter dramatically, and mysteriously, and

attempt to facilitate intercourse as swiftly as possible. If they lingered, there would be time to talk each other out of it. Well, she wouldn't be talked out of it, but he might be. They might fall prey to their old relationship and start goofing around, and then all they'd end up doing was raiding the minibar and watching *Letterman.* Boring. There was no way Leelee would allow this to be another missed opportunity. She was going to get her man if that was all she did.

The elevator pinged and Leelee got off and walked to her room. She fluffed her hair forward and fiddled with her skirt. It had been a pain to fly cross-country in high heels and stockings, and the skirt was just a little too tight, but she knew she wouldn't have time to change, so she had suffered for the sake of sexiness. She was even wearing a raunchy black garter belt underneath that she had just purchased at Victoria's Secret. Jack had often alluded to his penchant for garter belts in his joking e-mails.

"You came," said Jack when he opened the door. He looked more gorgeous than ever. He had obviously just gotten out of the shower, as he was clad in a plush white Ritz bathrobe and was drying his hair with a towel.

Leelee took one look at him and then jumped into his arms. In his surprise, he almost fell backwards, but held his arm out to stabilize himself on the door as she wrapped her legs around him and leaned in and kissed him passionately. Jack carried her into the bedroom and gently put her on the enormous canopy bed. She didn't say anything, just smiled. This was how it was supposed to be. She felt like Mrs. Jack Porter. She thought of Tierney and giggled. She had always hated her. As she and Jack embraced, alternating between long, wet kisses and shorter, more urgent ones, she realized that this was a better form of retribution against Tierney than her previous schemes. As Jack penetrated her, she thought of her previous pathetic acts of vengeance. They brought her only anger, not pleasure like now.

When Leelee was forced to move to L.A. she decided that she needed to overcome her rage toward Brad if she was going to spend her life with him. Instead, she channeled her venom toward Tierney. Whenever Leelee was having a bad day every few months or so, she'd drive down to the Kinko's in Manhattan Beach. There she would Xerox a copy of a letter that she had written using cutout letters from various newspapers. She'd make one copy, using the plastic gloves that she'd gotten out of a L'Oréal hair color box, and then tear the original to shreds. She'd place the letter into an envelope and then into a larger envelope addressed to a post office box in Dallas, Texas, that she had found online. When the letter was received in Dallas, the person there would remove the second letter and mail it so that the postmark would be from Texas. No one would have any idea that the letter originated with Leelee.

On her way back home, driving up the congested Lincoln Boulevard, Leelee would experience a surge of joy when she let her imagination run wild. It was such a pity that she couldn't be there to see the letter recipient open yet another piece of anonymous hate mail from Leelee. But she could imagine Tierney's contorted face and only hope that she'd brought her a tenth of the pain that she had caused Leelee. This was revenge, after all.

With a sudden surge, Leelee flipped Jack over. She made love to him passionately, her thoughts now focused on his wife. When she was done, she collapsed on the bed and closed her eyes.

"Knock, knock—you still there?" asked Jack, gazing at her intently.

Leelee realized that she had zoned out. She rolled over

toward him and rubbed her hand across his chest. "Totally. I'm just so happy."

Jack gave her a crooked smile and leaned back on the bed, his arms folded behind his head. "I know. It's weird."

"Weird?" asked Leelee, suddenly worried.

"Not weird bad, just weird. I mean, come on, after all these years."

"I know. You bastard, you made me wait way too long!" she said, teasingly punching him. They had always had such a light-hearted rapport. It would be strange to change the way they interacted now that they were lovers.

"But wasn't it worth it?" said Jack, his eyes shining brightly. "I mean, aren't I the best?"

"You are, Jack," said Leelee, beaming.

·· 24 ··

"Did you say something to Anson?" Helen asked Daniela, anger rising in her voice.

"What are you talking about? Of course not," she said calmly, taking a sip from her cosmopolitan. Her giant green eyes coolly returned Helen's stare.

"Then what is this?" asked Helen, thrusting the *Palisades Press* in her lover's face. It was a blind item in Anson's column: *Producer Daniela Fox has been squiring a lovely Asian lady around town. She looks familiar, like someone I might know, but then, I'm not sure. Good luck on your new relationship, Daniela!*

"It only mentions my name. There's nothing about you," said Daniela, her demeanor still relaxed and composed. That was actually one thing that Helen didn't like about Daniela: nothing seemed to rile her. In fact, she was completely blasé about everything. It made sense that she was a successful producer, as she never appeared flustered or lost her cool.

They were at Father's Office, a bar on Montana in Santa Monica, and it was beginning to get crowded with the singletons looking for beers and babes. Helen was supposed to have dinner with Daniela, but she was over it. They'd been together less than a month, but Daniela wasn't worth the risk of exposure, and obviously she wasn't as discreet as Helen had thought. It was odd, because she had believed that Daniela was not a gossip, but apparently that wasn't the case. Unless it was one of her friends who'd told Anson. Now that would make sense, realized Helen suddenly. After all, he had mentioned Justin last week.

"Sorry," said Helen. "I'm suffering from fear of detection."

"No problem," said Daniela. "Have a drink."

It was more of an order than an offer, and Helen felt compelled to say yes. Truth be told, Daniela scared her a little. After things didn't work out with the guy from YAS, Helen had thought that maybe it was men in general who couldn't give her what she needed. Maybe because her mother was cold and her biological mother abandoned her, she needed to find the care and love of another woman to satisfy her. It sounded sick, but she felt like she ought to try. But Daniela was more like a man than any man she had been with. She was very demanding in the bedroom—almost more aggressive than a man—and she had taken to calling Helen and telling her what to *wear* on their dates. At first it was titillating and sexy. She enjoyed being ordered around, and it was fun to wear the flirty little dresses that Daniela preferred. Not to mention that Daniela was very attractive, with curly red hair and creamy skin. But the more they had sex, the more she realized that she wasn't completely satisfied being with a woman. She needed to be penetrated, *deeply,* and gadgets didn't do it for her. Being with someone who had breasts was an initial novelty, but there was only so much you could do with them after a while, and it had been a month already. Although Daniela could spend hours playing with hers, which eventually got old. Not to mention that she hadn't found any of the tenderness or bonds that she had thought would come out of being with a woman. And then she had run into Parker, an old lover whom she had been with before Wesley, and they had a long conversation about how time had passed so quickly and how life was so ephemeral, and then one thing led to another and they had actually had sex that morning, which was awesome and once again confirmed that it had to end with Daniela.

"I need to end our . . . relationship," said Helen timidly.

Daniela's eyes widened as if she had heard something appalling, but that was the only part of her face that betrayed emotion.

"You're never going to find what you're looking for," said Daniela icily. "You're too broken, incapable of emotion. You think it should all be handed to you, but you don't realize you need to *participate* in a relationship in order for it to work."

Helen was dumbstruck that Daniela was so vicious. "Um, that's not really true . . ."

"Yes, it is," said Daniela coldly. "I mean, look at you. You can't relate to your husband, you're scared to death of your daughter, and you're as cold as a fish in the sack."

"I'm not scared of my daughter," said Helen, her voice rising.

"Yeah, right," said Daniela, beginning to cackle.

"What's that supposed to mean?"

"You stay away from her. You avoid her. You don't know how to be a mother to her."

"I don't know why you'd say such horrible things to me," said Helen, pushing back her chair and standing up. "I didn't think you were so cruel."

Daniela smiled calmly. "I'm not cruel. I just tell the truth."

Helen couldn't get out of there fast enough. How dare Daniela say those horrible things? To make up all those evil lies just because she was getting dumped. She should have known not to get involved with a woman. Women were such bitches! And to say that about Lauren. That was a joke. She wasn't scared of Lauren.

Helen unlocked her car and pulled out of the parking spot, still ruminating over Daniela's comments. Scared of Lauren? Absurd! Okay, yes, she let Wesley take the lead in her upbringing, but she was always *there* for Lauren. Okay, the truth was that she didn't want to fuck her up. Lauren was a good kid. She deserved a good mother. And Helen didn't know how to be a good mother. No one had ever told her. It had never even occurred to her that she'd have a daughter; she'd always thought she'd have sons. And after a very difficult delivery that turned into an emergency C-section, when the nurse held up the baby and pronounced her a girl, she was in shock. She had been so sure it was a boy that she hadn't even bothered to find out the sex. And there was this tiny little girl, who had only seconds before had an umbilical cord wrapped around her neck and was close to death, and now Helen was supposed to be responsible for her? She panicked. It didn't mean she didn't love her daughter. It didn't mean that she was a bad person. She was trying to be the best person she could be for her. That was all she could do.

"**More flowers for** you, Missus," said Juana, placing a vase of roses on the dining room table.

"Thanks, Juana," said Eliza, walking over to the table to tear open the card. Please, she prayed to herself, let them be from Declan. But of course they weren't. The card was signed *Thanks for your support.* Eliza sighed deeply as she tore the card to tiny pieces and let them fall into the garbage. Tyler Trask.

"Can I call you?" he had asked as she was leaving his trailer. He held on to her arm as if he didn't want her to leave.

"No, please . . ." she said, not looking at him. She was embarrassed. It had been a mistake to reinitiate contact.

"What about e-mail?" he pressed.

"God, no. Please, I can't . . ."

She felt the tears well up in her eyes. She stared at the ceiling, wishing them back into her tearducts but feeling them slide down her cheeks. Tyler softly turned her body toward him and wiped away one of her tears with his fingers.

"Don't cry," he said softly.

"Sorry," she said, still not looking at him.

"You did nothing wrong," he said, reassuring her.

"Right," she said. She did everything wrong. What was she doing here? How was this her life? He tried to pull her toward him again but she resisted now.

"I need to know how to get in touch with you. I don't want to disrupt your life, but I can't just cease contact," he said.

"I don't know, I don't know," sighed Eliza. God, this was so messy.

"I'll send you flowers."

"No! Declan will see them," she protested.

"I won't sign the card in my name. I'll pretend it's something else. And I'll only send them when I'm thinking of you. I want you to know."

What could she do? "Fine," she said, relenting. She felt too weak to argue. She was emotionally exhausted. She wished she could just crumple up in a ball and collapse in Tyler's bed. But she couldn't. Life was serious, and she could not afford to be frivolous.

"I gotta go," she said, pulling away from him.

"Eliza, wait," he said, not letting her go.

She turned and looked into his eyes. She almost changed her mind.

"Let me kiss you good-bye," he whispered.

"No," she said, wiping a tear away with the back of her hand.

"Please."

"No," she said. Yes! Yes! Kiss me—hold me in your arms and take me away to Happily Ever After Land. Where I'll always feel that fluttery feeling when I see you and there will be no pressures, no sense of reality, just . . . happily ever after.

He sighed and looked at her. Then he leaned in and kissed each of her eyes. And then she left.

He had said he'd send the flowers only when he thought of her, but he had sent them every day. That both worried and exhilarated her. Every day, a steady stream of roses with a different card. All from him. She was scared that Declan would see them, but deep down she was more scared about when he would stop sending them. When he would stop thinking about her. She couldn't stop thinking about him. But it was a fantasy.

She was glad she'd told her editor she couldn't write the piece. Somehow she didn't think she could maintain a poker face in the article. Someone would know. She felt as though everyone already knew.

Could her friends be trusted, really? *Never tell your friends everything.* Isn't that what Mr. Matthews had told her back in high school? It was her friends then who had told people of her affair with her teacher and gotten him fired. She had never believed they would, and it wasn't done in harm, but it was gossip, it was salacious, and that sort of information inevitably gets out. Since then she had tried to be the pearl of discretion. She refused to make any derisive comments about Declan, even when she wanted to throttle him, because she knew her friends would remember. And now they knew all about Tyler.

"Who are the flowers from?"

Eliza whipped around. She hadn't heard Declan come in. What was he doing home this early?

"Um, a woman on the school committee. Just a thank-you for . . . um, you know, helping with the silent auction," she said.

"Nice," said Declan, walking over to the refrigerator and opening the door. "Except you hate roses."

She stared at the flowers. She did hate roses. She had forgotten. "Yeah, you're right. So what are you doing home?"

"Had a meeting in Santa Monica that ended early and wanted to come home and see you guys," he said, taking a container of leftover pasta salad out of the fridge. "Where are the kids?"

"They're outside with Juana. I should go check on them."

"Wait a second. Stay and talk to me. Before the madness enters," he said, digging through the salad with his fork. He was avoiding peas, she knew it. He hated them. God, they knew everything about each other. She hated this flower, he hated that vegetable. There was so much history. Suddenly she realized that she had been looking at it from the wrong angle. Maybe it wasn't such a bad thing. Maybe discovering someone else, or getting that shivery feeling when you see someone like Tyler wasn't all it was cracked up to be. Because soon you inevitably do learn a person's idiosyncrasies, and likes and dislikes, and the unfamiliar wears off. And it's kind of sexy to have someone know you so well and still love you.

"Okay," she said, turning around. Her husband looked cute in his blue and white striped shirt, blue blazer with gold buttons, and khakis. He pretended he was Mr. Bubble when he gave the kids baths. He called her throughout the day, so many times that it sometimes annoyed her, but he needed to hear her voice and share everything with her. He told her she was the love of his life, often. He wanted to hold her when they slept, even though the hair on his arms tickled her. He said to her, "If I died right now, I'd be happy because I was married to you." The fluttering heartbeats were all there, just spread out over years.

"Tell me about your day," said Declan.

·· 26 ··

It is difficult to remember time when you live in Southern California. There are no seasons to break up memories. It is almost always perfect weather: no blizzards, thunderstorms, or hurricanes to frame an event. People go swimming in January. School often runs into July. Existence there is like one giant watercolor, where all of the paint has run and blurred into a smeared colorful jumble, leaving the images indecipherable.

The girls in the pact knew what they wanted to do, but picking the moment was difficult. What day or month would be *the* day? What would differentiate that day from any other day? They had lives, routines, patterns. Everything was cyclical, continuous. Life was for the most part pleasant, stable. How then, to choose the moments to make your mark? Often you had to wait.

Victoria knew the means and effort that it would take to get rid of Wayne and had enlisted her friend as an abettor, but the timing was becoming a problem. It needed to go down at Wayne's house. There was no other way she could search for the videotapes. But first he had a friend staying with him and now there was a little construction project on the kitchen, so Wayne was camped out at the Peninsula. She had hoped that everything that was going on would distract him, but he was more demanding and more insistent than ever, and frankly she was terrified. Wayne forced her to show up at events with Justin and then made her sneak off and have sex with him practically in public. Her fear of detection seemed to titillate him no end. She tried to refuse, but he was a bully, and a freak, and would threaten her and even knock on her door some evenings if she had not complied. So far Justin had no clue—thankfully he was never home—but she couldn't live on the edge like this anymore. Every time the phone rang she jumped, every doorbell ping was like a dagger stabbing her heart. She feared for her children and she feared for herself. The more Wayne threatened to upset her life, the more she loved her life. She could kill herself for getting into this mess.

But now all she had to do was wait. Wayne would be back in his house the weekend before Thanksgiving, and she would make her move. And she would take her revenge on him in a big way. He would pay. He would feel pain. And then he would never be in her life again, all memory of him erased.

On a Saturday morning in October, Victoria had to put all thoughts of her illicit life out of her mind and escort Justin and the boys to a birthday party for the son of a big Hollywood producer. Austin and Hunter, who were only two and a half, had never even met the boy, who was turning five; nor had Victoria ever met the producer or his wife. But that was standard at these events, which were more about adults making connections, exchanging business cards, and checking out competitors' spouses, than the child who was blowing out his candles. Victoria went to so many of these parties that she kept a closet full of wrapped birthday presents neatly organized by age and sex. If it was a really important child (meaning the parents were really successful), he or she received a gift from the top shelf, which were mostly electronics such as PlayStations. Real friends, the ones that they actually spent time with and knew, received presents from the bottom shelf, which were mostly board games, puzzles, and picture books (although never books about animals acting like humans; those drove Victoria *nuts*).

"Come on, we're gonna be late," Justin bellowed as Victoria finished buttoning Austin's shirt. Although most of the kids showed up in ragtag outfits to these events, Victoria refused to dress her boys accordingly. If it was a party, they would wear crisp Papa D'Anjou button-down shirts tucked into neatly pressed Ralph Lauren lightweight cords. She was from the East Coast, after all. That is how people dressed. It always amazed her how casual people in Los Angeles were. Most of the adults put their sons in sports outfits, even for special occasions, and there would be wimpy pale boys wearing giant Lakers jerseys and shorts, as if the parents refused to believe their child was incompetent at athletics and thought instead that one day little Preston would surprise us all and play basketball like Kobe Bryant. It was pathetic. And the girls were always clad in animal prints and weird leggings. Animal prints on children? It made Victoria shudder.

The getups on the parents were worse. The mothers still believed they were sixteen, and though Victoria agreed that they all had sensational Pilates figures, she didn't think that lowrider jeans with lacy pink thongs hanging out every time they bent down (which was as much as possible) was a good look. Her friends back in Greenwich would be appalled. The fathers were no better. At the party they went to the previous Sunday—it was held on the beach, at the club—one father had been wearing a T-shirt that said FORGET THE HORSE, RIDE THE COWGIRL! Victoria had wanted to vomit.

"Come on. I don't want to be late," snapped Justin when Victoria walked down the stairs holding Austin's hand.

"You know, you could have gotten up with the boys and gotten them ready," said Victoria defensively.

"I was working out," said Justin, opening the front door and pushing Hunter and Austin outside.

"I would have loved to work out," sighed Victoria with bitterness. "Unfortunately, there was no time. Someone has to look out for the boys."

"You're their *mother,* Victoria. Why do you resent everything you have to do for them? You act like it's everyone else's job. We're not doing you any favors."

"Whatever," said Victoria, snapping Austin into his car seat. She didn't want to admit it, but Justin was kind of right. She did resent that she had to do everything for her boys. They were so dependent on her. She had to feed them, dress them, get them into schools and the right playgroups. If she didn't, no one else would. Of course, she had a nanny, but they usually wanted Mommy. And sometimes that just pissed her off. She wanted to relax, read a book, take a vacation. She loved her boys and she wouldn't trade them for anything, but sometimes it all seemed like too much work. It made her cranky. Like she had permanent PMS.

"Okay, who are these people again?" asked Victoria.

"Russell Novotsky. Big, big producer, on the Paramount lot, just did *Drag Race Three,* which grossed one hundred and thirty-seven mil domestic, one ten foreign," said Justin, reciting the box office figures by rote.

"And his wife?"

"Haven't met her. Know she worked at Oliver Peoples on Sunset, think she's an Orange County girl. She's his second wife."

"Lovely."

"He wants Tad for his next movie, but Paul Walker's also up for it, so I need to nail it down today," said Justin, turning up the air-conditioning. He was always hot, even when it was fifty degrees outside. "Maybe you can make nice with the wife, have lunch or something. The kid goes to Brightwood—couldn't hurt to make more connections."

"Right." It amazed her how much Justin knew about everyone he considered important, even if he barely knew them. He remembered names, birthdays, what schools they went to, what clubs they belonged to. He had some internal spreadsheet in his mind, as if he had swallowed Excel.

The party was in Brentwood, at a large brick Georgian-style mansion with an enormous front lawn, which now had two fire engines plopped on it. Upon further inspection, Victoria could see through the fence that there was also a petting zoo, a Sponge-Bob jumpy castle, and an In-N-Out burger truck. Fancy. The valet took their car, and Victoria and Justin both took one child's hand, plastered on fake smiles, and entered the grounds.

"Hi!" said a fake-boobed blonde with a pretty face. "I'm Cindy, Atticus's mommy!"

"Hey, Cindy. Justin Coleman, my wife, Victoria, my boys, Hunter and Austin," said Justin smoothly.

"Glad you could make it! Come on in. The present table is over there," said Cindy, motioning to a large rectangular table that could seat twenty and was now covered in gifts of all shapes and sizes for little Atticus. "And we've got a jumpy castle and everything else. You boys can go on a fire truck—we've got *real* firemen here!"

"Great, thank you," said Victoria. "Where is the birthday boy? We'd love to say happy birthday."

"He's over there," said Cindy, proudly pointing to a thin, pale boy clad in a Dodgers tank top and Adidas sweatpants, riding a pony.

Victoria and Justin moved on toward the attractions, guiding Austin and Hunter onto the fire engine and listening as a *real* fireman explained how he used his ladder. Justin kept his eyes darting around for someone he knew or had to ass-kiss, but even though there were crowds of people, there were few he recognized.

After sampling the In-N-Out burgers, holding the baby chicks from the petting zoo, and getting cotton candy for the boys, Victoria and Justin both had that odd sensation that they were lingering too long at a party where they knew no one. Justin seemed disappointed; he had assumed it would be more of an A-list crowd. Obviously so had the hosts, because there were three photographers on hand to snap photos. But aside from a few sitcom stars who hadn't been on a hit show in ages and were reduced to making guest appearances on CBS comedies, it was slim pickings.

"Can we leave?" asked Victoria with a deep sigh.

"In a minute. I just need to say hi to Russell. There's been a shit-long line of kowtowers all day, it's been hard to get a second with him," said Justin, anxiously staring at the host, who was talking with a couple.

"Well, get cracking, please, 'cause I want to go. Go stand in line if you have to," said Victoria.

She was tired from smiling blankly at strangers and avoiding some of the women who were in her "Tiny Creatures" baby group the previous year. When the twins were a year old, the wife of one of Justin's golfing buddies had insisted that she join Tiny Creatures, claiming it was the *best* group on the planet. The class was not the best. It was located in a very comfortable Craftsman cottage in Venice and was led by a woman named Evangeline Brimmer, who was a dour, humorless hippie who was fanatical about breast-feeding children until they were four, cosleeping, vegetarianism, and avoiding discipline at all costs ("because it hurts their little spirits"). The ladies in the group, who were all pretty much trophy wives with giant fake breasts, fake tans, and too much jewelry, all took her word as gospel, nodding profusely at every word of advice Evangeline spouted ("Let little Ava sample the poison detergent herself and she will learn on her own that it is dangerous"). The woman had practically no education, Victoria was certain, and no right to be teaching the class, and yet she charged an exorbitant five thousand dollars for six months and had a two-hundred-person waiting list, or so she claimed. Victoria went to about five classes before bailing, four more than she would have liked, but she felt guilty about the money. Justin didn't care, but he encouraged her to hang on as long as she could to see if any of the women were married to someone he needed to know for business. Victoria quit before telling him that one of the women was the third wife of the latest studio chief at Fox.

"Be right back," said Justin, bolting toward Russell as soon as he saw an opening. He didn't notice that he'd left Hunter hanging off the edge of the fire engine. When it came to business he had a one-track mind.

Victoria watched as Justin greeted Russell, and knew how the whole conversation would go down. Bullshit, business, more bullshit. It was always the same.

"Is he your husband?" a voice behind Victoria asked.

She turned around and saw a very thin brunette who looked like a younger, darker version of Diane Keaton. She was clad in a purple and black floral dress that Victoria knew was from Marni, and held on tightly to the edges of the dark purple cashmere cardigan that she wore over it.

"Yes," said Victoria.

"You're married to Justin Coleman?" she asked, skeptical.

"Right. I'm Victoria Rand. And you are?" she asked, holding out her hand. No one in L.A. shook hands, but Victoria refused to acclimate.

"I'm Ruthie Marmon," she said, shaking Victoria's hand limply. "I used to be married to Wayne Mercer."

Victoria felt the blood rush to her face as she carefully maintained eye contact with this woman. She couldn't read her tone. Did she know about her and Wayne? Or did she just know that Wayne hated Justin? Her mind started to race.

"Nice to meet you," said Victoria.

"I always wanted to see Justin's better half," she said, again her tone neutral. What did that mean? Victoria kept her eyes on Ruthie, but she couldn't gauge anything from her expression. She didn't arch an eyebrow or emphasize her words to make "better half" sound bitchy. She spoke flatly, without any inflection.

"Oh." Victoria laughed nervously. "Why's that?"

Ruthie lifted her head higher and finally a small smile appeared at the corners of her mouth. "Because he's such a son of a bitch."

She said it without venom, as if she had just stated a fact, such as that it was supposed to rain tomorrow.

"Ha ha," said Victoria, fake laughing. "I guess you could say that about a lot of people in this town. That's what I heard about Wayne also."

"I'm sure you heard that," said Ruthie, her eyes narrowing. She emphasized the "you," thought Victoria. Didn't she? "It's true," she said, shrugging. "That's why I divorced him."

"Oh," said Victoria.

"But you're still with him," said Ruthie.

"With who, Wayne? Don't be crazy," said Victoria, her blood pressure rising.

Ruthie gave her a quizzical look. "I mean you're still with Justin. Are you with Wayne, too?"

"No, no. I didn't know what you meant." Shit, shit!

Ruthie stared at her in disbelief. "Right. Well, bye," she said, turning and walking away as quietly as she had come.

Victoria was shaken. As soon as Justin returned she scooped up the boys, turned in the valet ticket, and gathered them in the car when it came. She didn't let out a breath until then. Shit, now this Ruthie thinks I'm with Wayne. But what was that whole thing about? How dare she call Justin a son of a bitch! He may be, but who is she to say something? Unless . . .

"Do you know Ruthie Marmon, Wayne Mercer's ex-wife?" she asked, turning to Justin.

A small smile crept across Justin's face. "God, I haven't heard that name in a long time. Was she there?"

"Yes. Answer my question."

"Yeah, I know her."

"Did you fuck her?" asked Victoria.

"Vic! The boys are in the backseat!"

"Answer me," hissed Victoria.

"Jesus, yes, but a long time ago, before us."

"When she was married to Wayne?" asked Victoria.

"Yeah," said Justin, rubbing the back of his gelled head against the seat. He was obviously relishing the memory.

"You are scum," said Victoria.

"It was before we were married. What do you want?"

Victoria remained silent the rest of the trip. So maybe Wayne knew who she was all along. Maybe this was all part of his revenge. Congratulations, Victoria. Great job.

·· 27 ··

Since her weekend in Boston, Leelee was a new woman. She had never felt like this before, so euphoric, so complete. She now knew what the phrase "walking on air" meant. She had forgotten how good sex was, and she had forgotten how great Jack was. Every mundane activity became bearable because Leelee knew that it was merely temporary. She and Jack had been talking, he had poured out his soul to her, and he had admitted that he couldn't continue living his life with Tierney anymore. It was all a lie, anyway. He confessed that they lived entirely separate lives. She was obsessed with going out all the time; there was not a charity ball or store opening that she would miss. She was hellbent on becoming a fashion and society icon. She was the most superficial, dull, shallow girl he had ever met, and they had absolutely nothing in common. She was blowing through his money on her couture clothes and Verdura jewelry (although it would be hard to "blow through it" considering he had multimillions), and he had had enough. He wanted someone with character, someone who understood him and took care of him. He wanted Leelee.

It was just a matter of picking the right moment for their escape. They agreed that they should wait until the holidays were over and then take off together to start their own life. Jack loved her girls; it was another bone of contention with him and Tierney that she refused to get pregnant. She was confident that he would be a spectacular stepfather. Leelee had secret hopes for a honeymoon baby, perhaps a little boy. How cute would a miniature Jack be? Sure, Brad would be hurt, but he knew. He knew deep down that she and Jack were meant to be.

When Leelee returned home from Pilates class (she was making an extra effort to look good these days) she was humming "Sweet Child o' Mine" and fantasizing about her future life. She took a long, hot shower and decorated the Oval Office in her mind (for she just knew Jack would follow in his father's footsteps and become a senator and later even president) and didn't hear the door to the bathroom open. When she slid open the shower curtain she was startled to see Brad standing there in the steamy bathroom.

"Who's Cooldude?" he asked quietly.

God. Cooldude@dude.com was Jack's user name! How did Brad know that?

She feigned nonchalance and reached for a towel. "What are you talking about?" she asked calmly. "And what are you doing home already?"

"I got home early. Who's Cooldude?" he repeated.

Leelee knotted the towel around her and then picked up

another to dry her hair. She flung her head down and wrapped the second towel in a turban around her head before she answered.

"I don't know what you're talking about," she said, reaching for a bottle of cream on the counter and pumping a small drop into her hand.

Brad stared at her, carefully watching her reaction. "I went to send an e-mail on the computer and there was a message in your in-box from some Cooldude. Talking about running away together, how annoying his wife was, love . . . does this ring any bells?" he asked, his voice rising.

Leelee stopped and stared at him. Should she tell him now? He looked so pissed off, it would be so easy to pull the plug, to say Cooldude was Jack and he was taking her away from her measly little life forever. But she watched as Brad waited, and she stopped herself. Jack had said to wait. So she would.

"If you have to know, then okay. Cooldude is Victoria's lover. They've been having an affair for months. She uses my computer to e-mail him so that Justin won't find out."

Brad squinted his eyes slightly to study Leelee's face more carefully, but she retained her poker face. Finally his shoulders sagged.

"That's despicable. I can't believe Victoria would do that to Justin," said Brad, his eyes still glued on Leelee.

Leelee calmly spread the cream all over her legs in circular motions. "I guess. But remember, you thought that he was cheating on her anyway."

"Two wrongs don't make a right," said Brad. "You have to think of the children."

The children. Right, thought Leelee, her stomach sinking for the first time in ages. If she was to put her children first, she'd be stuck here in this crap house for the rest of her life. Charming, cozy, yes, but this is not how her life should be. She felt claustrophobic. Should she really sacrifice her happiness for theirs? And besides, it wouldn't be a sacrifice, because they loved Jack and he could provide for them on a much larger scale than their father.

"Yes, well, maybe Victoria just wants to be happy," said Leelee.

Brad had been walking out the door, but he turned around to look at Leelee. "Maybe she just has to grow up. Life isn't a fairy tale. There are no happily-ever-afters. No princes."

Leelee looked at him and wondered if he knew. Naw, there was no way. No way. Even if he found the e-mail, there was no way he knew it was between her and Jack. But she was a complete fool to leave it open and would have to be more careful.

"You're my prince, darling," she said with a smile.

Brad stared at her for a long time. "I was once," he said sadly. "I hope I still am."

He didn't wait for a reply, and left the bathroom.

·· 28 ··

After Daniela, Helen slept with Parker. He was great at sex, but that was all. It was almost sad. Her friends had given her carte blanche to express herself and tap in to her soul, to unleash her inner woman that had been suppressed for so long. And yet, she didn't feel unleashed. She didn't feel liberated or exhilarated or satisfied in any way. In fact, she was starting to feel kind of dirty.

She had been so preoccupied with her new love life that she had not spent much time with Lauren (or Wesley, for that matter), so when she found herself near Lauren's school at two-forty she called Wesley and told him that she would pick her up for a change. His surprised reaction pissed her off. She was a good mother—was he implying otherwise? She felt herself getting madder and madder as she parked the car and walked up the steps to Lauren's school. She watched as the other mothers greeted each other. Obviously they did this every day. She felt a little left out—no one stopped to chat with her and some barely even said hello. It was as if she had committed a crime by not picking Lauren up every day. Well, unlike these ladies, she had her art to pursue. Her photography. If they were doing something important, they might not be so judgmental. She stood up a little higher, looking haughtily at the other ladies, all in their workout clothes, until she saw Martha West. She was an environmental lawyer. Well, there was one working mom who made it to pick up her kid, but she owned her own firm. Then she saw Hannah Tassin, and Melanie Lutz, and Brooke Pelham. They all worked. And they were all here. Helen slunk down a little.

"Where's Dad?" asked Lauren as soon as she saw her mom.

"Dad's at home. How are you, sweetie?" said Helen, reaching down to kiss her daughter on the cheek.

Lauren looked at her oddly. "Is he okay?"

"Of course! Why wouldn't he be?"

"What are you doing here then?" she asked suspiciously.

Helen felt her face burn. "Can't I pick you up from school? Is it so unusual?"

Lauren gave her mother a quizzical look, but then softened. "Sure. I'm just used to Daddy getting me. Are you going to take me to ballet also?"

"You have ballet today?" asked Helen. She realized she knew nothing about her daughter's life. Sure, she'd scheduled all of these classes, but she'd never taken her. She couldn't remember the last time she actually spent time with Lauren. She looked at her beautiful daughter, who had a long swinging ponytail and gorgeous chocolate brown eyes, and felt so sad that she thought her heart would burst. "Of course I'll take you to ballet. I would love to."

Her daughter took her hand in hers and they walked to the parking lot. She glanced down every now and then at this magical little creature with the Strawberry Shortcake backpack and couldn't believe what a fool she'd been. Being with her daughter made the numbness subside. All of those strong feelings that she thought she'd get with another man were nothing compared to what she felt now. This was home. She finally comprehended what she had to do. She had to drop out of the infidelity pact. She had to put her family together again.

She opened the car door for Lauren and was about to get in the driver's seat when she heard someone calling her name. She whipped around. It was Anson Larrabee.

"Hey, Anson, how's it going?"

Anson was wearing Nantucket Red pants and a large Irish sweater. He looked absurd.

"Hello, Helen, how are you?" he asked.

"Fine. Just taking my daughter to ballet," she said wearily. What did he want?

"That's fabulous. Everyone will be thrilled to see you with your daughter. You've been MIA for quite some time. Didn't know if you and your hubby had split or what."

"No, we're together," she said curtly. Who did he think he was?

"Lovely," he said, his blue eyes boring into her. He leaned in and whispered, "You're the one I don't know what to make of. It's a real hoot, 'cause I know Victoria's secret—pardon the pun. Oh, that's a funny one." He paused to laugh at his inane joke. "And I know Eliza's secret, and I even know Leelee's secret—the gem if you ask me—but I don't know your secret exactly. What could it be?"

Helen was more pissed than worried. This man was a pathetic human being who did not deserve one smidgeon of her attention.

"I don't know what you're talking about, but whatever it is, I'm sure you're totally confused," she said brusquely.

Anson laughed a hearty laugh and then stopped. "I'm not talking about the infidelity pact. I know y'all are cheaters. I'm talking about the secrets y'all are keeping from each other. Victoria has one, Eliza has one, and Leelee has one, and believe me, you would be surprised what they are. I'm just waiting on yours. And I'm sure I won't be disappointed, darlin'," he said, glowering at her dismissal of him.

Helen felt herself get panicky. "We have no secrets. You're confused."

"Don't lie to *me!*" he said, stomping his foot for effect. He wagged his finger in her face. "You think you're safe, but you're not. Your friends haven't told you everything. Your house of cards is about to come crashin' down. And when it does, I'll be there!"

He turned and walked away. He had a balloon butt, Helen noticed as she watched him go. That was all that was racing through her mind, because everything else was too impossible to consider.

"Who was that, Mommy?" asked Lauren when she got in the car.

"This loser," said Helen, backing up.

Lauren laughed. "We have one of those in our class."

Through the entire ballet class, Helen was haunted by what

Anson had said. What secret could her friends have that they didn't tell her? Anson knew about the infidelity pact—he knew the name, even. How? Who was his confidante? Had her friends all planned this together just to get her? She was getting paranoid. She tried to call them from her cell, but no one answered. That made her even more panicky. What if they were all together somewhere and plotting something? She decided to drive straight over to Eliza's after she dropped Lauren off at home.

Declan answered when she rang the doorbell.

"Hey, Declan—is Eliza here?" she asked.

"She had to go to a screening of the new Michelle Pfeiffer movie. She's interviewing her for *Chat*. Do you want to come in?" he asked, opening the door and running to the kitchen. "I'm making dinner for the kids. Juana ran out to get milk, and the stove is bubbling over . . ."

Helen followed his voice into the kitchen. Donovan and Bridget were watching television in the eating nook, and Declan was trying to manage the boiling water for the SpongeBob macaroni while taking out the chicken breasts from the oven.

"Sorry . . . hectic," he said.

"Can I help?"

Helen set to work pouring the powdered neon cheese and butter into the noodles and stirring them around. "This color is disgusting."

"I agree. I can't believe I'm feeding it to my kids. But they love it," said Declan.

"Gross."

After the kids were all set up with dinner, Juana returned with the milk and Declan was able to lead Helen to the living room.

"Want a drink?"

"No thanks. Wait, yes, I would actually," Helen said. She definitely needed something to take the edge off.

"Vodka? Wine? Beer?" he asked, motioning to the bar.

"Whatever," she said, flopping on the couch. "Vodka. Straight."

Declan went over to the bar and poured her a drink from one of the crystal decanters with a smile. "Rough day?"

Something about his sympathetic tone made Helen burst into tears. "I'm sorry . . ."

"Whoa," he said, bringing the drink over. "Rough day."

Helen did everything in her power to stop crying to get a hold of herself, to relax, but she was unable to. She had never realized what a profound effect her infidelity was having on her.

"Sorry," she said, between sobs.

Declan rose to get her a tissue, but when he couldn't find one, he grabbed a paper cocktail napkin from the bar and handed it to her. "It's okay. You don't even have to tell me," he said.

That made her cry harder. He was so sweet. All of their husbands were so sweet. Okay, except maybe not Justin.

"Hey, let's do a shot. Then we'll feel much better," said Declan. He went over and opened a bottle of tequila, and poured it into two of the small Irish shot glasses that had been a wedding present.

"I'm Irish, so taking a nip of the good stuff is like medicine for us," he said, attempting a joke.

She drank it quickly and the liquor burned her throat.

"I'm okay," she said between sobs.

"Can I help?" he asked. "Is it Wesley? Lauren?" he asked, patting her on the back.

"We've made a terrible mistake . . ." she said, crying. She was on the verge of telling him everything. How they all decided to cheat, how she felt like a slut, how it wasn't going as planned. But then a cold clarity seized her and she stopped herself. No, she couldn't break the pact. She had promised. Okay, so maybe she had promised to love, honor, and cherish her husband and not cheat on him and she'd broken those promises also, but she couldn't do it to her friends. At the very least, she could say that she was loyal to her friends.

Helen suddenly straightened up, wiped her eyes, and smiled at Declan. "Sorry, Declan. It's just been a bad day."

"Wanna talk about it?"

"No, if it's okay," she said, staring at him.

"Some days are just like that," said Declan, awkwardly patting her on the back.

·· **29** ··

"**I can't believe** I just lied to Declan. I told him I had to go to a screening tonight, and here I am staking out your lover's house," Eliza said to Victoria as they sat in the car outside Wayne's driveway.

"And I totally appreciate it," said Victoria. She was staring intently at the house, trying to see if she could decipher Wayne's whereabouts through the window.

"We've really gone to hell in a handbasket," said Eliza.

Victoria stopped and turned toward her. "I really appreciate your doing this. You can't imagine how psycho this guy is. If I had had any idea . . ." Her voice trailed off, and for the first time in months Eliza saw Victoria's eyes well up with tears.

"It's okay. After tonight, hopefully he'll back off," said Eliza, leaning in to give her friend a hug. Victoria was the least huggy person she knew, a true tactophobe, but this time she hugged back.

"Tell me honestly: do you really think Anson knows something?" asked Victoria.

"Yes. But what or how, I do not know," said Eliza, turning down the air-conditioning. Everyone in L.A. always had the air-conditioning running in the car, no matter what time of year it is, thought Eliza. She didn't want to think about Anson. It scared her.

"Do you think Leelee told him?" asked Victoria.

"Why Leelee?" asked Eliza.

"I don't know. She seems so immature. I kind of regret including her in this."

"But she's the one who is so gung-ho now. She's actually planning on leaving her husband for Jack."

"She's a fool. He'll never leave his wife. But that's the problem. Leelee is indiscreet. And she has all those irritating Junior League Palisades mom friends, who are like Valley of the Dolls, Stepford Wives. I'm sure she blabbed to them." Victoria shuddered at the thought of those clones.

"I don't think Leelee talked. Anson must have overheard us somewhere."

"He actually stopped me on the street the other day and said he wanted to talk to me," said Victoria. "I said another time. I don't want to deal with him."

"You didn't!" said Eliza, horrified. "You can't blow him off, Vic. We need to find out what he knows exactly, and what he's going to do with this information. He's becoming dangerous . . ."

"Look! He's here. He turned on the lights in his screening room. Let's go," said Victoria.

"I'm nauseous," said Eliza. "You know I'm a terrible actress."

"I'll do all the talking."

Victoria grabbed her bag and they both got out of the car and walked up to the house. When Wayne answered the door, he looked surprised.

"Today's your lucky day, baby," said Victoria, giving him a wet kiss. "This is my friend. She wants to do the threesome with us."

Wayne gave Eliza the once-over. "Great, come on in," he said.

He disgusted Eliza. How could Victoria sleep with this sleazeball? She sure had terrible taste in men.

Eliza glanced around the modern living room, noticing at once that Wayne had an obsession with all things electrical and went in for all that black leather furniture that single men love. Gross, she thought, as she sat down on a wingback chair.

"Let's get this party started," said Wayne.

"Let's get some drinks. Then we'll get started. Oh, and maybe some blow?" she asked.

Eliza's eyes turned into saucers, but Victoria gave her a disapproving shrug. *Don't worry,* she mouthed.

And she was right. Wayne ended up doing all the cocaine himself. And after about four gin and tonics, he was totally wired. Luckily he was an egotist, so he was perfectly content maintaining a diatribe throughout the entire evening about all of the celebrities that he was best friends with and how important he was in Hollywood.

"I need to use the restroom," said Victoria finally.

"You know where it is, baby," he said, not interrupting his story about Ben Affleck. Eliza was pretending to be *really* impressed to keep him talking as long as possible.

Victoria made her way to Wayne's bedroom. She had been able to do some snooping around in the past, so she knew where he kept his videotapes, but she had never had enough time to find the one that she needed. What a scumbag. She walked over to his bookshelves and pushed aside the fake bound books. Classy. Only a guy like this would have props in his bedroom. Behind them was his stash of videos, and Victoria popped one in the VCR. Eliza had been warned to say "I'd love ice cream!" really loudly if Wayne was approaching, so Victoria sat on the edge of the bed to watch.

The first tape was boring. It was Wayne ordering some red-headed bimbo to strip for the camera. Victoria popped it out of the VCR. She thought she heard something so she walked over to the doorway and listened, but she could still only hear Wayne's voice in the living room relaying his favorite Val Kilmer story. Victoria crept back to the bedroom and put in another tape.

"Yeah, baby, yeah baby!" said the woman on film as Wayne pumped her.

Gross. But it wasn't Victoria. Victoria watched in disgust for a second and was about to switch it off when the woman flipped over. Hmm . . . she looks familiar, thought Victoria. An actress? That chick from *Entertainment Tonight*? Victoria squinted closely. Oh. My. God. Gold mine! It was Shelly Forrester. Wife of Dick Forrester, the founder of Wayne's agency, now head of a major studio. One of the biggest power brokers in Hollywood, if not the biggest. Wow. What a fool! And Wayne was now ogling at the camera, winking at it as he rode Shelly cowboy style. People are so stupid, thought Victoria. She wasn't, though. She was going to take this tape and blackmail Wayne with it. Make him fork over any tape that he had of her and more. She wanted him to suffer the way he made her suffer. And this was her ticket to revenge.

Victoria walked down the stairs, clutching the banister but keeping her eye on Wayne as she descended. *People like him don't deserve to live.* She watched as he became more and more animated in his story, relaying some meretricious anecdote in which he was inevitably saving some celebrity's life. *Those men are all alike. Beasts. Subhuman.* His eyes were dancing and he was furiously gesticulating, and Victoria had to do everything to control her revulsion. Even from ten feet away she could see the little drops of saliva that came flying out of his mouth as he talked faster and faster. She had been on the receiving end of that saliva storm, and it wasn't pretty. *This man doesn't deserve to live.* It was all going through her head again and again. *No one would miss him if he were gone.*

"Eliza's having second thoughts. We're going," said Victoria quickly as she grabbed her bag and walked to the front door.

"What?" asked Wayne, popping out of his seat.

Eliza stood up and mutely followed Victoria to the door.

"We're out of here, Wayne. Good-bye," she said.

"You can't go!"

"Yes, we're going," said Victoria.

Wayne ran over and tried to bar her from opening the door, but he was too drunk and out of his mind to stop her.

"Bye," said Eliza meekly.

"Cocksuckers! Teases! Whores!" he screamed at them as they walked down the path.

"Right back at you!" said Victoria.

"Did you get it?" asked Eliza.

"Got even better," said Victoria.

When Eliza got home that night the house was dark and she expected Declan to be asleep. He usually went to bed early on work nights—he couldn't even make it to Jon Stewart. She put down her keys and purse and was about to go upstairs when she heard a voice in the living room.

"How was the movie?" asked Declan.

"You're awake!" Eliza said, startled. "Why are you sitting in the dark?"

She walked over and sat down next to him.

"Just thinking. How was the movie?" he repeated.

"Great," said Eliza lamely. "How are the kids?"

"Good," said Declan.

He studied her face carefully and she returned his gaze with curiosity.

"Is everything okay?" she asked.

"Yup," he said, rising. "Let's go to bed."

·· *30* ··

Anson was offended that none of the ladies of the infidelity pact had come courting or begging after his blind items in the newspaper. He had expected flowers, tears, dinners, trinkets. But nothing. And even worse, they had either continued to ignore him or been outright rude.

"Victoria," Anson had called out on a recent morning. He was standing on the end of her driveway watching her maneuver grocery bags out of her car.

"Don't let your dog piss on my lawn," ordered Victoria, glowering at Samantha.

"Good morning to you, too," he sniffed, irritated on behalf of Samantha. "Since I know that you have undue influence on your husband, I was wondering if you might ask him to take a look at a screenplay I've been tinkering with."

Victoria's eyes narrowed and her nostrils flared ever so slightly. "Yeah, right," she snapped before she slammed the trunk of her car shut and stomped into her house.

Anson was speechless. Had she not read the blind items? Was she not worried? How could she dismiss him like that? It only fueled him further.

Anson knew that in order to build a case you needed to gather information and ammunition on your enemies. The baby monitor tapes were obviously a smoking gun, but he needed photographs or other supplementary evidence in order to get the death penalty. So he took to following the ladies. It was kind of fun, sneaking around after them. Their lives were actually pretty dull—carpool, dry cleaner's, workouts—until they did something naughty. Something with one of their lovers. Or so he suspected.

He watched the flowers arriving almost daily at Eliza's and knew that Tyler was wooing her no end. He also knew that Eliza was rebuffing him, because as soon as the van marked VELVET GARDEN drove off, Eliza walked around to the garbage bin outside and dumped out the roses. Getting rid of the evidence. In an effort to be completely thorough, Anson waited to walk Samantha until Declan had wheeled down the trash to the corner of the driveway to await morning pickup, and idled until Samantha pooped and he could throw out the doggie bag in their trash can. When he leaned into the can, he subtly grabbed the discarded note that came with the flowers. He'd call the flower shop and find out who was behind the note that said, *Thanks for your support.*

Every piece of information that Anson gathered on the girls was put into a file marked under their name in the leather cabinet in his office. He loved to read through those files. To think what those girls would do if they knew what he had on them! He would often make checklists of things that he felt were missing, that would be the so-called cherry on the top of the sundae. For one, he wanted to get his hands on an advance copy of Eliza's in-

terview with Tyler that would appear in *Chat* magazine, but his
initial attempts had been unsuccessful. And that was what led
him to his theory about Eliza, which he now believed to be true.
And he was certain her friends had no idea.

He also had photos of Helen and Daniela, but only of them
walking down the street, and he wasn't sure if that was enough.
Two women could always claim to be friends. It was hard to prove
lesbianism, especially when one had no track record of Sapphic
love. He wasn't sure what to do about Helen. Her file is still sort
of empty, thought Anson, discouraged.

Leelee was the one that perplexed him. He had followed her
down to Manhattan Beach twice and knew that she was up to no
good when she was there. Through his binoculars, which he
looked through from across the parking lot, he could see that she
was Xeroxing what looked like a ransom letter and then destroy-
ing the evidence, but he wasn't quite sure whom she was mailing.
Jack? Brad? No, she didn't want the recipient to know it was
her—why else would she wear those crazy gloves? He was still getting to the bottom of that one. But he realized that he didn't have
to know exactly what Leelee was doing. He could always bluff.
She'd probably spill the beans when she thought he knew something. Pictures were unnecessary in this case; all he needed to do
was make an anonymous call to the *New York Post* and the press
would be all over that. But he relished being the sole press person
on the case, and hated to relinquish that power.

It was definitely time to up the stakes. And there was only
one way to do that. Get the husbands involved.

As Helen was estranged from her parents ("*adoptive* parents" she would always say) and Wesley's family resided in England, they were essentially holiday orphans, particularly on American holidays. They often traveled for those "Hallmark occasions," as Wesley referred to them, but this year they had accepted an offer to celebrate Thanksgiving with the Gallahues, believing that it might be nice for Lauren to actually experience one such event. In a spurt of ambition, Eliza had also invited Victoria and Leelee, but the former was hosting her in-laws from Long Island and the latter was hosting her parents from Boston, and although both had agreed to stop by for a drink, Eliza knew that Victoria would but Leelee would not. It didn't really matter, for what Eliza was particularly excited about was that her best friend from Chicago, Claudia, and her husband, Morgan, had accepted the invitation to join them for the long weekend.

After a long, wine-soaked Wednesday-night dinner at Capo, while Morgan and Declan talked business and she filled Claudia in on every aspect of her life (except Tyler Trask), Eliza once again came to the conclusion that nothing beats old friends. Really, truly. It was that comfort level, that shorthand reference guide, the fact that any statement she made or opinion she expressed was contextualized. For example, politics. If Eliza said she might vote for a Republican governor, Claudia didn't immediately attack her for being anti-choice, pro-gun, and subhuman the way her other friends would. Eliza considered herself a moderate, but her more democratic friends associated that with devil worship. Affirmative action? They wanted that, of course. It was the right way. And yet if their child's spot at St. Peter's was taken by a black or Latino child, they were first in line at the admissions office to register a complaint (and then get ten board members to write threatening letters). Often Eliza felt as if everyone in Los Angeles was so knee-jerk liberal, but in the most self-aggrandizing, unthoughtful, and pedantic way. "Liberals are the most intolerant," Declan always said, and he was right.

Even just discussing politics with Claudia was a luxury. Eliza had gone to Georgetown, majoring in political science, and even interned at Senator Simon's office, and yet she found herself never discussing politics in Los Angeles. Sure, there was the small pocket of women who worked with the National Resources Defense Council and were happy to tell you how they were cleaning up the environment, why hybrid cars are better (and why their driving them counterbalances their flying in private jets), and *how you can help,* but for the most part, people just wanted to gossip. Celeb gossip, local gossip. Perhaps it was like that everywhere, although Eliza didn't remember her parents sitting around gossiping.

But more than just having a friend with whom she could discuss politics and current events, Eliza was most happy to have Claudia because with her she could be her totally relaxed, silly self. Claudia and Morgan had only recently married and still didn't have kids (Claudia also worked hundred-hour weeks at her law firm), so Claudia was totally indulgent in letting Eliza show off Donovan and Bridget (her goddaughter) and talk her ear off about their latest toddler accomplishments. They in turn loved their "Auntie" Claudia, whom they called Auntie Boom-Boom because of her big, hearty (booming) laugh. Everything about Claudia was big, which she credited to her fine German stock.

She stood a good five foot eleven, and had long legs, large breasts, and thick, long auburn hair and giant green eyes. Claudia was guileless and totally open on almost every topic, refreshingly un-jaded. She was as excited as a child when they were seated next to Larry David at the restaurant and on her last visit to Los Angeles could not stop raving about how totally cool it was to see the stars on Hollywood Boulevard. It was funny to Eliza that she was known as such a shark in the courtroom. She couldn't see it at all and promised herself to one day fly to Chicago for the sole purpose of checking out her friend in action.

On Thanksgiving morning, Declan and Morgan were dispatched to the golf course (they were classified by their spouses as useless in all culinary matters) and Eliza, Claudia, and Helen decamped in the Gallahues' kitchen to prepare the feast. Eliza was not a gourmand, and usually relied on Barefoot Contessa cookbooks when she was doing any sort of entertaining, but all the years of living far away from her parents had forced her to learn how to put together Thanksgiving dinner. Helen sat on a chair, peeling potatoes and letting the starchy strips of skin fall into the garbage can between her legs. Claudia was assembling the brussels sprouts, Parmesan cheese, and heavy cream that went into her favorite Thanksgiving dish, which she *promised* would be good and even to those who didn't like brussels sprouts—she'd make converts of them tonight. Eliza had already put the turkey in the oven that morning, filled with her favorite cornbread stuffing, and was now caramelizing baby onions on one range, while monitoring the peas and wild mushrooms that were sautéing on another.

"Okay, I'm obsessed, so please continue," commanded Claudia. She was in a dark red turtleneck sweater that clashed with her auburn hair, and couldn't have appeared more opposite of the small-boned Helen sitting across from her.

"You're so funny. What else can I tell you?" asked Helen, jerking her head to the side to flip the errant strands of hair that were getting in her eyes.

"I don't know. I guess . . . *everything*," said Claudia.

"You created a monster," said Eliza from the stove. "She's a lawyer, remember? She'll want all the details."

Within ten minutes of meeting her, Helen had told Claudia that she had been sleeping with a woman. Eliza's pupils had dilated and she looked alarmed, but Helen gave her a reassuring look as if to say, *Don't worry*, your *secret is safe with me*. And Eliza believed her. She knew that Helen wouldn't rat her out to other people, and she was fine with Helen discussing her infidelity as long as she didn't mention the pact. Eliza had thought about confiding in Claudia and couldn't believe she actually hadn't, because they had known each other since they were seven and she told her *everything*, but Claudia adored Declan and would never have approved. It was fine if it was other people, but not people she regarded as family.

"Okay, first I want to know, what is it like with a woman? Do you think you're a lesbian? Does this make you want to have a threesome?" asked Claudia, pouring milk into the casserole dish.

"Look at you! All these questions!" Helen smiled, unperturbed by them. "Okay, no, it doesn't make me want to have a threesome. You bring someone else into your bedroom and that's inviting trouble."

"Who wants to have a threesome?"

They turned around. It was Victoria. They hadn't heard her come in.

"Hey, Victoria," said Claudia rising and giving Victoria a big hug, from which Victoria slightly recoiled.

"Hey, Claudia. Welcome back to town," said Victoria, marching over to the wine rack on the kitchen counter, taking out a bottle of pinot noir, and studying the label.

"Can I open this?" she asked.

"Sure," said Eliza, opening the drawer and handing her a corkscrew.

"Isn't it a little early?" asked Helen.

"It's never too early when my in-laws are in town," said Victoria, twisting the handle and popping the cork out. She took out a glass. "Anyone else?"

"Well, I'm on vacation, so why not?" said Claudia, with mock guilt.

"If I have any now, I'll pass out," said Eliza.

"Helen?" asked Victoria.

"Sure."

Victoria poured the wine and brought it over to the other girls.

"What's wrong with your in-laws?" asked Claudia.

"Don't get me started," said Victoria, unlacing the mostly decorative wool scarf that she had around her neck (it was sixty-five degrees outside) and sliding out two chairs, one for her and the other for her feet. "First of all, my father-in-law? The guy literally sells aluminum siding. Could he be more white trash? And his accent is like Archie Bunker or some Mafioso, all 'dems' and 'dis.' He dyes his hair jet-black but it kind of has a bluish tint to it, and his clothes have lapels the size of airport hangars. Justin wanted to take them to Mr. Chow's for dinner but I said no way am I going anywhere with them where we might actually see people we know, so we took them to Peppone, which is the darkest restaurant in town. Of course my mother-in-law complained the entire time. She's the most passive-aggressive person I know. It's all, 'I don't care where we go, anywhere you want,' and then when we go to a place she's like, 'Of course, you know I had Italian last night, but it doesn't matter.' I can't deal."

Claudia was amused watching Victoria rant. For such a physical beauty, she always seemed to be spewing the most venomous, cutting remarks. Claudia couldn't imagine what she was so angry about.

"That's a drag," said Eliza from the stove. It was such a popular sport, bashing the in-laws, that she sometimes felt people did it more out of a sense of tradition than real feelings. She was lucky with Declan's parents. They were really sweet, good with the kids, and didn't interfere. They also had eight other grandchildren and lived in Baltimore, so that helped. Of course Eliza could find fault with them if she tried, but what was the point? They were there to stay; you can't change them. It seemed that as soon as some of her friends married their husbands they went on the offensive, armed and ready for battle with their in-laws, cataloging every irritation and small offense. Let it go.

"My in-laws are horrid, but thankfully they're in England," said Helen, stopping her potato peeling and taking a big swig of her wine.

"All right, I totally want to talk about this, but please, before the guys come back can we finish with your comments on your girlfriend?" asked Claudia, putting her hands under her chin and leaning in.

"You're telling her about Daniela?" asked Victoria, her eyebrow arched.

"Yes," said Helen.

Victoria glanced over at Eliza, who gave her a reassuring look.

"Anyway, what more can I say? It's been interesting, but not as fulfilling as I had imagined," said Helen.

"I just can't even imagine what it would be like," said Claudia, with Midwestern naïveté. "Do you do everything?"

"Um, not really. The whole thing is kind of boring, actually. I thought it would be so exciting and racy, but really, for me, just the idea of it was exciting. I don't know . . . it hasn't changed my life."

"And did you tell your husband?" asked Claudia.

"God, no," she said with disdain. "It's *our* little secret."

"Who has a secret?" asked Lauren, entering the kitchen with Donovan and Bridget trailing after her. Lauren was a gorgeous child, and she looked particularly cute today, dressed up in one of the fancy smock dresses that Wesley's parents had sent, with a silk bow in her hair.

"No one," said Helen, dismissing Lauren.

"I want a secret," said Donovan, coming up to Eliza and putting his arms up. He was an extremely affectionate child, with the largest hazel eyes anyone had ever seen.

"Okay, here it is," said Eliza, whispering in Donovan's ear. "I love you."

"That's not a secret!" Donovan giggled.

"Yes it is," whispered Eliza again, tickling his tummy. "I love you to the sky."

"I want a secret!" said Bridget, jumping up and down. Eliza leaned down to her and whispered in her ear, "I love you to the moon."

Bridget burst into giggles.

Lauren, who was normally quiet and reserved, was relaxed enough to break into a smile and approach Eliza. "Can I have a secret?" she asked politely.

Eliza leaned toward her and whispered in her ear: "I love you to Jupiter!"

Lauren began laughing also. Helen watched as Lauren followed Eliza, Donovan, and Bridget to the kitchen cabinets and waited for Eliza to retrieve and distribute mini bags of Goldfish crackers for each child. Then Lauren said, "Come on, guys," and the two smaller children followed her into the family room to continue their tea party. Eliza had such a natural way with children, thought Helen, burning with jealousy. She was never like that, never playful or goofy with Lauren. Yet it was obviously what Lauren needed because whenever Eliza was around she was like a barnacle to her side.

"Lauren is so sweet with the little ones," said Eliza.

"She's a natural," added Claudia, nodding. "She's only, what, seven? And she's already a little babysitter."

"That's the thing with girls," said Victoria, stretching back in her chair. "Their maternal instincts are there from the get-go. I can't believe how some of my friends who have girls are able to let them play together for hours without disturbance. My boys would trash the place and be at each other's throats. If I ask one where the other is, he runs away and I hear a slap, crash, bang, and a wail, and then he comes back without a word. But when I was over at my friend's house who has girls, she asked her four-year-old to check on the two-year-old, and the girl came back holding the younger one's hand and reported that she had been playing with choking hazards so they needed a new activity! It's crazy."

All the women laughed and agreed.

Later that evening, when all the men had arrived and everyone was showered and dressed and ready for cocktail hour before dinner, Claudia had a moment alone with Eliza in the kitchen.

"I can't believe your friends," said Claudia.

"I know."

"I mean, Helen? Cheating on her husband?" she said the last part with a whisper, eyes fervently darting at the door to make sure no one overheard. "That's just *crazy*. I mean, I only just met him, but he seems like a sweet guy."

"Yeah," said Eliza, giving the mashed potatoes a final stir. God, if Claudia only knew.

"And it's sad she's so not into her kid. She kind of gives her these looks like she's dealing with an alien," said Claudia, handing Eliza a pot holder so she could pull the turkey out of the oven.

"You're right," said Eliza.

"I think if she spent more time with her, she'd get the satisfaction that she's trying to find elsewhere. But what do I know?"

"No, you're right," repeated Eliza. Could she get extra satisfaction spending more time with her kids? No, that wasn't what it was with her. She felt she had a great relationship with Donovan and Bridget. And Declan as well. What she had wanted was to feel special. It was silly, really.

"And Victoria is a card!" said Claudia, laughing. "She's really angry about something, every time I see her. Now there's someone who maybe *should* consider divorce."

"Yeah, her husband's a jerk."

"But what do I know? They must be awesome people, because they're *your* friends," said Claudia, grabbing a plate of cheese and crackers and taking them with her to the living room.

Eliza stood for a minute, hands stuck deep into pot holders, steam from the hot dishes curling around her face, and tried to view her friends with detachment. It was too hard. Sometimes it takes an outsider to really tell you what's going on.

———

Meanwhile, over at Leelee's house, Thanksgiving was the tense affair that it had become in recent years. Leelee's mother, who had become pettier and more disheartened with her life as she aged, had on her usual sour face as she surveyed the dinner with her critical eye. "Now tell me, why don't you have a dining room again?" she asked several times, apparently not liking the response that they seldom entertained so it was better to turn the designated space into a toy room for the girls. "And when are you thinking of moving?" she'd ask, as if she had a tin ear to the fact that Brad had not earned any extra money to facilitate a move. Her disappointments ran deeper than her daughter's, but they both agreed on one thing: had Leelee married Jack as planned, life would be better. Well, there was still time.

·· *32* ··

Thanksgiving ended as quickly as it began, with people eating more than they should have and vowing to burn it off after the holidays. Sure enough, the gyms filled up the Monday after, and the bicycle and jogging paths along the ocean were glutted with aggressive workout fiends, feverish in their efforts to burn off the extra helping of sweet potatoes that they had regretfully sampled. All of the girls were back in their routines, dropping children off at school, taking them to classes, and dealing with their own extracurricular romances.

"Can I use your phone?" asked Leelee when Victoria opened the door to her house.

"Sure, and hello to you too," said Victoria, letting her in.

Leelee carefully wiped her shoes on the second floor mat, knowing Victoria was a stickler for dirt tracked into her house.

"Sorry, it's just, Brad is on my case ever since he found an e-mail from Jack, and I don't want him to find out yet," said Leelee.

"He's going to find out sooner or later," said Victoria.

"Well, I need it to be later. Where is the most private spot?" asked Leelee, glancing around. She didn't want to ask Victoria for a favor, but Helen wasn't home and she didn't feel comfortable doing it at Eliza's, because even though Eliza was on board, she still seemed a tad bit too disapproving of the whole thing.

"You can use my room or the twins'," said Victoria, motioning to the second floor.

"Thanks," said Leelee, bolting up the stairs.

"Do you want something to drink?" asked Victoria.

"No thanks," yelled Leelee, who was already out of sight.

Victoria sighed and returned to her desk, where she had been opening mail. Leelee was a great friend to go out with, have a few laughs, gossip, and discuss children with, but she was totally inappropriate for this endeavor. Victoria would never have included Leelee if she weren't so tight with Helen, and quite honestly Victoria hadn't believed that Leelee would ever find someone to cheat with, but she had obviously been proven wrong. And now her friend had turned into a monster. Leelee was so convinced that she would marry Jack Porter and be this high society first lady figure that she had become smug and vain. She had always had that propensity to come off as "to the manor born" because she was a Swift and in the *Social Register,* but now that she would finally have another swanky last name and some dough to go with it, she had become impossible to deal with. But Victoria wasn't so sure it would all end up going Leelee's way. She had a suspicion that it was one-sided, and Leelee in fact might be bluffing.

Victoria tore open a letter that was addressed, much to her annoyance, to Mr. and Mrs. Coleman. Who the hell didn't remember that she'd kept her maiden name? It was so irritating. She glanced at the picture of two smiling blond boys clad in identical blue Ralph Lauren sweaters, cuddling a big brown Lab. Someone was already organized enough to send Christmas cards? She flipped open the cover and read *Happy Holidays love, Dave, Nicole, Matty, Jasper, Duchess and Dander (not pictured).* It drove her nuts when people credited their animals on their Christmas cards. People, they are not human. It was so tacky. And especially those people who just sent out a Christmas card featuring their dog or cat, with no children. Ridiculous, thought Victoria, throwing the card into the trash bin. They should be committed. It shocked Victoria's friends that she discarded Christmas cards as soon as she looked at them instead of doing what everyone else does and display them on her mantel. Why the hell would she do that? Half of the people's kids she didn't even know, and often a lot of those kids were downright ugly. She didn't want to junk up her house with that clutter.

Victoria went through more bills and was about to call Verizon and ask them why the hell was her bill so high when she remembered Leelee was on the phone. God, she'd been on there awhile. She wanted to pick up the extension and eavesdrop, but surely they would hear her. Suddenly Victoria was seized by an idea. It was terrible, but hell, it was her house, so why not? She went and got the baby monitor from the kitchen and brought it into her office. The other extensions were upstairs and on as usual, so she would be able to hear Leelee's conversation.

The dial of the monitor turned and then a low static noise came out of the handset, until Victoria adjusted it on her desk and could finally hear Leelee's side of the conversation. She listened intently.

"I can't believe that, Porty, you poor thing," she heard Leelee say into the phone.

There was a pause where Jack was obviously filling her in on what had happened.

"Look, you were an idiot, eloping without a prenup, you bad boy, you! But I'm sure a judge will understand that you were young and drunk. She's not going to walk away with everything. You can buy her off with a few mil," said Leelee in her bossy tone.

So Jack was hedging, thought Victoria. Just as she'd suspected.

"She's such a bitch! No, I agree, wait until after the holidays, although it's strange 'cause it's not like you guys have any kids. Who cares if Daddy's home when Santa comes or not?" said Lee-lee. She paused.

"Right, well, but her parents are going to be just as disappointed *after* the holidays also, especially if you do spend all that time with them in Antigua . . ." continued Leelee.

This guy has no plan to leave Tierney, thought Victoria.

"Okay, love bug, I don't mean to be naggy-naggy! I just *miss* you. I love you to bits," sighed Leelee into the phone.

Victoria heard the phone click and she leapt across her desk to turn off the monitor. Minutes later, Leelee wandered into her office, beaming.

"It's all set," she said with a grin. "I just can't wait. I told him to delay it until after the holidays, and then we're good to go."

Leelee would never confide anything to Victoria that would be remotely negative about herself or her relationship. She felt as though Victoria sometimes looked down on her, as if she were a mere child, and that pissed her off.

"That's exciting," said Victoria, spinning around on her swivel chair. "Where are you guys going to live?"

"New York. First we'll go to Hawaii and then call our respective spouses, and on the way home I'll pick up the kids and head east," said Leelee.

"Are you at all upset about Brad?" asked Victoria.

"Brad . . ." began Leelee, but then stopped. "He'll find someone else."

"Right," said Victoria.

"Anyway, thanks for the phone," said Leelee.

It was still a bright day when Leelee left Victoria's house, one of those white December days that appear as if clouds have nestled around the city to protect it from snow and rain. Leelee couldn't contain her excitement. This is what it feels like to win the lottery. This is what it feels like to be elected president. This is what true happiness is. She did feel bad that she had to hurt some people along the way. But she truly believed everyone would end up happier.

Later that night, Victoria was on her way out to meet Wayne. It was the moment she'd been waiting for. She was going to present him with a copy of the tape she had made of him having sex with Shelly and then make him beg her for mercy. She had been savoring this idea for weeks now. He had called and harassed her and yelled at her and tormented her these past two weeks—he was particularly furious about the aborted threesome—but she had held him off in an effort to get him completely worked up. She wanted to shock him into submission and surprise him with her coup.

As Victoria got in her car, there was a knock on the window. She looked up. Anson Larrabee. What the hell did he want now? She rolled down the window.

"Hi, Anson," she said without a smile.

"Going out?" asked Anson.

"Yup, looks that way, doesn't it?" she asked sarcastically.

Suddenly Anson's face contorted and his manner turned severe. "I'm tired of y'all dismissing me like this. I know all about your infidelity pact. I know about you and Wayne," said Anson.

"Whatever," replied Victoria coolly. She didn't want to appear as if she cared. That was exactly what he wanted.

This further infuriated Anson. "I'm going to tell Justin! I'm going to tell everyone," said Anson, sounding like a spoiled child who wasn't getting his way.

"Go ahead," said Victoria. "He already knows."

Anson glared at Victoria and wondered if it was true. It could be. Justin was never home, and it actually seemed as though he and Victoria lived separate lives. It had been eons since he'd heard them having sex.

"Oh yeah? Well, what about your girlfriends?" asked Anson.

"What about them?" asked Victoria.

"Do they know about you and Wayne?"

Victoria stared at him coolly, not wanting to confess or confirm anything.

Anson smiled more broadly. He had got her. And it felt finger-lickin' good! "Do they know that you and Wayne were having this torrid affair for months before you brought them into this pact?"

Victoria continued staring at him, but he saw something flicker across her face that told him everything.

"Do they know that you created this entire scheme, this whole 'infidelity pact' "—he used his fingers to make air quotes—"so that their hands would be dirty, too, and then they wouldn't be judgmental about helping you out of your mess?"

It was all coming together now when he said it out loud. He had wondered why she'd suggested the pact at first. She certainly wasn't the type of gal who needed her girlfriends to follow along. And why extend the affair with Wayne when he was obviously terrorizing her? He had listened for weeks to Victoria pleading with him to back off. But now he understood. She needed help. And the only way to get friends to help in that type of situation was to put them *in* that type of situation.

"You're insane," said Victoria flatly. But her voice inadvertently shook. How did Anson know all this? *No one* knew this part. And it was true. She *had* started sleeping with Wayne two months before she'd gone out with her friends and gotten them to cheat on their husbands. And then when he went nutso, she enlisted them so they could help extricate her from this mess. She had gotten in over her head, but her pride wouldn't allow her to just confess to her friends and ask for help. Because goddamn it, she, Victoria Rand, was not the sort of woman who asked for help. But now that they were all a team—and all supporting each other, embarking on the adventure together—it was okay to ask Eliza to come with her to Wayne's. Eliza had already sold herself to the devil with her affair with Tyler Trask. She could never give a condescending look to Victoria again. No, none of her friends would ever have anything on her. And because Victoria was competitive and proud—yes, this she would admit—this was the only way she could have it. But they were never supposed to find out.

"I don't think I am," said Anson, backing away from the car. "And I don't think they'll think so either when I tell them."

"What do you want from us, Anson?" asked Victoria, exasperated. "Is this just a game to you? You want us to be scared of you? Or is this because you are so small and petty that you want us to be your best friends? No, Anson. You'll never be our best friend. You'll never insinuate yourself into our lives. Because you're a gossip columnist, and a petty loser!"

Victoria turned around and backed out of the driveway, leaving Anson slack-jawed. Screw him, she thought as she glanced at him in her rearview mirror. Then suddenly she squinted. What was that? Damn. Justin was pulling his car into the driveway. And he was waving to Anson. Should I turn around? she thought. No. Just keep on going.

·· *33* ··

"**I was reading** Lauren a book about pandas. Fascinating creatures. Do you know anything about them?" asked Wesley.

"No," said Helen, twirling her spaghetti. They were having a cozy dinner at Caffe Delfini at Wesley's suggestion. It was an intimate restaurant, with tables so close that you could reach over to the plate of the person at the next table and steal a bite of his gnocchi, the type of place where you could hear everyone's conversation. A perfect place to ask for a divorce because your unsuspecting spouse wouldn't make a scene. That had to be the reason that Wesley asked her there, Helen was sure. They had done nothing together in ages, they were virtual strangers, and suddenly this morning he asks to go to dinner? It didn't make sense. Helen was paranoid. She didn't want to get a divorce. It scared her, the thought of being thrust out there to nothingness. When she started this pact, she thought she might find someone to share her life with, that all the problems were because of Wesley. But she wasn't sure she felt that way anymore. She was partially to blame. She had recoiled as much as he had.

"Pandas are truly solitary creatures. They prefer to be alone and have to be coerced into mating. Wonky, right?" asked Wesley. "And they eat only bamboo. They consume pounds and pounds of it a year, and you know how difficult it is to procure bamboo? In actuality they should be extinct."

"Interesting," said Helen, looking down.

"And even the mother will attack her children, as will the father. Those bloody things mate, and then it's a delayed conception period—the sperm can just float about in the mother's uterus for months and they have no idea if she is impregnated. And then when the panda's born, it's only four ounces! Can you imagine?"

Wesley was truly amazed. That was Wesley: able to get very focused on something and research it to death until he knew everything about it. He was always finding something new to be fascinated about. Helen usually found this charming or irritating, depending on her general feelings for him at that time. But right now she felt an insurmountable sense of dread and foreboding. Was he trying to tell her something with this panda talk?

"Strange," murmured Helen.

"Is something wrong with the pasta?" asked Wesley.

Helen looked up. "No, sorry. Just not that hungry."

Wesley didn't even comment. He was used to Helen's odd eating habits. Through the years he'd been subjected to cleansing days, juice weeks, and every popular fad diet from Atkins to the Zone to that bizarre one where you ate only things your ancestors ate. He himself wasn't much of a foodie the way other people were, but he appreciated a good meal and a nice glass of wine.

"Wesley?" Helen asked suddenly.

"Yes?"

"Why do you love me?" She felt herself redden as she asked it. It was not a question she had ever asked him, and not the type of conversation that Wesley would enjoy engaging in. But she had to know.

"What do you mean? Don't be silly," he said, looking confounded.

"No . . . I mean, I need to know," she said, persistent. She'd usually let a conversation fall away if Wesley didn't bite, but this time she wasn't going to.

"I don't know—what an odd question. Are you going to one of those mad lectures again?"

"No, Wesley, I just want to know. Do you love me? Was I a trophy wife? What keeps us together?"

"Of course I love you. This is all silly, really," he said awkwardly. It's something Helen had noticed about British men. Or at least all of Wesley's British friends. They detested emotional conversation. They did not want to analyze feelings, opine on matters of the heart. It was both banal and frivolous.

"I need to know why," she implored.

Wesley looked at her. Then he sighed. "Helen, I don't know why. I just do."

"Why did you fall in love with me?"

"I don't get you, Helen. I just don't get you," said Wesley with a smile. Wesley would often say that to Helen. He'd shake his head and declare it not so much as a criticism as a fact, as if he was talking about a movie or a complicated scientific experiment. Helen puzzled him, and that was just their reality. It didn't seem to bother him at all. And the truth was, Helen didn't really get her husband. There was an abyss between them. Other couples had it. Some people thought that was exciting, the very essence of their relationship that made it work. It was their dynamic: they liked living with an enigma, finding it complex, titillating. But then there were those other friends, like Eliza and Declan, for whom there were no questions. They knew absolutely everything about each other: how they would react to things such as news, information, and what the other would do. There were never surprises because they told each other everything.

Well, except for the Tyler Trask part. But other than that, they were an open book. That was probably why Eliza wanted to try something different. And probably why Helen did also. She wanted someone to get her.

"No, seriously, Wesley. Don't be vague," reprimanded Helen. "Why did you fall for me?"

Wesley smiled. "It just happened," he said with finality. Topic over. Then he motioned for the waiter to bring him more mineral water.

It just happened. So that was it. Just like when she was thirteen and she found in her adoptive father's closet pornographic magazines with pictures of young Asian girls copulating. It just happened. And then when she fled outside to tell her older brother and he ran across the street to find out what was wrong and got hit and killed by a car. It just happened. And then she ran away from home and lived on the street for three days until her best friend's father brought her back to Orange County to live with them. It just happened. Dirk died. It just happened. She married Wesley. It just happened. She had Lauren. It just happened. Now she was unfaithful. It just happened. When would they take responsibility for their lives?

.. *34* ..

Christmas and New Year's came and went. Although Angelinos are confronted with perennial sunshine and not a lick of snow, attempts are made to create some semblance of a festive holiday atmosphere. Christmas tree lights are strewn around town, parties are in abundance, and stores decorate their windows in cheery red and green colors. Some people enjoy the season; others leave town.

Eliza and Declan went to Chicago the day after Christmas and returned the day after New Year's. Victoria and Justin took the boys to Cabo San Lucas for ten days, including Christmas and New Year's. Helen and Wesley went to Hawaii for Christmas but came back for New Year's. Leelee and Brad stayed in Los Angeles the entire time.

Eliza was thrilled to be away from town, anything to get her mind off Tyler Trask. He had left town but now there were traces of him everywhere, as his new movie just opened on Christmas Day and was a blockbuster sensation. She was sure he would roll back into town for press, and although she hadn't heard from him in a month, she feared that he would try to get in touch. She just wanted him out of her life for good. There wasn't room for him anymore. She usually had a Christmas party in December, but this year she couldn't get it together in time. Everything felt like high stress; the last thing she needed was to have to worry about hors d'oeuvres. But when she got back into town, she decided it would be fun to have a party. A cocktail party. Something to break up the monotony and gloom of January. She scheduled it for the fifteenth.

Victoria felt she deserved a much-needed vacation. For the past month she had been busy—yes, very busy indeed. Torturing Wayne Mercer. Her revenge was sweet. Once she showed him that she had possession of the tape, he went into a tailspin. He first threatened her but then begged her. When she ultimately comprehended that he was at her mercy, it was a humiliating experience for him and a moment of euphoria for her. She had wanted to get him at the jugular, so she forced him to do something he absolutely didn't want to do: part with a client. Justin had long wanted to represent Natalie Maddox, a young Hollywood ingenue, and was furious when Wayne signed her. Because she felt the slightest tinge of repentance toward Justin, she decided to give him Natalie. Well, more accurately, she decided to make Wayne give him Natalie. He refused for weeks, but when he saw her one day at the Ivy, marching over to his boss's table to greet him, he relented. He told Natalie that Justin would better fulfill her needs. Justin was ecstatic but had no idea it was all his wife's doing. That was okay, thought Victoria. For now.

Helen had her first real family vacation in years. Sure, she'd been on family vacations, but she hadn't done anything really to act like a family with Wesley and Lauren. She usually threw Lauren into the kids' camp and let Wesley take off and golf, and she'd plop herself on a chaise by the pool and read the latest Deepak Chopra. But not this time. It was a metamorphosis. The three of them kayaked, played tennis, went snorkeling, and did everything a normal family would do. And it felt good. This was connecting. This was a normal family. Because that's what she wanted them to be, that's what she would make them be.

Leelee remained in town for the first time in years because she thought of it as a last supper in a way. There was no need to go see family on the East Coast, because in less than three weeks she planned on living on the East Coast permanently. There was so much to be done: she needed to pack without packing, say good-bye to her friends without actually saying good-bye, and extricate herself from her life without letting anyone know. It was tricky and had to be done deftly, but Leelee prided herself on her discretion. There were so many lies in her life these days that she couldn't even see straight. It wouldn't matter soon enough.

Another blind item appeared in the *Palisades Press* over the holidays. It read: *A certain dashing young scion of a famous politi-*

cal family has been having relations with one of our own. Problem is, they're both married. How determined are they to keep their secret? Hopefully enough to put up the money for a wonderful script from a talented new screenwriter. Stay tuned.

·· *35* ··

Imelda felt marvelous. She had spent the morning in tennis clinic, making great improvement to her backhand and securing the attention of the handsome new tennis pro, and she had an afternoon of beauty treatments planned as a reward. Before walking to her car, she decided to cool off a little by proceeding to the playground to perhaps sit on the bench and take in some air. It was there that she saw Leelee Adams poring over a copy of the latest *Us Weekly* with great intensity.

Imelda watched her for a moment, recollecting how much Anson hated her. Well, all those women, really. He loathed them. Anson had been kind to Imelda, a good friend, and therefore she was inclined to be loyal to him. But she was also beginning to tire of his pettiness, his frequent mood swings, and his infantile behavior. She knew that soon their relationship would come to a conclusion, and she had already lined up a contender for his place, a certain Mr. Sebastian Falk who worked in the business affairs department at HBO. While not very glamorous, at least he held down a reasonable job and was, as far as she could tell, heterosexual.

Imelda entered the playground, her eyes still on Leelee, who had yet to notice her. She was about to sit on the other side of the park, far away from her, when she saw Leelee's daughter run up to her and whisper something in her mother's ear. Leelee smiled and patted her on the head, and the child then ran back and resumed her place in the giant fire truck that loomed over the playground. Something about that brief maternal interaction humanized Leelee for Imelda, and she decided to approach her.

"Hello there," said Imelda cheerily.

Leelee looked up. "Oh, hi, Imelda."

"What's this?" asked Imelda, taking Leelee's magazine out of her hands and studying the cover. Leelee felt disproportionate rage at Imelda's losing her place.

"You know, crack for adults," Leelee joked. Now give it back.

"This is so silly. Do you really care about Jessica Simpson?" asked Imelda with a laugh.

"I really do," said Leelee seriously.

Imelda laughed and handed Leelee the magazine, and then, much to Leelee's chagrin, sat down next to her. "It's a beautiful day."

"Yes," said Leelee. Ugh, could she not just get fifteen minutes to herself?

"This is such a nice park," said Imelda.

"Yes."

"Do you have any fun plans?"

"Not really." Was there a point to this?

"Listen, Leelee. I don't know you very well, and I pride myself on not getting involved in other people's business," she began with earnestness. She waited for Leelee to concur but proceeded when Leelee remained mute. "You know I adore Anson—we are such special friends—but I fear he's gotten a little irrational on the topic of you women."

Her speech sounded rehearsed to Leelee. Who speaks like that? She'd heard that Imelda watched a lot of soap operas in order to speak proper English, and it showed.

"Well, there's no love lost between me and Anson."

"I know. He despises you," Imelda said with a sigh, as if she was very troubled by it.

"That's too bad."

"The fact is, we both know that he has incriminating information on you and your friends. And I fear he is prepared to go to your husbands about it. I just thought I should warn you."

Leelee felt a sudden surge of adrenaline but didn't want Imelda to know. "I don't really know what he has on me and my friends. That's absurd."

Imelda smiled blankly. Leelee could not tell if she was being patronizing or nice or was just incapable of deep thinking, so she remained expressionless. "Well, my advice to you and your friends is to be charitable. Be kind. It wouldn't hurt any of you to help Anson with his career. He does have a brilliant screenplay."

"You've read it?" asked Leelee.

"No," admitted Imelda. "But he's so witty, I am sure it's fantastic."

"Right."

Imelda looked at her in anticipation. "So?"

"So?"

"You'll help him with the script?"

"Imelda, I have no Hollywood connections."

"Ta-ta," said Imelda, rising and waving her finger to shush Leelee. "I'm certain a smart girl like you can think of something. And you must. You really must before this all gets out of hand."

"That's not possible."

Imelda stopped and stared at Leelee. "He tape-records you,

Leelee," said Imelda with wide eyes. "He listens to you through Victoria's baby monitor. He knows everything. Be careful."

Leelee watched as Imelda walked toward the gate in her inappropriately short tennis skirt that showed off her thick legs. Should she trust her? Could it be true? It would explain how he knew so much. Now what? Leelee got out her cell and began to dial Eliza. She had to tell her that Anson knew everything, that they were all in danger. But suddenly she stopped. Who cared? She was out of here in a week. So what if he knew everything? Was it worth the drama? No, but she had to warn the others. It was only fair.

She left a message on Eliza's voice mail to call her ASAP and sent Victoria a text that Anson had blackmail tapes. Victoria e-mailed back at once, and her reply consoled Leelee: *So what?* She decided it wasn't even worth mentioning to Helen, who would get all bent out of shape for nothing.

.. *36* ..

Two days before Eliza's cocktail party, Helen brought Lauren home from ballet class and found Wesley reclining on the chaise in his office, flipping through a screenplay. Helen's New Year's resolution had been to make more of an effort with her daughter and her husband, especially demonstrating interest in things that were of interest to them.

"What are you reading?" said Helen, plopping down on the armchair across from Wesley and curling her legs under her.

Wesley bent down the side of the script and peered at Helen.

"It's the screenplay you wanted to talk to me about," he said. "What?"

"You know, the one by Anson Larrabee."

"Anson Larrabee?"

"Yes, I ran into him and he said he'd told you all about it and you thought it would be perfect for my next picture. He was surprised you hadn't mentioned it."

Helen felt her throat tighten. "Um, I guess I didn't have a chance."

"It's nice of you to take an interest in my work, darling."

"Yes, of course," said Helen, nervously twisting her wedding band. "So what do you think?"

"Well, he's a crap writer and the premise is tawdry as all hell. But if you sift through the rubbish, there are glimmers of truth that could be interesting if given to a better writer," he said.

"Really?" said Helen, trying to think, think! What to do? Does he know?

"Yes, I can't imagine Anson's truly serious about this, though. It's only thirty pages. Although, perhaps he wants it to be on telly. I don't know . . ."

"What's it called?" asked Helen.

Wesley flipped back to the title page. " 'The Pact,' " he said.

Helen stared at Wesley, whose face was still buried behind the script. "Is there something you want to tell me?" she asked softly.

Wesley put down the script. "Sorry, I just promised him I'd have a go at this and get back to him tomorrow. I want to get through and then I'm all yours."

"No, I'm not annoyed you're reading, I just meant . . ." She stopped. He didn't have any idea. "What's the screenplay about?"

"Four women who agree to cheat on their husbands. Absurd," he said.

Helen stood up. "I'll leave you to it, then."

"Thanks, love," he said.

"I have to pick up something at the store. I'll be back," she said.

She drove quickly to Victoria's house, dialing Eliza and Leelee along the way and ordering them to meet her there.

"This has to stop. He has to be stopped," said Helen furiously as she marched past Victoria into the house.

Victoria was in her workout clothes, eating a yogurt. "Anson?"

"Yes, Anson! He gave Wesley his script."

"Please. He's a loser."

Helen stopped and stared at Victoria. "How can you not care? He can destroy us."

"No, he can't."

Helen was irate that Victoria was so dismissive. How could she be so cavalier? "Yes, Victoria, he can. His script is about four women cheating on their husbands."

Victoria plopped down on her sofa and continued eating her yogurt. Helen was enraged. She was about to tear into her when the doorbell rang and Eliza and Leelee arrived.

Helen filled them in on what had transpired.

"I think Victoria is right. So what?" said Leelee.

Helen was aghast. "Eliza?"

"I think we have to talk to him. This is getting too dangerous."

"I agree," said Helen, nodding. "So what's our plan?"

Victoria and Leelee remained mute. Only Eliza appeared to be thinking.

"Guys, help me out. Victoria? You're the one who got us into this," said Helen.

"I got you into this? Oh, please."

"How dare you? Why are you copping out? I thought we were all supposed to have each other's backs here. Just because you don't care about your marriage doesn't mean I don't care about mine."

"Please," said Victoria.

"Really, Helen, calm down," said Leelee, for once glad to be on the same side as Victoria.

"I never should have agreed to this. You are both so selfish. You don't care anymore so you won't help me and Eliza," said Helen, beginning to cry.

Victoria sighed deeply and realized that even though she didn't care if her marriage was over, she did care if her friendship with Helen was over. "You're right, Helen. We'll deal with this. Won't we, Leelee?"

Leelee paused, swirling the Tiffany gold chain around her neck. She really couldn't be bothered. It would all blow over and she'd be living in New York. All she could think about was Jack, and this seemed like such a pain. But she'd have to do it. "Okay."

"So what's our strategy?" asked Eliza.

The ladies conferred for more than an hour and came up with a plan. They would invite Anson to Eliza's cocktail party and confront him there. They'd placate him in order to receive the tapes from the baby monitor, and all would be forgotten. That was the plan, anyway.

·· *37* ··

The next day was busy for Leelee. She wanted to spend as much time as possible with her daughters before she left with Jack, but she also wanted to say good-bye to her friends and make sure the house was in order. The plan was for her to meet Jack at the Santa Monica airport at two in the morning, when he would arrive by private jet and then whisk her off to Hawaii, where they would lay low until everything calmed down. They had been over the plan multiple times, but Leelee was so excited that she could have discussed it all day. Lately, Jack had been moody and a little more reluctant than usual to dissect every beat of their plan, which was fine with Leelee, because she didn't want to stress him out. She could envelop herself in euphoria and then when they were together it would rub off on him.

When she tucked her girls in for the night, for the first time she felt a pang in her heart, which she quickly dismissed. *No, no, this will be better for them. For all of us. For me.* She went downstairs and found Brad watching television in the living room, so she went and sat in the sofa across from him. As she nestled among monogrammed pillows, she realized she'd have to buy all new pillows and towels and stationery to fit her new initials when she married Jack. She'd get more expensive ones this time. So long, Horchow, hello, Leontine Linens. She glanced over at Brad, who was immersed in his program. One of the *Law & Order*s. She didn't know which one and had long ceased watching them, but Brad still loved them. It showed how provincial he was. They were all the same. And they always got the guy and had the murder weapon, but inevitably they had wrongfully attained the murder weapon and had to look for other clues to track down the killer. She found herself obsessing over the inanity of *Law & Order* and procedural cop shows in general, which she later found prescient.

"That's it, I'm beat," said Brad, standing up and handing her the remote. "You going to bed?"

"No, I think I'll watch Jon Stewart," she said turning the channel.

"All right," he said, and walked to the door of the room. Suddenly he stopped and turned around. "I love you," he said in a voice so low, she almost didn't hear.

She turned and looked at him. "I love you, too," she said, but she knew her voice was fake.

He looked as if he was about to say something but he changed his mind. Seconds later she heard him trudging up the stairs. After the show, Leelee went to her desk and began a letter to Brad. She was going to leave it on the commode in the front hall for him to find in the morning. He usually left early—at work he had to operate on East Coast time, so he was out the door by five-forty-five at the latest.

Dear Brad,

Well, what can I say? Let's not fool each other. We knew this time would come. I am finally leaving you. I am, and always have been, in love with Jack Porter, and I feel it is my destiny to be with him. Thank you, Brad, for our two beautiful daughters. You were a good husband, loyal and devoted. But we both know that we went into this marriage thinking our lives would be one way and everything turned out different. I cannot help but blame you. I am sorry that I am not a stronger person to get over that, but I had always promised myself that I would not make the same mistake that my mother did when she married my father, and yet I repeated history, and now I am leading a life that I fought so hard against. For this I cannot forgive you. Let's make this easy. I will give you the house and cars, the membership to the beach

club, and half of our bank account. I will send for the
girls next week and we will move to New York, to be
with Jack. Please don't make this difficult. Let's think of
Charlotte and Violet. Godspeed, Brad.

Leelee

She folded the letter carefully and put it in an envelope, on which she wrote *Brad.* She spent the next hour deleting e-mails, organizing her desk, and making sure her carry-on bag had ample reading (*Us Weekly, Star, People, In Touch*, and the new Mary Higgins Clark novel). When it was time, she called and ordered a taxi, directing it not to honk or telephone her to announce its arrival, but instead to wait on the curb. She took her bag out of the hall closet and placed the letter on the commode, and she opened the door when she saw the taxi's headlights. A gust of wind blew into the house, startling Leelee, but she kept going out the door. She had promised herself that once she opened the door she would never look back.

When she got to the airport she was beside herself with excitement. She looked around and finally found the waiting area, where she paced back and forth. Two o'clock came and went, and then it was two-fifteen, two-thirty, and finally two-forty-five. She tried Jack's cell but it went straight to voice mail, and the office was deserted except for a man with a mustache at the information desk, who was on the phone. When she finally got his attention, he told her that Jack's plane had radioed and said they would land at three-thirty. They'd gotten a late start from Teterboro. Late start? Leelee felt her stomach lurch but then remembered that it was January and on the East Coast there was fog and snowstorms, not ideal weather. Finally at 3:33 she saw a plane come into sight and gently touch down on the tarmac.

"Can I go out now?" she asked the man.

"Gotta wait until they bring the stairs," he said.

Leelee pressed her face to the glass and walked out to the steps to get a closer look. The air felt fresh, and it awakened her. *This is finally it! This is the fairy-tale ending.* Then the hatch opened and the stairs were wheeled up, and without thinking Leelee felt herself running to the plane. A flight attendant stood at the door talking to someone, and before she knew it, she realized the someone was Jack! *Jack!* Her Jack. He looked gorgeous, the handsomest man in the world. He was wearing a light blue jacket and jeans, and his hair was longish, just the way she liked it. He turned toward her and caught her eye and she waved.

But he didn't smile.

At first Leelee thought that he must be distracted, giving orders to the crew, asking how long they needed to refuel before they set off for Hawaii. She yelled "Jack!" and he turned again to her, but he still didn't smile. She saw him motioning to someone on the plane, and before she knew it Jack had stepped aside and gallantly let a woman get off the plane in front of him.

Tierney.

What the hell is she doing here? Leelee wanted to scream, but Jack kept his eyes averted, as if it took a tremendous amount of concentration to get down the stairs. Tierney, on the other hand, looked up at her and waved, and Leelee felt sick. What was going on? Did Jack want to confront Tierney together? Was Tierney so humiliated that she insisted on moving to California to avoid her friends and the press?

"Hey, you!" said Tierney, approaching Leelee and giving her an air kiss. "You are *such* a doll for meeting us out here in the middle of the night! Jack said you might, and I told him not to be crazy, that we'd see you in the morning, but he said you were so excited to see us that you were going to make it out!"

Leelee didn't look at Tierney and stared directly at Jack, who avoided her gaze. She was struck dumb. Literally. She now knew what the phrase meant. What was going on?

"There's the car," said Jack, and Leelee turned and looked to where he had pointed. A black stretch limousine was waiting by the gate, its engine huffing and steam floating out of its tailpipe.

"Let's go then. I'm freezing!" said Tierney, walking toward the car. "You didn't tell me that it gets cold here! It's California! Isn't it supposed to be, like, eighty degrees?"

"Not in winter," said Jack, walking behind her.

Leelee didn't move. She watched Tierney run and dive into the car, but Jack was halfway there before he noticed that she was frozen. He walked back to her.

"Wh-what is going on, Jack?" asked Leelee, looking up at him. Please say she just took it really well, and we're still going to Hawaii. Please say you love me.

"I couldn't do it, Swifty," he said with a sigh.

"What do you mean?" she asked, her voice faltering.

"I can't leave her. I'm so sorry," he said.

"I don't understand." She wasn't going to let him walk away like this. She had to know.

Jack took a deep breath. He was used to getting off the hook. He was not accustomed to having to answer for his actions, and he appeared put out. "It's just . . . look. Swifty, you and I—we will always have something. You're my best friend. But . . . I can't leave Tierney . . ."

"That's not good enough," said Leelee, irate. "Don't you love me?"

"I do, but . . ." He stuck his hands in his pants. "I want to run for office one day. A divorce won't look good . . ."

Leelee felt her face go red and the vein in her neck throb. "What? WHAT? I can't believe you, Jack Porter. You are a disgrace. A disgrace! You won't leave your wife because of that? You're a pussy!"

"Swifty, I knew you would . . ."

She cut him off. "Don't—DON'T Swifty me! You are disgusting. If you knew that, then why would you lead me on like this? Why would you send for me to come to Boston and then woo me and then promise me everything, a life together, and drag me out here in the middle of the night if you knew you couldn't do it? You are not a man!"

She was too stunned and furious to cry. She couldn't believe it! It was just not what was supposed to happen. She felt betrayed. She felt ill. She felt like a fool.

"I know, I know. I'm lame," he said, shaking his head. "But let's go now. We'll drive you home. Tierney's going to think it's weird that we're out here."

"Tierney? So now you care what Tierney thinks? I thought you told me she was an idiot who only cared about shopping. Now you care about her feelings?"

"Look, Swifty, enough. I know I hurt you, and I'm sorry. But let's walk away clean. Brad doesn't know, Tierney doesn't know, no one knows. Let's just end it quietly so we can pick up the pieces of our lives."

Leelee was suddenly seized by a thought. What bothered Jack more than anything was to have someone have something on him. He always wanted to one-up people, and he voraciously protected his secrets. "Other people know, Jack."

"Who?" he snapped.

"This guy in the Palisades. Anson Larrabee. He writes the gossip column. He knows and he hates me, so he'll do something about it."

"How can he prove it?"

"He has tapes. He tape-recorded us talking. He used a baby monitor. He has it all, Jack. It's out of my hands now," she said with a smile. Let him squirm.

"Where does he live?"

"Why, Jack? What are you going to do?" she asked, her eyes challenging him. "You're too much of a pussy to do anything."

"Look, I know you're hurt, but let's just get through this. Where does this Anson live?" he asked. She could tell he was nervous.

"In the Palisades. You look it up!" she said, walking to the waiting limousine. It was deserted in the airport and would take forever to get a cab. She had no choice but to take a ride home.

She heard Jack following her and she walked over to the gate and got her suitcase. The limousine driver put it in the trunk and she got into the car.

"Geez, what took you guys so long?" asked Tierney with a yawn. "I'm so tired."

Jack got in and sat across from Tierney and Leelee. He looked unsettled, at which Leelee couldn't help but smile.

"We'll drop Leelee off and then head to the hotel, sweetie," said Jack.

"Where are you staying?" asked Leelee.

"Shutters," said Tierney.

"Nice. Romantic," said Leelee, looking at Jack. "Not as romantic as the Ritz in Boston, but romantic."

"Yeah, it has a pool," said Tierney, resting her head on her arm and closing her eyes.

"Why don't *I* drop you guys off?" asked Leelee. "Your hotel is first."

"No, that's okay . . ." began Jack.

"Great," said Tierney. "I'm exhausted. And we're only here one day then off to Hawaii, so I want to make sure I hit Fred Segal before I go."

Leelee glared at Jack. He averted his eyes again.

When she dropped them off at the hotel, Jack leaned in to kiss her good-bye, but she turned her head. Tierney gave her a sleepy hug.

"I don't think I have time for lunch this trip . . ." she said apologetically.

"Don't worry about it," said Leelee.

"One of my best friends lives here, and I promised . . ." she continued.

Leelee motioned for her to stop. "I get it," she said as she started to close the car door. "That's why I insisted on coming in the middle of the night to say hi! I just knew it would be a whirlwind!"

"You're so sweet," said Tierney, already looking away. She was watching the porter unload her T. Anthony luggage onto the cart. Leelee's eyes focused on the giant gold monogram: T.H.P. *Bitch.*

"Hey, Leelee," said Tierney, her eyebrows furrowed. "Why did you bring your suitcase?"

Leelee smiled and leaned forward to the driver. "You can go now," she said.

The car drove away and Leelee didn't look back.

When she pulled up to her house, she looked at her watch. 4:47. Yikes. So late, or rather, so early. The driver carried her bag to the door and she let herself in quietly. She walked over to the hall closet and pushed her suitcase into the back, behind the long coats, and closed the door. She walked upstairs to the bathroom in the hall and changed into the sweats that she had been wearing before she left. She had thought she would never see them again, or at least not for a long time. She dropped the skirt and blouse and sexy lingerie that she had spent weeks obsessing over (her "going away outfit," she called it) into a ball on the floor. As she splashed cold water on her face she stared at her reflection. Life just isn't what you think it will be. She knew she should be grateful for all that she had, and she was, but all she could feel right now was very sorry for herself. She just wanted to curl up and die. She was humiliated, heartbroken, and rejected.

She flipped off the light switch and crept into her room so as not to wake Brad. But when she glanced at her bed, she realized that he wasn't in it.

"Brad?" she asked.

No response. Leelee walked over to the bathroom off their bedroom and looked inside. "Brad?" she asked.

Silence.

Suddenly a wave of panic crept over Leelee. She ran to the girls' room, but no Brad. Oh God, the letter. She ran downstairs and looked at the commode. The letter was gone. She looked down next to it. Brad's briefcase was gone. She ran into the living room then to the kitchen and even looked outside the backyard but no Brad. When she opened the garage door she saw that his car was gone. Brad was gone. He must have read the letter. Her life was now officially destroyed.

38

Victoria woke up early the morning of Eliza's party and immediately felt that something was wrong. She glanced over at Justin's side of the bed and saw that he wasn't there. *That's what it was.* Justin hadn't come home last night by the time she went to bed, and it appeared as if he'd never come home at all. Victoria sprang up, threw on her cashmere bathrobe, and went downstairs. No sign of Justin at all. *That bastard.*

Marguerita came and got the boys breakfast while Victoria took a shower. She turned the water so hot that it was almost unbearable, feeling her skin scream under its crush. The bathroom got steamy and Victoria closed her eyes and let the water pound on her until she could no longer take it and got out. When she left the bathroom, Justin was standing by the full-length mirror, adjusting his tie.

"Where were you last night?" asked Victoria.

Justin smiled and reknotted his tie. "Out."

Victoria rolled her eyes and threw the wet towel that she had been using to dry her hair back into the bathroom. "Out? Surely you can do better than that," she said with derision.

"What? You think I was with some bimbo? Sorry. It was work, baby. You know, I do everything around here so you can get massages and pedicures. I'm the one making the living and staying up talking Tad down from a coke bender until six in the morning."

"Gee, sounds like a nightmare," she said with a sneer.

He turned around and glared at her. "It was. And I would

like a little support and gratitude when I've worked my ass off all night. I don't want to come home to this!"

"You could have called," snapped Victoria.

"Right, right. I'm the one who did something wrong. You disappear all the time to God knows where, and *I'm* guilty. Listen, I own you now. I am your bread and butter. So don't mess with me. I don't want to hear complaints or whining or anything but a thank-you. I want my feet massaged when I get home, and I want my balls licked."

"You don't own me. I made you. You would be nothing without me. I'm the one who smoothed it over with your boss's wife when you were a dick to her. I'm the one who got our kids into the right school so you could suck up to those industry people there. I just got you your brand-new client."

"Who?" said Justin, approaching Victoria with anger. She stood there with her hands on her hips, steaming. "Who the hell are you talking about, Victoria?"

"Natalie Maddox," said Victoria.

Justin turned away and laughed. "Yeah, that's a joke. She came to me begging for proper representation. She knew where to get the best."

"She came to you because I made Wayne Mercer give her to you."

Justin narrowed his eyes. "And why would he do that?"

"Because I was tired of screwing him. And I was tired of his sadistic games. So I sent him away and made him give us a departing present. A new client for you, a new Jaguar for me. We're even."

She couldn't believe that she had told him this way, but it all made sense, actually. There was no other moment she could have brought it up, no more peaceful dinners where they confessed everything. Their lives were full of the most vitriolic, rage-fueled beats that it had to happen this way.

Justin looked at her and knew at once that she wasn't lying. His face contorted slightly, but before he got angry, he started laughing. And he laughed harder and harder. He turned around and faced the mirror again as he buttoned his suit jacket.

"Wayne got the short end of the deal. You're a lousy lay," he said merrily.

"You didn't think that before."

"Your own sister is better than you," he said, staring at her in the mirror. "Yes, your fat, stupid sister. I screwed her one night when we were all in Nantucket for your cousin's wedding. I was bored and she was there."

Victoria was enraged. "You got the short end of the deal there."

"In your dreams," said Justin. He had a propensity to sound like a middle-schooler when he fought. "I get pussy every day. My assistant, my hairdresser, all those stupid bimbos who want to be stars. I screw them everywhere. All the time. And I don't care."

Victoria knew it was true, had always known it was true, but she felt stung. "Well, let's get a divorce then," she said.

"Great," said Justin. "It's about time."

He was so cool and casual about the way he said it that Victoria freaked out. She ran over to him and started pounding him violently, slapping him on the head before he knew what was coming, and shoving him. Justin tried to grab her arms, but she flailed them around. Her wet hair smacked him on the face and he slapped her back. He tried to twist her arm but she dug her nails into his chest. She could feel each and every one of her nails snap off as she did that.

"You asshole!" she screamed.

"Bitch!" he shouted back.

She kept at him, punching and kicking until he overtook her and pushed her down on the bed. The next thing she knew they were passionately kissing, then he unzipped his pants and was in her. They had never had sex like this before. It was wild and crazy. It hurt, but the pain was so much deeper than any physical pain she had ever experienced. It was the pain of knowing that she had never meant anything to this man. She had taken him from a woman—his wife—only because it was a challenge, and he had always resented it and treated her as a conquest. Everything that was special or unique about her he didn't care about. He didn't want a wife with brains; he'd rather have a wife with big tits. So what that she had an MBA—he'd rather her father be head of Warner Brothers.

After they came, Victoria rolled over on her stomach and began to cry. She cried harder and harder, and soon she was wailing. She thought she was crying like a child, or an animal in the jungle. She moaned and sobbed as if she had been raised by wolves. She felt sorry for herself. Sorry that her dad had betrayed her and sorry that she was married to a man who didn't love her. She had never been loved by a man. When she finally calmed down, she noticed that Justin had dressed again and was leaving. She looked up at him through her tears.

"So, we're done," she said.

"Victoria, I don't want to be the bad guy in your life anymore. You have to grow up. I'm not your father. I'm your husband. I can't right every wrong for you."

Victoria sat up. She felt dizzy from crying. "But you never fight for me. You never, ever fought for me. I needed you to choose *me*, to fight for *me*, and you never did."

"You sound like a child! I chose you over my wife. I chose

you over other women. What else do you want?" he said with impatience.

Victoria thought. She needed him to prove his love to her. "I need proof. Go beat up Wayne Mercer! Go get the tapes from Anson Larrabee! Go tell all those bimbos that try to sleep with you that you won't because you're a married man."

"What does Anson Larrabee have to do with this?" asked Justin.

Victoria leaned back down on the bed. He didn't get it. It was all about the who-what-where-when-why with him. He lacked emotion. "Nothing. He just recorded tapes of Wayne and me on the phone. He eavesdropped through the baby monitor. Apparently the whole town can hear everything that goes down through the monitors."

"What do you mean?" asked Justin, aghast.

"I don't know. Apparently, every time we talk on the cordless upstairs, Anson's baby monitor picks up on it. He hears everything. He has it all on tape."

"That sneaky asshole!" said Justin, his brow furrowed. He became really agitated. "I can't believe that guy . . ."

"It doesn't matter. It doesn't matter—he's done. We're done. We'll go to Eliza's party tonight and tell everyone."

Justin stopped brooding and stared at her. "If that's what you want."

"It is," said Victoria, closing her eyes and pulling her sheets up over her. As she drifted off to sleep, she wondered what she really wanted.

39

Leelee was in a panic. She had no idea how she got the girls to school (did she get the girls to school? She didn't remember at all), but she headed straight for Eliza's as soon as they were gone. Eliza was unloading her car and appeared stunned to see Leelee.

"What happened?" asked Eliza.

"He bailed," she said. "He loves Tierney. Won't ever leave her. Wants to run for office . . ." Her voice trailed off and tears sprang to her eyes. She knew her face was a mess—her pale, freckled skin became the most unattractive pink color when she was upset, and lord knows what her makeup was doing, but she didn't care.

"Oh, Leelee," said Eliza, coming over and embracing her friend. "I'm so sorry."

Leelee started sobbing. "My life is over."

"Maybe this is for the best? Maybe you were never meant to be together. Maybe Brad is the love of your life," said Eliza, patting her back.

"No, that's the worst. Brad is gone. *Gone.* I've tried his cell phone, his office . . . he's not answering. He found the note. He left me," she said, her body shaking with tears.

Eliza led her into the house and poured her a cup of tea. She listened as Leelee wept and raged about her lover and her husband, stopping only to call Helen and Victoria and tell them to come over. Helen said she was on her way, but Victoria didn't return her call.

The ladies all sat in the living room, sprawled on the various so-
fas and chairs, in a daze.

"So, was it worth it after all?" asked Helen finally. "I don't
think so."

"Guys, this pact was doomed from the start. And I have a
confession to make. I don't know why I didn't tell you, but I may
as well. I didn't sleep with Tyler. I was going to, but I couldn't . . ."
Eliza's voice trailed off.

"I can't do it," Eliza said when he pulled her onto his lap.

Tyler looked at her and then swallowed. "Are you sure?"

"I can't do it. I thought I could, but I can't," she said, squirm-
ing away.

She knew she would cry because it would never be, and it could
never be. She had once been the sort of person to sleep with her
teacher and do something rash and unexpected, but times were dif-
ferent now. She was married. She had kids.

"Can I call you?" he asked.

"Hello, earth to Eliza?" asked Helen with a smile.

Eliza was immediately jolted back into the present. She had
been remembering her would-be moment. "Yeah. Sorry, guys. It
didn't happen."

"What do you mean?" asked Leelee.

"I never told you anything other than I went to meet him.
You all assumed," said Eliza, defensive.

Victoria suddenly laughed, high-pitched fake laughter. "I
should have known. You would never."

"Why not?" asked Eliza.

Suddenly, Helen, Leelee, and Victoria all collapsed into giggles. Then they started laughing harder and harder as Eliza
watched them with confusion.

"Why not?" Eliza repeated. "How can you be so sure?"

"You're not the type," said Helen.

"What do you mean?" asked Eliza. How did her friends know that about her? She didn't even know that about herself. Should she feel offended that her friends regarded her as so straight? She supposed not, because it was the truth. She had never really realized that about herself. She had learned a lot this past year.

"Why'd you lie?" asked Victoria, ignoring her question.

"I didn't lie, exactly, but I didn't tell the truth," said Eliza.

"Don't worry about it," said Helen.

"I also have a confession. I told Brad that Victoria was having an affair," said Leelee casually. "But it doesn't matter. Brad is gonzo, so you'll never see him again."

"Doesn't matter. Justin's gonzo too," said Victoria. And then she began to laugh hysterically, and Leelee followed suit.

"Any other confessions?" asked Eliza.

"No," said Helen.

Victoria's eyes darted to the side for a split second, and Eliza caught her. "Victoria? Do you have something to say?"

"Okay, yes, I have a confession," said Victoria. She glanced at all of her friends. They were so different and yet now they were all united. Helen in her diaphanous top and hands jammed with mood rings, appearing ditzy and so L.A. Leelee, preppy as can be in the mommy pants that cut above the ass and a ribbed green cashmere sweater. Eliza in her low-cut jeans and button-down oxford. These were her friends. They would understand.

"I was sleeping with Wayne months before the pact. I just brought you all into it so you could help me get out of it. I wanted you to reserve judgment."

There was a pause as if the air had been sucked out of the

room as her friends processed the information. Finally Helen broke the silence.

"You bitch!" said Helen. She was appalled and yet not. It didn't ultimately matter to her that Victoria had misled them. It was just a matter of time before she stepped out on Wesley.

Leelee threw back her head and laughed harder. "Figures. You're the most cunning of us all!"

Leelee was mostly happy that her often-negative opinion of Victoria had been confirmed. She'd always love Victoria but she'd always hate her. And it was so Victoria to try to manipulate the gang. But she should be thankful to her. She'd had Jack for a moment. And it had been amazing.

Eliza was surprised. It was very conniving of Victoria to trick them. Why couldn't she just tell them in advance and ask them for help? Why did she have to fool them? But she had learned a lot about people over the past eight months. Everyone was complicated, everyone was unpredictable. She herself had almost cheated, but when put to the test chose not to. And she was glad she had confronted her naked soul and figured out what road she would take. It made her love Declan more. It made her realize that any little doubt she had about him or them was just a little blip. He was the man for her. She couldn't break that tie.

They were slaphappy and emotionally exhausted, so that even though they were now furious at each other for various offenses, they started laughing. And laughing. And laughing.

"Yikes, I'm having a party in a few hours and I have to get ready," said Eliza finally.

"What are we going to do about Anson?" asked Helen. "What if he is still planning something? Isn't it risky to bring him to the party?"

"Yeah, like what if he makes an announcement?" asked Leelee.

"Let's proceed as planned. Maybe Imelda doesn't know anything. Maybe she talked to him before we did," said Eliza.

"I agree. Wait until he comes and then we can talk to him again and sort it out," said Victoria, rising.

"I guess I don't care," said Leelee. "Brad is gone . . ." She started to cry again. Was she sad about Brad? Or just embarrassed that he might leave her and she'd look like a fool? Or was it that Jack had betrayed her? All of the above. She felt sorry for herself, so she cried. But what made it harder was knowing that she would have to change. If she wanted to remain with Brad, which she did, she had to forgive him and move on. It was the only way.

"It will be okay," said Eliza, putting her hands on Leelee's shoulders. "Trust me. Brad will come back, and Anson will stop. Or be stopped."

The ladies all left and agreed to see one another in a few hours.

·· *40* ··

Hours before, when Anson was either dead or about to be, Eliza was still getting ready for her party. She returned home, after her makeup and blow-dry and found Declan already there, putting on his blazer and tie.

"You're home early," said Eliza.

"Yes, I had something I had to do, so I came home after," he said with a smile.

And then he did something he didn't usually do. He went

over to her and kissed her, and took her into his arms and gave her a big hug. It wasn't that they never kissed or hugged anymore; it just wasn't usually this impromptu or spontaneous. Eliza hugged him back. Hard.

"I have something to tell you, Declan," she said, pulling away.

He looked at her carefully, but his expression remained neutral.

She began to pace the room nervously. And then she launched. She told him about the pact, about all the various infidelities committed and what she had led her friends to believe.

"But the truth is, I never had an affair with Tyler Trask," she said. "You have to believe me. I'm sorry that I let people think I did. I don't know why . . ." She felt herself tearing up, but she didn't want to ruin her makeup job, so she fought it.

"I know you didn't, Eliza," said Declan with a smile.

"How?"

"You're not the type to have an affair. You're a good girl," he said.

"Do you really think so?" she asked, hopeful.

"Yes," he said.

"But how do you know? I mean, I thought for a second . . ." She didn't want to actually say that she'd briefly thought she would cheat. She couldn't say that to her husband. "I thought for a second that I wasn't a good girl."

Declan walked over to her and put his arms firmly on her shoulders. "You are a good girl. You have to get over that. You're not like your friends. You wouldn't jeopardize everything. I understand that you maybe want some excitement, that you get dramatic and want passion and fireworks, but come on . . . we're a team. Don't borrow trouble."

"You're right, you're right," she said.

"So let's just forget all this, okay?" he asked.

"Yeah," she said. Then she was seized by a small panic. "The only thing is that Anson knows. He tape-recorded us."

"I wouldn't worry about him."

"You're right," she said. "I won't worry about Anson anymore."

Then Declan kissed her on each eyelid.

Helen knew that she had to tell Wesley. She couldn't take it anymore. How was she going to explain to him why they had to pick up Anson for Eliza's party? He knew she hated him. How could she continue this charade? Even if Anson never told, she couldn't live under the threat of that possibility. No. She had to tell Wesley.

Even Victoria agreed with her. "Beg for his mercy," she advised. "He's a good man. He'll keep you." So that was the plan. Beg for his mercy.

Helen walked into his screening room and found him watching *Vertigo* on his black-and-white projector. The fading daylight meekly streamed into the room through the slats in the venetian blinds, and Hitchcock's characters danced on the screen.

"I cheated on you," said Helen, leaning against the threshold of the door.

Wesley turned and looked at her. "What?"

"I cheated on you," she said calmly. "I slept with a few people, I thought I could save myself, but I was wrong, and it's over and I want to be with you."

The silence seemed deafening. Helen watched as the veins under Wesley's temples flared ever so slightly. More blood being pumped into his brain to allow him to process this deceit.

"How do you know you want to be with me?" he asked, speaking at last.

"I . . . just know. Who else would I be with?"

"That's not a good answer."

"I don't know. I'm thinking that maybe all this searching . . . I don't know, all this looking around for fulfillment—maybe I'm not going to find it with someone else. We're happy, right? I think we just need to talk more." Was that it? she wondered. It had to be. She had to stop running away from facing everything. She had to form a bond. She had to work on it, and so did he.

Wesley took off his glasses and rubbed them on his shirt. "Are you sorry?" he asked, not looking at her.

"Yes," she said. "I couldn't be sorrier." She went to him and kneeled down next to him. "I love you. I betrayed you. Forgive me."

Wesley still wouldn't meet her eye. "Does everyone know? Am I a laughingstock, the cuckolded husband, the last to know?"

"Everyone doesn't know . . ." she said lamely. "Victoria, Eliza, and Leelee, but that's it."

Wesley started laughing sarcastically. "Oh, that's it. Just all your girlfriends."

"They won't tell."

"Right-o," he said. "So your girlfriends won't tell anyone, therefore it can all be forgotten."

"Anson Larrabee knows and he's been blackmailing us. That's why I have to pick him up and take him to Eliza's party. He wants us to be friends so he won't tell anyone."

"Anson knows . . . Now it all makes sense . . . the screenplay—of course. I'm a fool." He rubbed his eyes with his hands.

"You're not a fool," said Helen, going over to him. Her voice and face were even and composed, but she felt she was cracking inside. "I love you. I made mistakes, huge mistakes. I forgot my touchstones. Please forgive me."

"I can't take this anymore, Helen," said Wesley.

"Please, Wesley . . ." She burst into tears. "Let's forget it happened. Let's make it all go away."

"Right, that's what you need me for always, to make it go away. To clean up your messes."

"I don't expect you to clean up my messes! I can take care of Anson myself. I'll get those tapes somehow and I'll take care of him."

"Right, the way you did with Dirk?"

Helen collapsed into the chair. "Right. I guess I need you more than I realized. I know that now. I forgot . . ."

"Well, this time is different," he said, calmly rising and walking to the door.

"But what about Lauren?" she said softly. She had curled up into a ball and was clasping her knees.

Wesley paused by the door and she saw his shoulders sink. It appeared as if he was about to say something but he changed his mind. He walked out the door but suddenly reappeared.

"I'll always take care of Lauren," he said, and then turned and left.

·· *41* ··

Leelee was still incessantly calling Brad on his cell phone and at work, and he wouldn't answer. She felt disgusting. What if Brad left her? She would have nowhere to go. Ugh—how did he get her into this situation? Of course, she shouldn't have written a good-bye letter, but God! She did not want to go to Eliza's cock-tail party at all, but she knew she had to because of Anson. That was the deal. They would all get up his butt and act like syco-phants to kiss his pansy ass because he had all those tapes that he could flash to the world! If only she could ride off into the sunset with Jack. He used to be her hero. What an asshole he was. There was no one to save her now. She just had to put on a cute outfit and a fake smile and go try to save her life.

"You're late," said Victoria when Justin came home.

He didn't even stop to talk to her, instead made a beeline up-stairs until she heard the bathroom door close. God, what an ass. You'd think that at least for their last hurrah he could show up on time. All he had to do was go to the party and then they were done. Victoria waited fifteen solid minutes for Justin to come downstairs, during which time she bit off all her nails. She had ripped them off one hand earlier when they fought, and since she didn't have time to get a manicure she thought she'd just chew them off the other hand, down to the quick. She knew Justin hated that, when a woman's nails were jagged and bloody. The first thing he always looked at was a lady's hands—he always said that. "Well, have a good look at these babies," Victoria said out loud, holding up her hands. She couldn't imagine what was tak-ing him so long. He definitely was Mr. Product and Mr. Fashion, but usually he didn't need that much time to get ready. Especially when they were going somewhere with *her* friends. He was prob-ably doing it to piss her off. When he finally trudged down the stairs, she was about to get angry but refrained. It wasn't her prob-lem anymore. He wouldn't be her problem anymore.

"Let's go," he said, walking out to the street.

"You changed," she said, looking at his outfit. He had worn the dark Zegna this morning and now he was in the striped Armani.

"Spilled something," he said. "Are we walking or riding?"

"It's two blocks. I think we can walk."

"Fine."

They strode together in silence, Victoria walking slower than usual due to her high heels.

"Anyone good going to be there?" asked Justin finally.

"Good? You mean, like *famous*? Or *in the industry*? I doubt it," she said.

"You don't have to be such a bitch. I'm going, aren't I?" he asked.

"Yes, thank you, THANK YOU FOR THAT!" she practically screamed. What a martyr.

"Shut up," he snapped as they got to the front door. "You don't ever have to talk to me again. I should be at Koi with Tad, but I'm doing this for you. *One last time.*"

"You're such a great guy," she said, ringing the doorbell.

"Hello!" said Eliza, opening the door.

"Hi," said Victoria.

"Come on in," said Eliza, taking their coats and leading them into the living room.

They were all stressed and awaiting Anson's arrival with anxiety. Leelee was also on the lookout for Brad, whom she still hadn't heard from. Would he come? Did he even remember that there was a party tonight? Please let him come. Please let him come, she prayed.

Suddenly, across the room she noticed him enter. She was making idle talk with the bartender when she saw Brad greet

Eliza, Victoria, and Pam. He came! It seemed like a million years before he extricated himself from her friends and made his way over to her. She beamed when she saw him.

"You came!" she said.

Brad looked puzzled. "Of course I came. I'm just surprised you left without me."

"I was calling all day! You weren't at the office, I didn't see you before you left for work this morning . . ."

"I told you, I had to go to Irvine for a conference all day. And my cell phone is out—that's why you didn't hear from me. But where were you when I left this morning?"

"It was really strange, but I got sucked into the television and then I didn't want to wake you, so I slept on the sofa."

"Huh. I guess I didn't notice you when I crept out so early," he said.

"Yeah," she said quickly. "But I am thrilled you are here!"

She gave him a hug, which surprised him. Then Helen arrived and her friends called her away into the pantry to inform her that Anson was dead. The plan was to meet after the party outside of Anson's house and check out the scene. No one should say anything. Everyone should act natural.

When Leelee and Brad got home after the party, before she went to meet her friends, she waited until he went upstairs to change before she scanned the foyer for the note. She looked on the floor and under the sisal rug, but it wasn't until she pulled out the commode that she found the letter. That gust of wind when she left! It must have blown the note away. She quickly went into the kitchen and lit a match to burn it. She let all of the pieces fall into the sink before she turned on the garbage disposal. She let the water run and flushed them out of her life forever.

It was now three days since Anson's death. There was a memorial service rumored to be scheduled for the following week, but with no close relatives around, there was no confirmation one way or another. No one knew if he had been murdered or died of natural causes, but people were leaning toward the more salacious idea. It was just a question of who, and many theories abounded. Eliza, Victoria, Helen, and Leelee all held their breath that they would not be pulled into it, and most of all, that no one they knew had committed the crime. But they couldn't help but be suspicious of one another, which added wariness to their tenuous dynamic.

Wesley finally returned. Helen came downstairs early in the morning and found him sitting in the darkened kitchen. He startled her so much that she let out a yelp.

"Wesley!" she said.

He turned and looked at her and didn't say anything. His eyes looked sad and older, as if the past few days had taken an extreme toll on him, and she felt bad.

"Are you okay?" she asked. The tile floor felt cold under her feet, and she wished she had remembered to put on her slippers. In fact, the whole house seemed chilled. She was going to have to turn up the heat.

"I want us to be a family," he said quietly.

"That's fantastic!" she squealed and rushed to him. He put up his hand to stop her.

"But you have to do it *my* way now. No more lies, no more cheating, no more solo trips to go find yourself. I want you to find yourself *here*. I don't want you to leave this family, emotionally, sexually, or physically and embark on a journey of self-discovery. We have to be *partners* if we are going to make this work. That is the only way I'll have it."

For the first time ever, really, Helen felt a bolt of love for Wesley. He was a man. He took care of things. He was what she had been looking for all along. He was home.

"I love you, Wesley," she said, running and hugging him.

"I love you, too," he said.

Later that day, all the ladies converged at Victoria's to help her pack up Justin's clothes. It was heartbreaking to look at Austin and Hunter and know that their lives were about to change, but it was for the better. The atmosphere between their parents was too toxic to sustain.

"Where do you want us to put these boxes?" said Eliza.

"Geez, the man has serious duds. His closet is bigger than yours!" said Helen.

"I know. He's such a girl," said Victoria, who was on her knees, pulling out fancy loafers and suede cowboy boots from the back of the closet.

They continued packing the boxes in silence. Even though they had all declared their innocence the night Anson was found dead, each wondered about her friends. It was just too neat, too clean, that Anson had died. All of their problems were over, and it was as if it had never happened. None of them could really believe that any of the other friends was capable of murder, although . . . they did agree that Victoria would not react well to being ostracized by the neighbors for inappropriate behavior. If she was put into a position where she was deemed a laughing-stock, her rage would be uncontrollable.

"Wow, I invited you guys over so it wouldn't be gloomy. Come on, people, why so silent?" asked Victoria. She stared at her friends' faces and had the strangest sensation that they weren't meeting her eye. What was going on?

"Do you losers think *I* killed Anson?" Victoria demanded.

No one said anything for a beat too long. "Of course not," began Eliza and Helen at the same time.

But Eliza and Helen weren't that certain. They'd had a brief discussion about it before they both started to feel too guilty for thinking it and changed the subject. She wouldn't kill anyone over a slight. It was stupid to think that. But now it was out there.

"Liars," said Victoria, rising and putting her hands on her hips. "I can't believe you people."

"Victoria, we didn't say anything," protested Eliza.

"But you thought it," said Victoria with anger. "So just for the record, I want you to know that I did not kill Anson. Remember, I'm the one who didn't care what he had on us. Look around you—would I really have cared that he had tapes of me cheating? I mean, yes, it's unpleasant and it could jeopardize my divorce settlement, but I don't care anymore."

They believed her.

"This is stupid. We're all just on edge," said Leelee.

"You're right," said Helen quickly. "Now where should we put these boxes?"

"Let's put them in the garage."

They all carried them out to the garage and were standing outside loading them in when Leelee pointed at someone.

"Here comes Imelda," Leelee said.

They all looked and watched Pancake Face in her Juicy sweats approach them, obviously in a tizzy. "I don't care what they say! You ladies did it! You killed Anson!" she screamed.

"Whatever," said Victoria.

"Calm down," said Helen.

"Put a cork in it," said Leelee, laughing.

All of the girls dissolved into giggles, which enraged Imelda even more.

"You ladies!" she said, wagging her finger in their faces. "You killed him. I never should have told you about the tapes. Never."

"Imelda, we know you're upset . . ." said Eliza, trying to put an arm around her. Even though she loathed Anson, she felt genuinely bad for Imelda. It would be harsh to lose your close friend like that.

Imelda squirmed away. "The police are wrong! It was not an accident."

The ladies stopped laughing. "The police ruled it an accident?" asked Eliza.

"It's lies!" said Imelda.

Eliza, Victoria, Helen, and Leelee all looked at one another. Then they ran into the house, where Victoria placed a call to the police station. They put the phone on speaker so they could all hear.

"Yes, the coroner's report deemed that the level of alcohol and prescription drugs in his blood was so high that the probable cause of death was either accidental or suicidal. Most likely he tripped down the stairs and knocked into the porcelain flowerpot, which smashed on his head," said the officer on the other end.

"So that's that, then?" asked Victoria.

"Case closed," said the officer.

"Thank you, officer!" the ladies all squealed in unison.

As soon as they hung up they jumped up and down, hugging each other and screaming. Victoria brought out a bottle of champagne, which spilled all over the rug when they popped it, but they didn't care. They were ecstatic. It was over! It was finally over!

"To think, all that stressing for nothing!" said Leelee.

"I am elated, positively elated," said Helen.

"It's like, he's dead and we're free," said Eliza.

"Well, except for all those unanswered questions, like where are the tapes, what was that about all those files that he kept on us, and where are they, and everything else that may end up in the *Palisades Press* tomorrow. If he really did write a column like Imelda said," Victoria reminded them.

The women stopped celebrating. "Why'd you have to put a damper on it?" asked Helen.

"You know what? We could worry forever. I'm going to move on. I think we all should," said Leelee.

"Cheers," said Eliza, and they all clinked glasses.

·· *43* ··

They went to the memorial service. Imelda glared at them and whispered something to the anorexic with a face-lift who was sitting next to her, and she turned and looked at them all, sitting in the fourth to the last pew, but they didn't care. They had come to pay their respects. (Although Leelee had laughingly said that they really came to make sure he was truly dead.) After the five o'clock service, Eliza, Victoria, Helen, and Leelee all linked arms and walked together to Vittorio's, having agreed in advance to forgo the reception held in the community room at the church. They'd pay their respects—but they only had so much respect to pay. Besides, they needed a drink. It was time to move on.

"So what did we decide?" asked Eliza when they were seated in the outside patio and the waiter had opened the bottle of Chianti. "Was it worth it?"

"Ask me later," said Leelee.

"No," said Helen hastily.

"If it were done differently..." said Victoria, who then stopped abruptly. "I guess, no."

They all momentarily got lost in thought while they took a sip of their drinks.

"You know," said Helen. "Anson's article that Imelda promised never did come out in the *Press.*"

"Oh, I forgot to tell you," said Victoria. "They pulled his column when he died. I ran into Susan, who covers the Happenings section, and she said it would have been too creepy to do a postmortem piece."

"You could have told me that!" said Helen. "The last thing I want is for this to be stirred up again. Wesley has finally started to talk to me again."

"God, I'm glad this is over!" sighed Eliza as she leaned back in her chair and gathered up her hair, which she knotted into a casual ponytail.

"Shut up! You didn't do anything," said Leelee.

"I know—I did and I didn't," she said. "I entertained a thought and luckily didn't act on it."

"I'm not unhappy that we did this," said Leelee. "It was an itch I needed to scratch. It didn't have the happy ending that I hoped I would have, but at least I got Jack Porter out of my system."

"Well, what are you going to do now?" asked Helen.

"I don't know," said Leelee. "I guess stay with Brad. I guess I should learn to appreciate him a little more."

"Recognition is the first step," said Victoria. "See, a few

months ago you never would have admitted that anything was wrong."

"You're right," agreed Leelee. "I guess I wanted a superhero and all I got was an average guy."

"Hey, don't knock average guys," said Eliza. "The truth is, there's nothing better."

"Okay, so in conclusion, I'm getting divorced, I think . . ." said Victoria.

"You sure?" asked Helen.

Victoria nodded and swirled the wine in her glass. "I think that though I am sometimes obsessed with my husband—for example, currently, because he moved out—it's just too much of a sick relationship to continue. Especially as the boys get older."

"Well, don't decide anything now," said Helen. "You never know."

"Oh, I know," said Victoria. "But it's all good. Already I feel I can honestly and openly look around at other men and there's a lightness to me. I can pick and choose this time."

"Anyone caught your eye?" asked Helen.

"Everyone. I mean, geez, the boys had on *The Wiggles* the other day and I thought, Wow, that blue one is not half bad," said Victoria.

"Did you ever notice that he never does anything? He doesn't play an instrument, he doesn't sing, he's not like Jeff, asleep all the time . . . why is he on there?" asked Leelee.

"You're right," said Victoria, cocking her head to the side. "Maybe he writes it?"

"You guys, we're off-topic," said Helen.

"Right. It was pleasant for a second," said Victoria, focusing. But already her friends could sense that she was not as intense as she used to be. Maybe leaving Justin was a great thing for her personality. "Anyway, so I'm divorcing, Helen and Wesley are working on their marriage, Leelee and Brad are status quo, and Eliza is still totally happy with Declan and not 'fessing up about any problems—"

"Hey," interrupted Eliza. "Sometimes it *is* better to keep things to yourself. We all learned the hard way what happens when people share their innermost secrets."

"Well, we still don't know what happened with Anson's tapes," said Leelee mischievously.

"Okay, buzz kill," said Eliza.

"You totally stressed me out—thank you, Leelee," said Helen.

"Let's not worry about it," said Victoria. "Let's all make a new pact: the be happy pact."

"And let's never mention Anson again," said Eliza.

"Hear! Hear!" they all said, clinking glasses.

Leelee got home in time to give the girls a bath and put them to bed while Brad watched television downstairs. It took her extra long these days because they had let Charlotte watch *Monsters Inc.* on the ill advice of a classmate friend, and now she was terrified that there were monsters in her closet. That they were *friendly* monsters in the movie was lost on her. All she needed to see was that one-eyed Mike voiced by Billy Crystal and she was in tears. That meant more books to read before bed, and Leelee trudged through three Curious Georges until Charlotte was delirious with exhaustion and Leelee could finally take her leave.

After flipping out the lights ("Except for the closet, Mommy!"), Leelee ignored her instinctual pull to her office computer. It was strange not to be e-mailing with Jack anymore. As she put on her pajamas and washed her face, she stared at her reflection in the mirror and thought about how life doesn't go the way you want it to but maybe that is for the best. Maybe things would not have been all rosy with Jack. He was fun and exciting, but was he emotionally strong enough to sustain a family? Would he have been happy? Would she have felt he was always looking elsewhere? Probably what he loved about Tierney was that she never gave him the time of day. She was never unsatisfied and wanting more. That was probably comfortable for Jack. But Leelee wasn't like that. And she never could be.

"I did it," said Brad. He was standing in the doorway and staring at her reflection in the mirror. She had swirls of suds on her face, so she leaned down and splashed water up to rinse it off, then grabbed a washcloth to dry it.

"Did what?" she asked, walking past him out of the bathroom and untucking the sheets on the bed.

"I killed Anson," he said.

"Yeah, right," she said, still not looking at him.

"It's true," he said sternly.

Leelee turned around to stare at him. She studied his face carefully. His expression was that of serene confidence and determination. *Brad killed Anson?* "But the police said it was an accident . . . he drank too much and fell down the stairs."

Brad nodded. "I made it look like an accident."

Leelee was stunned. "But why?"

Brad walked toward her and stood right in front of the bed. "Come on, Leelee. I'm not an idiot. I knew Jack was Cooldude. That stuff about Victoria having an affair, well, I found out later that was also true, but I had a hunch. I found the e-mail and then I ran into Anson . . ." He stopped, unsure what to say.

"Go on," she urged.

"I know you've always loved Jack. I know you wished you'd married him instead of me. I know you were going to leave me for him. I found the letter, Leelee . . ."

"No, it fell behind the commode," she said, sinking onto the bed. It fell behind the commode and you didn't find it. I was so happy. Right?

"I put it there. I read it, and I got angry and I left, and then I got angrier, and I went to Irvine and sat in that conference room and brooded all day. And when I got back, I went straight to Anson's. I thought you were gone. And I thought Jack was gone. And Anson was the only one left who was a part of this. So I went, and I killed him. And when I came back, I saw the lights on in the house, and you through the windows, so I waited for you to go to the party and I put the note back."

"Oh my God . . ." said Leelee.

"I did it for you. To defend your honor. To be the man you wanted. That's all I ever wanted."

Leelee felt numb at first. It was so surreal. Brad killed Anson? She never would have put that together. She felt she should be disgusted or scared, but she didn't feel that. She couldn't place what the feeling was. Anger? Worry? No . . . slowly she realized what she felt: excited. Her man, the man she thought was a pathetic wimp for so long, the man she accused of not being a man, had actually gone and killed her tormentor. He had defended her honor. She had never loved him more. She walked over to Brad and kissed him passionately. She wanted him now. She kissed his hands and imagined them pushing Anson, punching him, making him suffer. Such sexy hands. She looked at his mouth and kissed it. This was the mouth that cursed out her nemesis. Brad kissed back and made love to her. Leelee was euphoric. He had proven himself and she couldn't get enough of him. Brad had finally become her hero.

He'd watched through the window as Anson poured himself a large tumbler of vodka. Through the paned glass he saw him walking between rooms—that damn dog yapping and snipping at Anson's slippered feet. He looked at his watch. It was almost time for the party. He had to get going. Like, really get going. Was this guy ever going to go upstairs and take his shower? He'd watched him the past few nights and knew that was Anson's routine, and he also knew that he was due at the cocktail party within the hour, so it was time to get a move on, buddy.

He wasn't nervous at all. You'd think he would be, for what he had planned, but for some reason it didn't seem at all wrong. He felt exhilarated. It was probably because he was so certain that what he was about to do *had* to be done. And he didn't worry about neighbors or anything like that. He knew them all, and if he said he was just returning Anson's dog, which he'd found roaming the streets, no one would question him. That's what he had learned about people, what made him successful in business: if you say something with certainty, people will have no reason not to believe you. Power is perception.

Finally Anson went upstairs. "It's about time," he sighed, as he crept around back and surreptitiously opened the side door. He heard the dog bark and come running down the stairs, but then Anson yelled to the dog, so it went back up. Luckily it was a windy night, with things rattling everywhere, so Anson wouldn't be fazed by any odd noise. He waited, not wanting to move, until he heard the pipes and knew that the shower was running. He walked into the living room and found Anson's sweating highball glass propped on the Chinese cabinet. He supposed it should feel odd that he was in this guy's house, with the guy upstairs having no clue, but once again, he was unmoved. He took the pills out of his pocket. The pills had been the only tricky part. Neither he nor his wife was a pill popper, so he had to wait until they went to a Christmas party so he could sneak inside the hosts' medicine cabinet (luckily everyone knew they were major pharmaceutical lovers) and steal the prescription pills. They would never miss them. He couldn't believe in a way that he was so devious—stealing, breaking and entering, and all that was to come—but it just seemed more like a necessary chain of events than a criminal act or acts. He carefully opened the plastic pill lid and dumped four tablets in the drink. That should do it. He didn't want to kill the guy; he just wanted to knock him out so he could come back later and find the damn tapes. He walked out the side door and knew none would be the wiser that he had been there.

That was his plan. He was going to make sure Anson was in for a long night's sleep, and then he would return after the party and have ample time to search the house top to bottom with no fear of discovery. It was time to end this. The guy was a first-class jerk. Who blackmails women? Regardless of whether they're faithful, what business is it of anyone's but their own and their husbands'? He thought adultery was appalling, but what people did was their own business. Why in the hell did Anson think he could appoint himself as moral judge, St. Peter himself, guarding the gates of heaven? The guy was no angel. And now it had to end. He didn't want Anson to keep blackmailing his wife and her friends any longer. If it meant that he had to steal those tapes, then that is what he would do.

He felt noble, defending his wife's honor like this. The funny thing was, he knew Eliza would never cheat on him. Since the day they were married, the day they met, actually, he knew that his wife was a good girl. She liked to talk herself into being a bad-ass sometimes, but she was no cheater. She was a good wife. Declan would do anything for her.

<h2 style="text-align:center">·· 45 ··</h2>

He couldn't believe it when Helen told him that she had cheated. How could he be such a fool? He'd never expected it. That was bad enough, but she also told him that Anson was blackmailing her. And he knew why she told him. It wasn't that she was scared; it was that she wanted him to sort out her mess again. Like with Dirk. Erase all the traces of her. Get those tapes. Those were the unspoken words. Either she was the most cunning bitch in the world, or she was just so hopeless that she didn't realize what she was suggesting. He actually wasn't quite sure.

One side of him didn't want to do it. Let her suffer. Let her squirm. Let her pick up the pieces of her life herself. But then there was Lauren. His adored, beloved Lauren. He would never hurt her. Ever. He wanted to protect her. And in protecting her, he had to protect his wife. It was difficult, but the fact was that despite everything, he did love his wife. And he supposed that he did love that she really needed him. He was born with money, status, even a title, but he had never felt as though he had accomplished anything on his own until he saved Helen. And he knew he saved her, and she knew it. So they were almost saving each other. That had to mean something.

"Sorry to bother you, Anson. I thought we might have a word," Wesley said as he stood on the threshold of the door. Although he had seen Anson through the curtains in the living room, it had taken him an extraordinary amount of time to answer the door, and Wesley had been compelled to ring the buzzer twice. And when the door was finally opened, it was with a large swing and then a bang, as if Anson were ripping it off its hinges.

Anson squinted and then spoke. "Wesley, old pal," he slurred.

Wesley noticed that Anson was swaying ever so slightly, and his grip was tightening on the glass he held in his hand. He must have had a lot to drink.

"I wondered if I could have a word," repeated Wesley, and without waiting he slipped past Anson and made his way into the foyer.

"Come on in," said Anson.

Wesley looked down at the sniveling dog nipping at Anson's feet and eyeing him suspiciously. A dog would not be a good thing now, especially if he was protective.

"Um, can you put that dog away? I'm allergic."

"Samantha? No," said Anson petulantly.

"Just for a minute. I won't take up more of your time," said Wesley, swooping down to pick up the reluctant dog, which squirmed in his arms. Wesley noticed a screened-in porch off the living room and walked over and put the dog inside.

"He'll be fine in there just for a second," said Wesley.

But Anson seemed to have already forgotten about the dog. "Can I get you something to drink?" he asked, making his way to the bar.

"No. Or . . . yes." Should he have something to drink? He didn't want to linger; his intention was to demand the evidence and then leave at once, then destroy it when he got home. In his mind he had envisioned the scenario as slightly hostile, in which

Wesley would defend his wife's honor and humble Anson in the process. But maybe it could be civil.

"Well, which is it?" said Anson, walking slowly to his bar cart. "I'll take it as a yes."

"Yes, sure, whatever you're having."

Anson twisted the cap off the scotch and took down a glass from the shelf. "Sit down. Relax."

Despite himself, Wesley sat down on the plush couch, sinking deeply into the pillows. He regretted it immediately, realizing that he should be calling the shots, not Anson. So he stood up again and walked toward the mantel, pretending to admire the oil painting that hung above it. He could feel the dog's eyes boring into him through the glass door.

"How's the movie biz these days? Did you see the new Woody Allen? I would say he's back," commented Anson while handing Wesley his glass.

"Let's cut the rubbish," said Wesley, his pulse picking up speed. He didn't want to make chitchat with this asshole, pretend all was nice and rosy when they both knew what he was doing to his wife.

"What's wrong?" asked Anson before plopping down into a worn armchair as if he didn't have a care in the world.

"I want the tapes," said Wesley firmly.

Anson stared at him, his face puffy from drink, his eyes watery. He didn't respond at first, but then a slow smile crept across his face.

"Sorry, my friend, but no can do."

Wesley felt rage slink through his veins. This bloke is really enjoying this. It's the only sense of power he's had in ages.

"I won't take no for an answer," said Wesley, walking closer to Anson, as if his slight figure could intimidate the larger man.

"You're going to have to," said Anson with a flourish, before taking a large gulp of his drink.

"Why are you doing this?"

Anson bent his head back and rested it on the back of his chair. He closed his eyes, and for a moment Wesley thought he might pass out. It was probably only seconds but it felt like minutes before Anson reopened his eyes, and when he did he looked startled to see Wesley.

"I gotta get ready for the party," said Anson groggily. He heaved his large body up out of the chair, an effort that required extra strength from both arms, and brushed past Wesley on his way to the staircase.

Wesley followed him. "We're not done, Anson," he said harshly.

Anson continued on his path but waved his arms at Wesley as if he were swatting away a mosquito. "Ah, patooey," he muttered.

"Anson," said Wesley, grabbing Anson's fleshy arm. He felt his nails seeping in to Anson's pale and flabby skin.

"Get off me," whined Anson, jerking away and stumbling toward the stairs.

He is totally out of it, thought Wesley. He must be seriously drunk.

"Where are the tapes?" demanded Wesley.

But Anson didn't respond, and he was now halfway up the stairs. But when he stopped and glanced at his reflection in the venetian mirror on the landing, taking a moment to smooth his eyebrows, it was the breaking point for Wesley. Before he realized it, he had lunged at him. Anson shouted out, but, weak with alcohol, his body was almost weightless, and Wesley's jab made him crumble. As Wesley saw the large figure dropping toward him, he instinctively moved to the side, causing Anson to fall even farther down the stairs. It was all done in seconds, and Wesley realized that he was staring at Anson's limp body at the bottom of the stairs.

"Anson?" he asked softly.

There was no response. Wesley ran down the steps and felt Anson's pulse. He was still alive. He couldn't be that hurt; he had only fallen a few steps. He had probably just passed out, Wesley reassured himself. What should he do? He tried to pick him up, but Anson was enormous and now dead weight. Better not to move him. He'd just go with the premise that he had left and Anson must have stumbled down the stairs, and anything else Anson would say was just the delusional ideas of a drunken man. There was no other way. But now he had to act quickly. First he ran to the living room, took his glass of scotch, and brought it to the kitchen. He found cleaning gloves under the sink, put them on, and carefully washed his glass, and the cabinet door handle as well. He kept the gloves on so as not to leave further prints, and walked through the house, finally locating the office and rummaging through the desk in an effort to find the tapes. He didn't find them, but in a dusty cabinet he did find a file that held incriminating notes on his wife and her friends. He scooped it up and slipped it under his shirt. He knew he had little time, so after opening cabinets and closets throughout the house and taking a superficial look, he decided to leave. He had done his job. He knew Anson would be okay, and probably accuse him of intentionally hurting him, but Anson was so drunk that he might not remember anything. Wesley could always say that he left when Anson walked up the stairs and didn't know what Anson was talking about.

Later, he felt a fleeting panic when he heard Anson was dead. It was as if a cold wind swept through his body. It was a surprise, but that was all. He couldn't say he was sorry.

Justin was sick when Victoria told him Anson had tape-recorded everything that went on in their house. He couldn't care less that people knew his wife—soon to be ex—was screwing around on him, but he was petrified that Anson had recorded some of his conversations with Tad Baxter's coke dealer. The fact was, Tad had gotten really messed up one night, and he wouldn't call it rape, but he sort of had sex with an unconscious girl and beat her up a little, and, well, if it got out, Tad's career was toast. That would be a huge blow to Justin. Even more so if he was the leak. He couldn't afford that.

He left his car at Palisades Park and walked to Anson's house on foot so no one would see his car in Anson's driveway. He knocked on the door and was discouraged that Anson didn't answer. He started to walk away, but the thought of some asshole like Wayne Mercer swooping in to poach Tad as a client made him turn around. On a whim, he tried Anson's door, and when it easily opened he took it as an invitation to enter Anson's house and search for the tapes.

"Hello?" Justin yelled cheerily, just in case Anson was home and on the shitter or something.

"Anson baby?" Justin yelled again, now waltzing into the foyer. Suddenly he noticed Anson lying on the floor by the stairs. He rushed over to him.

"Anson?" he asked, pressing on Anson's chest to see if his heart was beating. It was. He leaned over and peeled up one of Anson's eyelids, which revealed a bloodshot eye. Then like a slap in the face he smelled the alcohol on Anson's breath and recoiled in disgust.

"The old fag has passed out," he said, laughing. Perfect.

He stood up and started to walk around the house. It was very froofy. Funny how Anson wanted to pretend he was straight and then had a pad like this, with fringes and chintz everywhere. He leaned in to examine a picture of a young Anson with some old relative, maybe a mother or something, and smiled. Anson was in his late teens but clad in a sailor suit. That mom sure did a number on him. No wonder he was a fruit.

Where could those tapes be? Justin thought to himself. Where do I hide my porn? He made his way to Anson's closet and pushed through the racks of pastel pants and blazers. In the back he noticed a small safe, but he knew it was one of those dummy kinds that you could get at Target. A few yanks to the dial and it would open no matter what, which is exactly what it did. Score. He felt the same rush he got when he snorted a good line. There were packs of neatly labeled and organized tapes, which Justin grabbed. He saw an old L.L.Bean tote bag with Anson's monogram and stuffed them all in there. If anyone ever asked, but he knew no one would, he'd say that they were a short Anson wanted him to look at.

Justin heard a dog barking downstairs and knew he had to get out. On his way down the stairs he stared at Anson splayed on the floor. He started to step over him, but suddenly Anson's hand grabbed his foot. Startled, Justin screamed and lurched back, attempting to grasp the wall for support. Anson was moaning softly, and when Justin steadied himself on the sill of the window that looked over the yard, he noticed a small Chinese vase holding flowers. He looked down at Anson and back at the flowers and knew he had to get out now. So with his small white fingers he delicately flicked the vase, which smashed on Anson's head. Justin wasn't sure if he had wanted to kill him. If he really thought and did some soul searching, well, then yes, he'd probably decide that he had. But he could always rationalize that he had just wanted to knock him out again. And he didn't know that the vase would land with such force on his head, breaking his skull. But such is life. "Accidents" happen. The bastard deserves it, he told himself. You get what comes to you.

He'd never tell Victoria, because first of all, she'd think he did it for her and then she would want him, and second, let her squirm. After all, she had cheated on him. Why the hell should he tell her that her secret was safe? So that was that. Anson died. Sorry, but no great loss. No one could say the world wasn't a better place without Anson. He'd done everyone a favor.

·· 47 ··

There was a fifth person who went to Anson's house that night, and he'd been the only one with the actual intent to kill him. It turned out to be the easiest job he'd ever had. The guy was dead when he got there. And it looked like an accident. He saw no use in reporting that to the man who'd hired him, though. It would just confuse things. Take the money and run.

He wasn't sure who had hired him, but he'd been used by this middleman before and it was always some sort of political thing. The victim was usually more high profile, though, and the crime would end up in the papers. He had his suspicions of who was calling the shots, and they were all high-ranking government officials. A certain senator from Rhode Island seemed to benefit the most. But in his line of work it was better to know less than more. This was a funny one. A gossip columnist in California. Who knew that those people could still piss people off?

Acknowledgments

I would like to thank my editor, Stacy Creamer, for all of her excellent guidance. Jennifer Joel and Amanda Urban for their agenting expertise. Special thanks also to Laura Swerdloff, Katie Sigelman, Josie Freedman, and the amazing Joanna Pinsker. Many thanks to Christina Mace Turner for being an early reader.

I am grateful to my aunt Maureen Egen for all of her notes, assistance with my panic, and overall enthusiasm.

I have been really fortunate to have a fantastic writing partner. Even though I wrote this book alone, it never could have been written without Jill Kargman (who makes going to work every day so much fun). Thanks for everything, especially coming up with such a great title!

And lastly to my family: Mom, Dick, the Careys, the Hammams, the Huitzes, and the boys at home: Vas, James, and Peter. *Merci* and Love.

© Donna Newman

About the Author

Carrie Karasyov is the coauthor (with Jill Kargman) of the best-selling novel *The Right Address* and *Wolves in Chic Clothing*. After spending several years in Santa Monica, California, she's back in her native New York along with her husband and two sons.

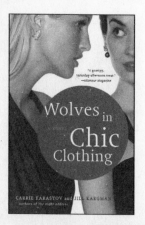